Sixth Cycle

Darren Wearmouth
& Carl Sinclair

Copyright © 2013 Wearmouth & Sinclair

ALL RIGHTS RESERVED This edition published in 2014 by Phalanx Press. This is a work of fiction. All characters and events portrayed in this work are either fictitious or are used fictitiously. Any similarity is purely coincidental. All rights reserved. No part of this publication maybe reproduced, stored in a retrieval system, transmitted in any form or by any means without prior written permission of the publisher. The rights of the authors of this work has been asserted by him/her in accordance with the Copyright, Designs and Patents Act 1988.

Chapter One

Captain Jake Phillips lay flat on his back, surrounded by a quiet electric hum. He parted his lips and attempted to take a breath. His body failed to respond to his brain's command.

He panicked and forced open his heavy eyelids. The surrounding blur formed into an enclosed space. A familiar light pink glowing sarcophagus. Waking from stasis wasn't supposed to be like this. Flight Lieutenant Mills, the second in command for his Orbital Bomber shift, was supposed to supervise his procedure and open the pod.

Jake struggled against his inert muscles and stared at the hazy, thick plastic lid above. A distant synthetic female voice mumbled something. He fought with his body. Winced as he flexed his legs. Attempting to cry for help only produced a weak croak.

A moment later his system responded, and he gasped for air.

Fully conscious, Jake regulated his breathing. Mills would get his ass kicked for this. He was normally reliable. A solid partner for their six-year mission in space.

He thumped his trembling fists against the lid three times. No response.

To his left, a series of cherry red circular buttons ran along the internal wall, lit up by a thin blue neon striplight. He pushed his elbow against the one circled in yellow. An emergency opening button he thought he would never have to use.

The lid groaned, shook and raised several inches with a penetrating screech. It smoothly slid to one side with a pneumatic hiss. The overhead lights in the stasis chamber were out. Cool air flooded into his pod. Jake tensed his cramped arms around his body and shuddered.

He remembered the instructor's words during stasis training: *Waking after two years is gonna feel like the worst hangover in the world.*

Jake grabbed both sides of the pod, pulled himself to a sitting position, and scanned the chamber. A console at one end cast a thin blue glow around the basketball-court-sized room. Out of the twelve pods, his appeared to be the only one with power; the rest looked like metallic tombs.

The lack of light suggested a skeleton mode power configuration. A crash landing procedure that channeled the energy cell to only the vital parts of the ship after grounding. The stasis chamber to preserve life, and the main communications console that sent out a distress signal.

If the other eleven crew members escaped or were recovered, why did they leave him here?

He glanced back inside his pod at two compartments by his feet. One stored a reintroduction support pack. The crew used to joke about using it; Jake certainly never expected to quench his thirst with the water inside.

He slid open the thin plastic compartment door and pulled out a white metal drawer. It contained a bottle of water, nutrient tablets and two foil energy gel sachets.

A synthetic voice mumbled again, sounding like somebody trying to talk with a pillow stuffed over their face.

Jake grabbed the water and twisted off the cap. His fingers stung against its grooves. He popped two tablets out of their foil casing and swallowed both with a mouthful of water. His stomach initially protested and tried to force the liquid back into his throat. He tore the corner off a gel pack, squeezed blackcurrant-flavored slime into his mouth, and swallowed with an exaggerated gulp.

The other compartment contained a weapon. He flipped up the long thin door, grabbed a rifle he personally zeroed on the range before takeoff, and slammed home a full thirty-round magazine.

Once Jake established his location, he could inform HQ of the ship's position. They couldn't have known because he was still here, unless he was in enemy territory. That might explain the lack of crew. Nothing else made sense.

He staggered over to the steel bench in front of the console and flopped down. Most controls and readings were out. A few on the central panel remained, but were indecipherable below the faded, formerly transparent shielding.

The unintelligible voice spoke again. Something about 'resources'.

He pressed the console speaker button. It initially resisted, then cracked down after he applied more force. "Captain Jake Phillips. Endeavor Three. Status."

The allies kept four bombers constantly in orbit as the threat of nuclear war loomed large. Six-year missions. Crews of twelve. Two always on duty. They rotated in stasis to allow them to stay in space for extended periods. It cut costs significantly and provided an excellent deterrent. He and Mills were the sixth cycle.

Something had gone wrong. The year was 2075, or it had been when he'd last entered stasis.

"Fleet Control. Do you copy?"

Nothing. Not even the confidence ping that confirmed successful transmission.

Jake groaned on standing and limped to the closest stasis pod. His olive green flight suit felt loose. He tightened up his belt and folded up his collar, protecting his neck from the chill.

On closer inspection, the pod gleamed. Its black casing and silver trim were polished to the kind of standard he expected. He hadn't been left here for long.

Unnatural shapes ran across the floor from his pod to the door. Jake knelt and instantly recognized muddy footprints. Hundreds of them. All with zigzag tread. Somebody, or somebodies, had visited the stasis chamber. The mud confirmed they were on dry land. The trail confirmed him as the person of interest.

There was no way to tell the freshness of the marks. A hundred-year-old footprint was still visible on the moon. The thought occurred that the ship's core power could survive two thousand years on skeleton mode. Drip feeding the essential areas. Stasis fried the brain after several decades. All of Jake's senses were returning.

Whatever the age and wherever they were, Jake felt an increasing sense of urgency building inside. He needed to understand his situation and react accordingly. The Fleet taught him survival skills on top of his flight training, but this was new territory.

He shouldered his rifle and decided to move.

* * *

Jake's stiffness and pain reminded him of the morning after his first day of grueling activity at Fleet Academy. His body adapted to the regime as time went along. He told himself this would get easier.

His right knee buckled, and he dropped to a crouch. He paused to compose himself and squinted through the gloom at the exit pad next to the door. Fingerprints smudged across its shiny black surface.

Jake reached down to the bottom of the door. A draft gently blew against the back of his hand. The sign of a compromised outer structure, and not the comfortable climate control system that pumped around a fully working ship.

He shook his head and pressed the pad with his thumb.

The door vibrated. Seconds later it jerkily screeched along its rails and banged open. Not the smooth mechanism he remembered that confidently punched open at a consistent speed.

He took a sharp intake of breath and propped his arm against the wall for support. The corridor outside ran along the side of the ship on the front upper deck, with a long external viewing window. It used to be a bright, well-lit space where he and Mills would eat while gazing at the stars.

White emulsion splashed across the high-temperature quartz glass windows. In a few places where the paint had cracked and fallen off, thin shafts of light streamed in, providing an eerie ambience. The formerly white walls were a filthy cream color. A mud trail led from the stasis chamber to the end of the sixty-foot corridor, where a larger area of light shone through. One of the emergency exits.

A breeze gusted through the opening, echoed along the corridor, and whistled through a crack in the roof. A dry leaf danced along the floor.

Jake pressed his left hand against the wall for support, held his rifle against his right hip, and shuffled forward.

Thirty feet along the corridor, he came to the entrance of the Endeavor's food locker and twisted the handle of the thick steel door.

Its hinges groaned and it opened a few inches. Jake shoved his shoulder against it to widen the gap.

Natural light shining through cracks in the paint illuminated the stall-sized room. Painted wooden carvings of his ship and a stasis pod were neatly stacked on the metal shelves. A straw broom and red plastic bucket sat in the corner. He cursed under his breath. *What the hell is going on?*

The place looked like a second rate souvenir shop. Somebody must be having a cruel joke at his expense. He wondered if his parents even knew he was back on Earth and MIA. They would be the ones that worried about him. To the rest of society, he was probably long forgotten. The isolated career of a bomber crew saw to that.

Perhaps they were in enemy territory, and the crew were being taken out one by one for interrogation. If so, he would need all of his escape and evasion skills. Guards might be stationed outside.

He crept to the emergency exit, took a deep breath, put a round in the chamber, and swung to face the outside world.

The sun beamed through a gap in the gray could sky.

His eyes immediately shot down. A wooden staircase, four feet wide, ran from the emergency exit to the ground below. Fifty steps were supported by large planks of wood in a lattice formation, like an old railroad bridge he'd seen in twentieth-century films.

At the bottom of the structure, in a small clearing, a large signpost faced away from him. A well-beaten trail disappeared into woodland behind it.

Beyond the trees, three industrial metal chimneys poked out of the top of a red brick building. White smoke belched out of the middle one and drifted away on the breeze. This wasn't like any factory Jake had seen before.

To the left of the factory, rows of smaller brick buildings with hipped slate roofs formed in neat lines of ten. Maybe five hundred houses in all. A huge stone wall surrounded the whole area, with square towers at regular intervals. Jake's ship was also inside the perimeter. Definitely a foreign place. Maybe one of those old industrial towns in Eastern Europe. It had that kind of feel.

Jake scrambled away from the door, crouched against the wall of the ship, and tried to think of a plan. The perimeter wall looked around ten yards high. He needed to find a gate and surprise any guards. Staying in the ship wasn't an option, and he had to move fast to avoid detection. Whoever was outside probably thought he remained safely secured in stasis.

If he could get to the cockpit, the communications console might still be working. It could give him a time for when the other crew woke up and a GPS reading. An idea of his location might give a clue to what kind of people he faced outside.

To his left, at the end of the corridor, a door led to the cockpit located at the front of the ship. Its aluminum coating had split and curled away in parts, leaving strips of dark red rust in its place.

Cobwebs covered the waist-height, square black entrance pad. Jake swiped them to one side and thumbed the pad. Nothing happened.

At the right-hand side of the door, behind a small hatch, a winding mechanism provided a way to manually open the door, in case of power failure. Jake knelt and squeaked the decaying bolt up and down. Specks of corrosion dropped as he eased it open.

The hatch swung out with a swift tug.

On the inside, an arrow on a faded sticker pointed in a clockwise direction. He reached in and grabbed a handle attached to a small wheel with cable coiled around it.

The mechanism creaked, but didn't move. Jake sat with his knees up on either side of the hatch and placed his feet against the wall for leverage. He pulled with as much force as he could muster.

The handle snapped.

He fell backwards and his shoulders bounced against the cold floor.

Tools would be needed, but Jake didn't want to hang around any longer.

With his mind made up, he decided to move with conviction. He hadn't shot up the ranks by messing around. If something needed to be done, he was the man for the job. This was his own personal job. Improvise, adapt and overcome.

The platform at the top of the staircase felt sturdy. Jake surveyed the areas below through his sights and descended, placing his feet gently down on each step.

Trees rustled in the breeze and birds tweeted, but he couldn't detect any human sounds. As he got lower, the trees obscured the buildings.

Halfway down, he glanced over his shoulder at the ship.

The black exterior of the three-hundred-foot, arrow-shaped vessel had turned charcoal gray. The ships markings were enhanced with white paint. None of it made sense.

Something clanked in the distance, like a hammer striking a block of iron.

Jake moved with urgency to the bottom of the staircase. He sprinted across the clearing and ducked behind a large tree next to the trail. Footprints led to and from the town. At least he knew the location of the visitors, but who and why remained a mystery.

He looked back at the signpost in front of his ship and gasped. An arrow pointed to the staircase, and the words 'Come and see Earth's oldest man!' were daubed below it in green paint.

Chapter Two

Skye Reed passed the dead oak tree and shivered, an unwelcome reminder that she was home. The warm humid air ignited the scents of wet moss and pinecones. Fresh rain hid the usually strong stench of decaying undergrowth and clay. The downpour softened the pine needles, masking her progress through the forest. They would not hear her coming.

Three people passed this way less than an hour ago, dragging another. To an untrained eye it would be impossible to tell. Skye had tracked this forest for years. A stone out of place, a broken twig or muddy imprint would be missed by most. Not by her. For Skye, the signs of recent human disruption were obvious.

She kept low and moved from tree to tree, never staying still for more than a moment. Nobody would follow her to this part of the forest. The people she tracked wouldn't realize they were being stalked.

A gust of wind blew through the forest. Something moved in Skye's peripheral vision. She ducked behind the nearest tree and pressed against its rough bark.

Shadows cast from the canopy played with rays of sun to create the illusion of movement. Satisfied nobody was there, she continued her pursuit.

Light rain began to fall. She couldn't wait for summer. The stronghold needed water for crops and drinking, but the endless cycle of being soaked and never quite drying out grew tedious.

Skye's sodden leather boots squelched against the ground. She moved further away from the safety of her tower and focused on her prey.

She hated being this close to her former settlement. Painful memories of that night always flooded back. They refused to remain buried and still vividly scarred her mind after ten years.

The charred remains of the western watch tower appeared through the undergrowth. Now just a pile of stones and brittle black timber.

Overgrown fruit trees, long recovered from fire damage, littered the landscape. The bountiful home of her youth had been transformed into a graveyard in two vicious hours.

People had traveled dangerous routes to taste her mother's famous harvest. Those roads were now overgrown and the settlement avoided at all costs. Citizens in Omega called it the bone orchard.

Skye knelt and inspected the foliage. Pine needles scattered near the base of a large trunk. A struggle had taken place between the men and their captive, that much was clear from the spread and pattern. A crimson smear stained a nearby rock. She brushed her finger against it. Fresh blood.

They were within striking distance.

The footprints had no tread. A sign of wastelanders or outlaws, not citizens of any of the eight strongholds, who had the recognizable patterns of Zeta-produced shoes. Those outside of society often had little to lose. It made them dangerous.

The tracks separated after the watchtower. Two sets of prints had scrapes in the dirt between them. An unconscious third's heels, dragging along the ground. They headed north away from the settlement. The other person headed for the central ruins.

Skye removed her standard-issue pistol from her hip holster and followed north, conscious that she might be facing a threat from two directions. If they did suspect they were being followed, one might be waiting to deal with her.

Thunder cracked in the distance. Heavy rain battered her head and shoulders. She had a decision to make.

She could turn back to the tower and avoid punishment, follow the single set of prints to the ruins, or head north after the group. She didn't have time for more than one.

Her head told her to turn back, her heart to go into the ruins. Skye always followed her gut instinct. This was more than a dispute between outsiders. A citizen's life was at stake.

* * *

The forest thinned and the trail became more obvious in the saturated thick grass. Skye paused behind the settlement's crumbling north tower and made sure the person heading for the ruins wasn't following.

Raised voices echoed ahead of her. They could not have been more than forty yards away, coming from inside a tightly packed copse.

Skye thrust her pistol forward and crept within twenty yards. Still no visual.

She felt a mix of trepidation and excitement. Climbing a tree to gain a better vantage point was out of the question. It would pin her to a single location if they spotted her first.

In one move she pushed off her heels and dashed over to a large boulder. Only fifteen yards away now, and she could smell their body odor.

Two men casually talked in broken English, unaware of her presence. She leaned around the boulder's slippery surface and pushed a damp fern to one side.

A tall, stocky man propped his arm against an oak. Grime plastered the upper half of his weather-beaten face. A thick graying beard covered the rest.

A mixture of mismatched light leather armor and dark pieces of cloth stretched around his bulky frame. His boots, as suspected, looked handmade. Dark leather laces crisscrossed over his calves.

He shouted something unintelligible and roared with laughter.

His partner remained obscured by the tree, apart from a filthy hand that gestured toward the first man. She could see no sign of their hostage. These men were wastelanders from the edge of the fallout one.

The first wastelander picked up sticks and pinecones from the ground and piled them up in the small clearing. The second moved from behind the oak and helped him. He looked much the same as the first, although a few inches shorter with no sign of graying. Starting a fire would be hard in these wet conditions, and a curious thing to do, given the time of day.

"Get bigger sticks," the taller one said.

"I not your woman. I no take orders from you."

"For now you do. Sky Man says so, until we done."

A chill ran up Skye's spine. The last man to mention that name had cut her father's throat seconds after. She'd hid under their cart and watched her father's hair being ripped back. *Sky Man sends his regards.*

She ran hours that night after watching her settlement being systematically slaughtered by a group of organized wastelanders. Eventually she came across sanctuary in the form of Omega.

Skye spent ten years dreaming of a faceless man coming for her every night. Six years hunting him every day to get her revenge.

She decided to hold off her attack and see if these two revealed any information about his whereabouts.

Nobody believed her story. The woman who ran the small orphanage told her it was a child's mind dealing with a horrific event. They had been outlaws, not a drilled invasion force of wastelanders. It wasn't considered possible. They didn't coordinate in groups.

Ross was the only other survivor that night, and he never supported her version of events. He claimed he fought off and killed six men before finally abandoning his post. If he had, he would know the truth. They were no simple outlaws of society; they were mutated abominations of men on a mission.

Ross ran like a coward. He wasn't the hero that presented himself at Omega. Finding Sky Man would prove her right.

"I don't care what he says," the younger wastelander said. "I am free man. I do what I please."

"He says we come here. Take north man and burn him. Start problem with other stone city."

"Why?"

The older wastelander laughed and slapped him on the shoulder. "Make them all easier to kill. Then we live in stone city with Sky Man. Own their food and tools. So stop argue and get more sticks, idiot."

If their motivation was to cause unrest between two strongholds, they were doomed to failure. They didn't count on a witness.

With the rain continuing to fall, soaking her regulation uniform, Skye decided not to waste any more time. A citizen could be dying close to their location. The trail of blood didn't look good. The longer she delayed, the less chance she had of saving this poor soul.

She had the element of surprise and couldn't see any weapons. Wastelanders usually carried knives, axes or spears. No match for her pistol at this range.

A footstep squelched on the forest floor behind her.

She spun and faced a man, like the other two. He lurched forward. She raised her pistol to fire. He swung his thick muscular arm and smashed it out of her hand with his fist.

He clamped his right hand around Skye's throat and squeezed. "You listen to my friends. Now means I have to kill you early."

She struggled to prize away his hand. He slapped her across the face with his left palm.

How could she have been so stupid and forget about the tracks that led to the ruins. She never made these kinds of mistakes. Talk of Sky Man had distracted her.

She refused to panic and raised her knees. The others were only yards away. Taking three would be impossible at close quarters while he still had her in a firm grip.

"Stay still, you. I don't want to smash your head until I have proper kiss. No pretty girls like you where I come from."

In the corner of her eye, she could see the other two had stopped building their fire and focused on her. Thankfully these were the northern variety, otherwise all three would be instantly attacking. Wastelanders were migrating from the south in increasing numbers, and brought an extreme and unquestioning form of aggression.

Skye thrust her feet against his chest and pushed out as hard as she could. His grip momentarily loosened. She sprang forward and gouged her thumbs into the corners of both of his eyes. He roared in pain and swung his fists. Both wild punches sailed over her head.

She reached for her boot, pulled a dagger free and rammed it under his jaw. His eyes bulged and he collapsed to the ground, clutching his throat.

The larger wastelander pulled a spear from behind a tree. He hunched like a bull preparing to advance, growled and charged. Skye skidded to one knee, grabbed her pistol, aimed and fired.

His head snapped back after the round punctured his forehead, and he thudded face first into the boulder she initially hid behind.

The younger one ran at her, his face contorted in rage. He jabbed the rusty barbed point of his spear forward and bared his rotting teeth.

Skye aimed and fired. The chamber clicked, but nothing happened.

She pulled the trigger again. Nothing. "Shit!"

He lunged at her with his spear. She sprang to her left, stuck her leg in front of him, and used his momentum to plant his face in the dirt.

Skye stamped on his hand with the heel of her boot and ripped his spear free. He tried to wriggle away. She thrust her boot at the side of his head. He screamed and desperately tried to grab her ankle.

She raised the spear in a two-handed grip and rammed it into his back. He let out a wet croak, and his arms relaxed by his side.

She stooped next to his head. "Say hello to Sky Man for me."

Skye searched the immediate area and found the abducted man propped against a trunk. His glazed eyes stared blankly to one side. Blood stained his uniform and face. She recognized him as one of the new tower recruits, Jai Lee. Early this morning he'd left with a message from Omega to Sigma.

Everyone in a tower spent time as a messenger while being trained. Somebody had to do this dangerous job, and the less experienced the better. They hated losing an experienced number off the clock.

She checked his pulse, but knew deep down it was too late.

Taking a moment to catch her breath, she surveyed the scene of carnage. Nobody could deny this compelling evidence that outside groups were making a move against them. She tore Jai's Omega-issued dog tags from his neck and stuffed them in her trouser pocket.

Before leaving the scene, Skye retrieved her dagger from the larger man's throat, wiped it clean on his shirt, holstered her useless pistol, and searched the wastelanders for evidence. The younger one was still alive, but he didn't deserve a quick death. She had to get back to Omega and inform them of the impending threat.

Sky Man had returned.

Chapter Three

Jake staggered deeper into the woodland cover and tried to process what he had just seen. The sign, written in English, and wooden carvings in the ship only led him to a single bizarre conclusion. He was being used as a tourist attraction.

The ship must have come down in another English-speaking country. Possibly his only bit of good news since waking. The UK, Canada, Australia, New Zealand and Ireland were also part of the Allied Alliance. The chill climate suggested he wasn't anywhere near the Caribbean.

An oily burning smell hung in the air, probably from the factory.

The buildings were only two hundred yards away, making Jake acutely aware that he could be quickly and easily spotted once he decided to make his move.

The breeze wrapped a sheet of yellowing newspaper against the base of an oak tree. He moved across to it in a crouching run and picked it up.

His eyes immediately shot to the date on the top right-hand corner. *Epsilon Monthly, April 2205*. It seemed impossible that he spent one hundred and thirty years in stasis, but it did provide an explanation for the sign and the state of the ship.

The headline on the article read: *Stronghold facing fight!*

The top two paragraphs were still visible, the rest faded to a blur.

> *Due to the declining popularity of Phillips, Epsilon requires a solution in order to maintain the clock at three thousand. The Trader will not sanction an increase of weapons exports, so the Beth and Barry are currently looking at our alternatives. Suggestions so far include an offer of new sets of pots for the other seven strongholds, or a commissioned statue of their choosing.*
>
> *At the moment, we still have space for seventy more citizens. If a cut is required, Beth and Barry have assured this paper that it will be done through natural decline and recruitment from outside will be frozen.*

Not only was Jake a tourist attraction, it looked like he wasn't even a good one. From what he could gather from the article, the size of this stronghold's population linked directly to their economy, him being part of that. Who were these people?

He had to get the hell out of here and contact HQ. If they still existed. The realization hit that he might not know a single person alive, although they knew him.

Part of Jake's basic training taught him how to live off the land. He needed food and water to help build his strength, but his priority was getting over the high stone wall, away from this place.

A twig snapped to his front. He ducked behind a tree and peered around it.

A young boy, about six years old, walked through the trees, wearing a brown woolly sweater and black trousers. He held a carving of the Orbital Bomber and made a whooshing noise as he swept it from left to right.

Jake lowered his rifle. "Hey, kid … Over here."

The boy froze.

He held out his remaining blackcurrant gel pack. "Would you like this? Tastes good. You can have it if you answer a couple of questions."

The boy dropped his ship, pressed his hands against his cheeks, and screamed. He ran for the town without looking back. Jake considered chasing him, but that would clearly lead him toward trouble. His walking, talking self might not find friends around here. He decided to find a place to climb the perimeter wall.

He sprinted to his left, away from the housing area and factory, bounding over the soft ground while swerving between trees. Adrenaline pumped through his body, allowing for easier movement. The perimeter wall wasn't far away.

Jake's right foot tangled in a thick knot of weeds. He flew forward and twisted to his side. His shoulder crashed against the ground and skidded through a thick layer of damp pine needles.

The twenty-foot-high, dirty stone wall was only thirty yards away. An eighty-yard rampart ran between two red brick towers on his left and right. It looked like the defensive wall of a medieval town or fort. He understood why the newspaper called this place a stronghold. A gravel track ran around the inside of it.

A low metallic clank, like a Swiss cow bell, repeatedly chimed from the main center of the stronghold. The same noise echoed from the tower on Jake's right, shortly followed by the one on his left. Others rang around the perimeter. It sounded like a herd of wild cows on the loose. That would be preferable to the probable reason behind the collective noise. An alarm to signal his hunt.

Jake took a deep breath, sprang to his feet, and wiped pine needles off the side of his rifle. He ran to the edge of the track and glanced in both directions.

The wall and track curved into the distance on either side. To his immediate right, a wooden ladder was propped against the rampart. He could jump over the wall from there, if the drop on the other side wasn't potentially fatal.

A male voice shouted from the left tower. Jake couldn't make out the words above the clattering bells.

Other voices called out behind him. He looked over his shoulder. Ten figures moved through the trees, dressed in dark blue jumpsuits, the closest carried a hammer. He had to go for it.

He slung his rifle over his shoulder and rushed for the ladder. A voice from the tower bellowed again as Jake's boots crunched over the gravel track. He immediately grabbed the smooth wooden ladder rungs and ascended. He hurried to the top, pulled his rifle into his shoulder, and carried out a quick visual sweep.

Six men and four women appeared through the trees and stopped on the track below him. They gaped up, and one whispered something to another. Thunder rumbled in the darkening sky.

A steel door on the right-hand tower creaked open, and a bearded man, also in a blue jumpsuit, stepped onto the rampart, no more than thirty yards away. He trained his strange-looking rifle on Jake.

The bells stopped ringing.

"Drop your weapon and put your hands on your head," the bearded man said in an unrecognizable English accent.

Jake edged back until his back pressed against the ramparts. He peered over it. A twenty-foot drop on the other side. Tree stumps peppered the ground twenty yards in front of the wall, only a short distance to cover to reach the forest's edge.

"Don't even think about it," beard said. "If you move, I fire."

Jake decided to gamble that they wanted to take their tourist attraction alive. Beard's aggressive expression and threat added to his burning desire to leave.

Jake earned his parachute wings during basic training. At the time he thought it was a pointless relic of hundred-year old armies, but the landing technique would avoid him twisting an ankle or breaking a leg. As soon as his feet hit the ground, he would throw himself sideways to sequentially distribute the landing shock along five parts of his body. His feet and the sides of his calf, thigh, hip and back.

He didn't hesitate and vaulted over the wall.

The ground rushed toward him and he thudded against it, went to his right, and rolled in the damp grass. His right ankle twinged, but he didn't have any serious damage.

A shot split the air and thumped in the ground a few yards away. The bearded man aimed over the wall. Another man joined him.

"Stay right where you are. It's dangerous out there."

Jake would rather take his own chances. These lot didn't seem the friendliest bunch. He darted for the forest, zigzagging between tree stumps, expecting to hear gunfire at any moment. None came, and he entered the densely packed forest.

* * *

Jake decided to find some clear ground to try to establish his location. Maybe he would see a recognizable landmark, an Allied vehicle or craft, any sign of familiarity to help him plan his next moves. If it really was 2205, and he had his doubts that a human could survive so long in stasis, the world would be changed significantly. Alliances might have shifted, the balance of power changed.

On current evidence, civilization had regressed rather than advanced. At least people spoke his language. The newspaper mentioned seven other strongholds. If they were in close proximity, Jake might have a chance of capturing an individual and asking them questions. At the moment, it didn't feel safe to approach one of these places without knowing their potential to be a threat.

He headed for the sound of running water. A foaming, twenty-yard-wide river cut through the forest and snaked down a gentle hill, gushing over rocks that jagged above the surface. Following one of these in any survival situation usually led to civilization or a coast, although the distance could be vast. Wherever the river flowed toward, it was away from Epsilon.

Jake knelt on the bank, splashed his face, cupped his hands and drank. He felt the cool refreshing liquid run through his body, and followed it up by eating his last blackcurrant gel pack. The boy not accepting it was a blessing in disguise, as the pack provided some much-needed carbohydrates.

Gentle rain began to fall as he trudged a mile along the bank. Jake had no idea of the time. He didn't need a wristwatch in an Orbital Bomber; they'd had digital clocks everywhere. The newspaper didn't look too old, and this wasn't atypical of a spring day in April or May in the northern hemisphere.

The dark forest on either side looked uninviting and claustrophobic. Thankfully the river helped with his orientation. The forest eventually thinned to Jake's right, and he noticed the shattered remains of a village amongst the trees.

He approached to investigate. A broken wall surrounded an area the size of a football field. Two sides were reduced to piles of rubble. The four towers on each corner were little more than collapsed ruins. All thirty stone houses inside were burnt-out shells. Black scorch marks covered stone lintels above the smashed windows. Slates collapsed through the roof, leaving only charred timbers.

In the center of the settlement, weeds and small trees sprang out of the gaps in a cobbled square. To the left of the houses, eighty wooden crosses poked out of the undergrowth in various states of decay. All crudely constructed out of two stakes lashed together with rotting rope, apart from two: varnished pine crosses at the end of the back row, with names carved on them. Bunches of wilted flowers lay on the trimmed grass at each of their bases. Jake read the closest inscription.

Thomas Reed. Died 2195.

Somebody still cared about him and still visited this place, although it must have been years since people lived here. It also made Jake finally believe the date on the newspaper. Two pieces of matching evidence from separate areas, coupled with the odd stronghold and the state of his ship. He didn't believe in coincidences.

The situation blew his mind, but dwelling on what he now knew to be true wouldn't solve anything.

A groan came from Jake's left. He dropped to one knee and swept his rifle across the settlement.

A groan again. It came from behind the closest ruin.

He crossed the square, keeping his steps light, and edged around the building's mossy stone wall.

A man coughed and spat.

This could be an opportunity to talk to an individual, although he sounded in serious strife. Better than negotiating with an armed force in blue jumpsuits.

Jake twisted around the corner and aimed at four bodies.

A man propped against a tree stared to one side with lifeless eyes. He dressed the smartest of the four, in a gray jumpsuit with a diagonal zip across the chest. Another, in a strange mix of leather and thickly woven cloth, had a stab wound under his bushy chin and must have quickly bled out. The filthy-faced third, in similar attire, had a gunshot wound in his forehead. The only one left alive was dressed like the previous two and had a spear in his back.

Jake quickly checked the immediate vicinity and returned to the man.

He stopped two yards short and crouched. "Who are you?"

The man grimaced. "You die."

"That's far more likely to happen to you. What country are we in?"

"North."

"North what?"

"North people die."

The man gurgled and rolled onto his front. His speech suggested English wasn't his native tongue. For a person on his last legs, Jake also found his behavior chilling. Rather than ask for help, he issued a death threat to a stranger.

If Epsilon contained North people, maybe the warning the guard shouted about it being *dangerous out there* meant the three people here who looked like they'd never seen a bath or razor. The one left alive must be confusing him for one of his tourists.

Something moved in Jake's peripheral vision. He snapped his head to the right. A bearded man, dressed like the three next to him, charged with an axe raised over his head. When Jake locked eyes with him, he roared and threw his weapon.

The axe spun through the air. Jake dodged to his left. It whistled over his shoulder and slammed into the tree next to him.

Jake curled his finger around the trigger. The man continued to advance and drew a knife from a leather scabbard on his belt. He reached within ten yards.

He aimed at the man's torso and fired twice. The man grunted and collapsed to the ground. Jake's shots echoed through the forest.

In the distance he heard a collective scream, like a wild battle cry.

"Holy shit."

He turned and ran, vaulting over weeds and rotten logs, veering between trees.

The cries sounded closer every second. They weren't giving up the chase and were gaining on him.

A gravel road appeared on the right, cutting through the forest. The river curved away to the left. He could see another stone wall through the trees straight ahead.

A high-pitched siren began wailing ahead.

Jake glanced back. Figures advanced through the trees. Perhaps civilization was a good idea after all. He sprinted for the wall.

Chapter Four

Skye broke out of the tree line toward the wall, exhausted after spending the last hour running through the forest. Sweat dripped from her face, and her heart pounded against her chest. If those savages were an advance party, Omega needed to prepare.

She headed straight for the main guard post. The miserable borderland station that had become her home.

The twenty-foot-high wall, built with large blocks of cut stone, wrapped around the two square miles of the stronghold. Governor Finch upgraded it to be ominous for anyone attempting to access the central town without permission. *We are powerful. Try if you dare* was its intended message.

A roughly cut staircase, made from discarded construction blocks, provided the only external way into Omega apart from the cast-iron main gates. It climbed both sides of the wall at a forty-five-degree angle and met on the internal rampart. Forces needed a way to deploy other than the main gates, but it created a weak point.

Finch addressed this by building two concrete pillboxes either side of the steps on top of the wall, twenty feet apart. Eight rifles bristled out of the thin slits. Four men patrolled between them on the rampart.

Skye raised her hand to the left pillbox and trudged up the steps.

Sam Bennett waited at the top. He tucked his rifle over his shoulder, brushed his sandy hair to the side and smiled. Skye loved his sparkling green eyes. He took his duties seriously, unlike most others who treated the wall as a chore.

"You're in deep shit this time, Skye."

She stepped onto the rampart and sighed. "Don't tell me. Ross?"

"He sent out an order for you to report to the tower three hours ago."

"I've been out doing some real work. We've got wastelanders in the area."

Sam shrugged. "There's always one or two."

"I came across three, carrying out received orders. They killed Jai."

"You're kidding me?" Sam said and unslung his rifle. "Are they close?"

"An hour north. You don't need to worry about them, but stay alert."

Sam gave her a single firm nod. Skye knew him well enough to understand that he would take her words seriously. "I'll send word along the rampart. Did you recover Jai's tags?"

"Yep. Ross in his office?"

"Did you need to ask?"

Skye didn't respond. The coward would be in the captain's tower. She decided a few years ago to push the thoughts of him running from their settlement to one side, until she had proof. Regardless of her feelings toward him, they still had a job to do.

She hurried down the steps on the other side. Two guards stood at the bottom. One nodded at her. The other retrieved a hip flask from inside his jacket and drank. Skye smelled alcohol as she passed. It wasn't even lunchtime. Attitudes had to change if they wanted a robust defense.

A pillbox team of four walked out of the windowless concrete barrack block and headed to relieve the current shift. Finch had the barracks built behind the stairs to ensure they could be quickly reinforced if required. Skye had a bunk in the building, but tried to avoid it. The place stank of sweat. The plastic corrugated roof made it feel like a greenhouse in the summer, although the solar panel heating system kept it warm in winter. Nobody complained about that trade.

A well-beaten path led across a grass field to a wooden mess hall and the hexagonal five-story captain's tower. Ross deployed a sniper on the tower roof, providing further protection for the steps.

It would take a small army of organized wastelanders to overrun this area. Most thought they were too crazy to coordinate anything outside of their own small groups. Skye knew differently.

SIXTH CYCLE

Wheat and barley gently swayed in the small fields surrounding a central area, where the main population lived in tightly clustered wooden houses. The inner ring, a six-foot wall, marked the old perimeter until Finch expanded out to include crops and livestock to boost the stronghold's economy. The Omega Force patrolled the buffer as well as the ramparts.

Two new recruits, male and female in their late teens, stood guard outside the tower's thick wooden door. They were easy to spot because they still had smart uniforms and hadn't slipped into downtrodden complacency just yet. It wouldn't be long. Ross was an expert at sapping morale. Members of the force nicknamed his office *the ivory tower*.

Both eyed Skye's officer epaulets and stiffly saluted in turn.

"The captain's in a meeting," the woman said.

"He asked not to be disturbed," the man added.

"Stand aside, please. I need to speak to him immediately."

"The captain told us—" the woman said.

"I'm not gonna start ordering you about, but trust me, it's in all our interests that he hears what I have to say."

They looked at each other. The man fidgeted with his rifle. Skye realized they were in an awkward situation, worried about annoying their new commanding officer by disobeying his request.

"I'll tell him I commanded you. Now please …"

The pair seemed to relax, and the woman opened the door.

She bounded up the spiral stone staircase to Ross' office on the fifth floor and paused for a moment outside the entrance. Even looking at his brass nameplate, screwed to the hardwood door, managed to raise her blood pressure a few notches.

Skye considered knocking, but only briefly.

Ross bolted upright when she walked into his cramped semi-circular office. A woman sitting on his knee closed her brown satin robe and looked away, no doubt embarrassed about being caught in a trade with the *hero*. He placed a whiskey bottle down on his solid hand-carved desk, scowled and jabbed a finger at Skye. "Who gave you permission to enter?"

"I've got important information to report, sir."

He encouraged the woman off his knee and closed his purple bathrobe, hiding his rolls of flab. "Where the hell have you been?"

"An hour north. What I have to tell you isn't for civilian ears."

Ross rolled his eyes and held the woman's hand. "Until tomorrow?"

She mumbled a positive acknowledgment, turned her back on him, and dressed in a light blue uniform of the laundromat in town. Skye knew exactly who she was. The only woman in Omega that carried out this type of historical and creepy transaction.

Five crates sat to Ross' left, no doubt stuffed with luxury items to pay for his personal service. It made Skye's skin crawl.

While Skye waited for the woman to leave, she gazed at the paintings hanging on the curved wall. Most dated from before the Great War. A nineteenth-century navy ship in rough seas, a silhouetted skyline of one of the former great cities, and a family scene with a working television. Only Governor Finch had an office with more decorations.

Skye realized she stood on one of the five full animal skins stretched around his office floor, and stepped to one side. The woman shuffled past.

As soon as the door closed, Ross folded his arms. "You've gone too far this time. Finch won't defend you for this. How dare you go out again without permission?"

He glared at her. She maintained eye contact but thought it best not to mention Sky Man at this stage, and try to reason with him first. Ross would immediately dismiss it. He went out of his way to discredit her story ten years ago to preserve his hero status.

She took a deep breath and composed herself. "I found a dead citizen. Three wastelanders killed him, under orders."

"Lying is not gonna get you out of this—"

She fished the bloodstained dog tags out of her pocket and threw them across the desk. "See for yourself."

Ross turned the metallic tags in his hands, licked his finger, and wiped away the dried blood. "Ensign Jai. Tell me again how you got these?"

"Three wastelanders abducted him. I'm not sure when. I picked up their trail and tracked them north. They were planning to blame it on Epsilon, or so they said. Sounds like they're trying to cause unrest."

"Sounds like total nonsense. They don't have the mental capacity."

"I can assure you they do, and more might be coming," Skye said and placed her pistol on the table. "We need to order a full weapons test. This one jammed after the first shot. I'll use my crossbow until I find a reliable gun."

"The hell you will. You're an officer and need to lead by example. Those pistols are standard issue and high quality. The Trader assured us of their expert craftsmanship."

"If this is his idea of expert craftsmanship, I'd hate to use his poor quality stock."

Ross rubbed his eyes and groaned. "What are we going to do with you, Skye? Why can't you just fall into line like everyone else on the force?"

Skye looked through the window behind Ross. A road ran from the main gates of the stronghold to the inner ring, through its modest cluttered houses to Governor Finch's stone villa.

"If an attack comes and we're unprepared, do you want them knocking on Finch's front door?"

"Governor Finch to you."

"Whatever. The wastelanders said …"

Skye trailed off. Ross wasn't listening. She had to tell him the truth. Anything to shake him out of his arrogant malaise. It didn't just risk her life, it risked the lives of everyone in Omega.

"They said what?" he said.

She pressed her hands on the desk and leaned toward him. "They said they worked for Sky Man."

His eyes widened, just a little, but enough for Skye to notice.

Ross drank from the whiskey bottle, slammed it on the table, and shook his head. "Not this again. Your mysterious Sky Man has come back to kill us all? I'm having you put away for good this time."

"I'm being serious, Ross."

"Captain Ross or sir to—"

The attack siren warbled.

* * *

Skye spun and rushed out the door. She clambered up the metal ladder that led to the sniper's nest on top of the captain's tower.

The circular metal hatch at the top squeaked open, and she crawled onto the roof. A guard lay in the prone position and peered down his telescopic sight. The gun cracked and he pulled back the bolt handle to eject the shell case.

"Damn it," he said. "It's impossible from here."

Hitting from a range of three hundred yards in a gentle breeze should be easy for a trained sniper with a decent rifle, but Ross kept a slack force, and the Epsilon weapons were questionable.

"What's going on down there?" Skye asked.

"Wastelanders attacked the stairs. Twenty of them. Largest group I've ever seen."

"Did any make it to the rampart?"

"They retreated for cover after we opened fire. Looks like they're testing our defenses."

Rifle fire echoed from the pillboxes. Figures moved between the trees outside the wall. The guard wiped sweat from the brow of his bald head, reloaded, and planted his eye against the rubber eyepiece of the scope.

"Hey, do we have any scouts out today?" he said.

"Don't think so, why?"

"They're attacking somebody near the road. He's shot three of them."

"Let me see."

He leaned over and passed Skye his rifle. She noticed a pair of spectacles poking out from his right top pocket and wondered if he traded with Ross to land a position on the tower instead of the cramped confines of a pillbox.

She knelt on her right knee, adjusted the scope, and scanned the area outside the wall.

The remaining wastelanders were being distracted away from the stairs by a man dressed in dark green. He crouched behind a large rock and fired as they approached him, taking single aimed shots. Cool under pressure, she thought.

He didn't wear a stronghold uniform she recognized, but she knew it. His light brown hair and clean-shaved face joined the pieces in her mind. Her parents had taken her to see him on three occasions as a child.

Captain Jake Phillips, the oldest man in the world.

She couldn't figure out why one of Epsilon's former prized assets was fighting on his own outside Omega's walls. Whatever the reason, he needed help as the remaining wastelanders rounded on his position.

Skye handed the rifle back. "I'm going out there. Whatever you do, don't shoot after I go over the wall."

He frowned. "It's my job."

"It's my life."

She gripped the ladder rails and slid eight feet to the stone floor below. Ran down the spiral staircase, running her hand along the metal rail to keep her balance, and burst through the door at the bottom.

"I need to borrow your rifle," she said to the female guard.

"Are you sure? I was taught to always keep my personal weapon—"

"We haven't got time for debate," Skye said with firm sincerity. "Your weapon, please?"

She pulled her sling over her head and held out the rifle. Skye put a round in the chamber and sprinted for the wall.

Sam knelt at the rampart and turned as she bounded up the steps. "We pushed them back, but it looks like they're heading for the main gate."

Skye took a moment to catch her breath. "They're after Phillips. He's on the edge of the forest, a hundred yards to our left."

"Phillips?"

"You ever been to Epsilon?"

Sam raised his eyebrows. "The guy in the ship? I didn't even think he was alive. What the hell's he doing here?"

"No idea, but he's being surrounded. Are you coming?"

Sam turned to the two other guards on the rampart. "We're going out. Give us some covering fire."

Rounds whizzed into the forest, ripping through leaves and smacking into trunks. Skye shouldered her rifle and descended the outer steps. Thunder rumbled overhead.

She could hear Sam's footsteps behind as she kept close to the wall and quickly moved toward Phillips' location.

Five wastelanders ducked behind trees around him, only about twenty yards away. Phillips dropped one who made a run for him. He must've run out of ammunition because he grabbed his rifle by the muzzle and held it like a club. She had to draw attention away from him.

Skye reached within thirty yards and fired at the closest wastelander. The round hit him in the small of the back. He dropped to the ground with a twist.

A spear sliced through the air and whistled between Skye and Sam. It clanked against the stronghold's wall. Sam returned fire and hit two wastelanders who broke from the trees and charged with axes raised.

The remaining two circling Phillips watched their comrades fall, looked at each other, and took flight to a deeper part of the forest.

"Captain Phillips. Get over here. Now!" Skye said.

He turned from watching the wastelanders flee. "Who are you? Who are they?"

"I'll explain after we're back behind the wall."

Or at least explain to the best of her ability. Phillips probably had a thousand questions. Who wouldn't after being woken up centuries after going to sleep? Skye knew she wouldn't have all of his answers, but at least they could take him to safe ground.

He paused for a moment, looked down, and shook his head before jogging over.

Sam gave him a reassuring pat on the arm. "This way, Captain Phillips."

Phillips edged away. "I take it you've *visited* me?"

A bloodcurdling scream echoed in the distance.

"No time for this at the moment, Captain, follow me," Skye said.

She quickly returned to the entry point. Phillips tentatively followed, and Sam covered the rear. The guards at the rampart all stared open-mouthed at their new arrival. Skye felt sorry for him as he cast nervous glances at the pillboxes. She led him past more uniformed guards down the internal steps. They whispered to each other and glanced at him.

Sam stayed on the rampart to organize the defenses in case of a secondary attack. Ross, now fully dressed in his tightly fitting dark blue tunic and matching trousers, strode along the path from his tower, flanked by two guards.

"Don't be afraid," Skye said to Phillips. "We're not bad people here."

"Depends on your definition of bad. Seems like you've all enjoyed treating me and my ship as a freak show."

"It's not like that."

He grunted. "Thanks for saving my ass, by the way."

The two guards stopped a few yards short. Ross looked Phillips up and down. "Is it really you?"

"I'm Captain Jake Phillips from Endeavor Three. Where am I?"

"Omega. I'm Captain Wendell Ross, commanding officer of the stronghold force."

"I don't know Omega, and I don't know where I am. I know it's 2205, you've been using me as an attraction, and there's crazy people in the forest. You need to help me out here."

"Not until Governor Finch has decided what to do with you."

"For God's sake, at least tell me what country I'm in?"

Ross raised his finger and gestured the guards forward. Both ran either side of Phillips and raised their rifles. He glanced back to the wall, no doubt thinking about running. Skye would do the same in his shoes.

It was typical of Ross to take this approach. He wouldn't be considering Phillips' mental state. He would be thinking about his value and how that could benefit him.

Skye stood in front of Phillips. "He helped us defeat the attack. I saw him kill wastelanders."

Ross grimaced. "Meet me back at my tower after I've finished with Governer Finch, Skye. I haven't finished with you just yet."

He turned and walked away. One of the guards jerked his rifle in the direction of the inner ring. "Get moving, Captain."

Ross spun around. "I'm the only captain in this stronghold. Don't call him that again."

Phillips looked at her and half smiled before being led away. As strange as this meeting had been, Skye had larger things to worry about.

Chapter Five

Jake followed the man named Ross while the two guards continued to silently encourage him along with their rifles. Leaving the forest gave him a sense of relief, and these people didn't seem half as crazy as the ones outside. At least not Skye and her male partner who rescued him from his sticky situation. He still couldn't quite put his finger on their accent. North American at a guess, but not one he'd ever heard before.

Hopefully the governor would be able to answer the main questions swirling around his head. His location, the whereabouts of his crew, what happened over the last 130 years, and an idea of the current situation on the ground. He didn't know if the Fleet even still existed. Somebody around here would surely have the patience and knowledge to explain.

Pillboxes and guards were evenly spread every hundred yards along the rampart that surrounded crop fields. He now understood the reason for it. The psychos in the forest weren't the type to negotiate.

A paved road led from a double set of iron gates at the perimeter to a centrally located residential area. A smaller internal wall, six feet in height and constructed with rocks and cement, ringed it, although Jake doubted it provided much protection. Ross led him toward it along a dirt track between two small fields growing carrots and turnips.

They joined the paved road and headed straight for a Georgian-style white mansion in the center of the stronghold, around three hundred yards away. Jake wondered if the governor was playing Lord of the Manor and had organized his own form of feudal system in exchange for safety behind his walls.

Wind turbines lined the route to the mansion. Their blades lazily rotated in the breeze. It looked like a poor man's version of the Champs-Élysées in Paris. Jake took his last vacation in Europe before his mission, and loved traveling to sample different cultures. This trip gave his hobby an ugly new twist.

Paint peeled off the scruffy wooden bungalows jammed tightly together along both sides of the road. Not half as spacious or well constructed as the ones in Epsilon, although by Jake's estimate, this place was twice the size.

Similar roads led off to the left and right. A group of small children dressed in green linen shirts and trousers played hopscotch along one street. A couple of solid-looking unbranded SUVs were parked on another.

Omega had weapons, vehicles and electricity. Not all that bad if the world outside had turned to shit.

Within a hundred yards of the mansion, the houses turned to basic-looking stores. The signs overhead simply said *Vegetables, Dairy, Meat, Clothes* and *Bathroom*. Nothing on the tables outside had a price attached. A woman stuffed spring onions, peas and a cauliflower into a straw basket and acknowledged somebody inside the store with a wave. She glanced at Jake being escorted down the road and hurried away.

Ross entered the mansion's wrought-iron gates and turned to the guards. "Wait here until I call you. Don't let him out of your sight."

He crunched up the gravel drive.

"Is he always like this?" Jake said.

The closest guard, a young man with a wispy mustache, sighed. "Pretty much. Easier to just do as he says."

"Can I ask you an honest question?"

"Sure."

"Am I in danger?"

"From Governor Finch? No, he's all right."

The guard spoke genuinely, which put Jake's mind slightly more at ease. He guessed the earlier theatrics near the wall were only to avoid the wrath of Ross. Every army or small force he encountered over the years had their own little Napoleon. It didn't take long to meet Omega's.

"How long have you been here?"

"Omega? Since I can remember. I was born in the Zeta maternity unit, most citizens are."

"Is there a reason why the strongholds are named after letters in the Greek alphabet?"

The guard tilted his head. "Greek alphabet?"

"Forget it."

Jake looked at the house again and noticed four white plastic numbers 5973 attached to a metal bar hanging from the central window ledge on the second floor. "Do those numbers mean anything?"

"It's our population clock."

"How does that work?"

"Please, Captain, stop asking me questions. You'll get me into trouble."

A woman in a crisp white dress met Ross before he reached the main entrance. They held a brief conversation. She pointed at a dark alley to the side of the mansion.

He turned and gestured the guards forward. "Bring him to the garden."

"This way, Captain Phillips."

Jake followed the guard over the gravel drive. The other trudged behind. He thought their royal blue uniforms made them look like toy soldiers, or extras from a theater production, although Skye and her partner showed that these people were far from useless. They carried out a quick extraction move without any fuss and efficiently dealt with the enemy.

The path at the side of the house led to an acre-sized garden at the rear of the property. A seven-foot-high, darkly stained shadow box fence gave it privacy. The immaculately manicured lawn had a stone bird table in the middle of it. Evergreen shrubs stuffed the surrounding borders.

These first signs of familiarity since waking felt abnormal. The scene here was out of place against what he had witnessed so far.

A man with slicked back gray hair, wearing a purple turtleneck sweater tucked into his black trousers, sat on one of the chairs of an iron bistro patio set. He held a magnifying glass to his eye and gazed down at a cabbage white butterfly resting on a piece of black paper.

Ross cleared his throat. "Governor Finch. This morning we captured Captain Phillips of the Epsilon display outside our walls during a wastelander attack. I believe he wasn't part of their force, but have brought him here under armed guard as a precaution."

Jake decided to bite his lip for the moment. It didn't take long to see exactly how Ross operated. A good leader of men would've found out the details from Skye and her colleague, and praised them. Instead, he kept the story generic, probably wanting to take any credit that might be coming.

Finch placed his magnifying glass on the table and stood. "A wastelander attack? Are you sure, Captain Ross?"

"Positive. My guess is that it's random. A one-off. But we'll stay alert, as usual. I'm more worried about Skye Reed spreading rumors about Sky Man."

Finch nodded in understanding. "Very good, Captain. I'll speak to Skye. You keep up the excellent work."

"Do you want me to leave now?"

"No. Stay here with the guards until I've finished with Captain Phillips."

"Yes, Governor."

The whole exchange felt incredibly false. Their tone and body language suggested they were friends. Ross clicked his heels together and took a couple of paces back.

Finch extended a hand to Jake. "Welcome to Omega. I'm Alexander Finch."

He gave it a firm shake. "Captain Jake Phillips. I've got a lot of questions."

"I'm sure you do," he said and held his hand toward the bistro set. "Take a seat. I'll be happy to tell you what I know."

A young teenage boy brought out a jug of water and two glasses on a tray. Finch poured them both a drink and passed Jake a glass. "I've seen you a few times during my visits to Epsilon. Did you escape, or did they throw you out?"

"They chased me out. Fired a warning shot, but I think they wanted to capture rather than kill."

"Understandable. You account for twenty-five percent of their population."

"How does that work? I've seen your population clock. Do you all have those?"

"Have you ever seen a caterpillar turn into a butterfly?"

Jake frowned. "Not sure what you're getting at?"

"Let me explain," Finch said. He crossed his legs and folded his arms behind his head. "The transformation of a caterpillar into an airborne creature of beauty is a perfect metaphor for change and improvement. For this to happen, it has to eat and grow in a safe environment."

"I'm not sure I'm with you."

"You better take a drink of water before I tell you the next part."

Jake tasted a hint of lemon. He glanced over his shoulder at Ross and the two guards. They looked bored. One of the guard's eyes followed a fly around the garden. Maybe they'd heard Finch's butterfly story a hundred times.

"Does this have anything to do with your clock or what happened to the world?" Jake said. "I don't know anything after 2075."

"I was getting around to telling you, but if you want the blunt version, so be it."

"Blunt is good. I'm flying blind."

Finch gave him a fake smile. "In January 2077, the world descended into nuclear war. Don't ask me the politics; you'll have to go to the library in Theta if you want to read the finer details. The Alliance struck most of the Axis' silos and dumps in retaliation after a tactical strike in South America. In a final act of spite before admitting defeat, they fired every conventional warhead available at the United States, Canada, the UK and Australia. The leadership and most of the populations of the Alliance were wiped out."

"So the Axis won in the end?"

"You seem to be forgetting the sealed envelopes that are carried in the safes of your orbital bombers and nuclear submarines. They were opened, and the instructions told them to fire on the enemy. After the dust settled, three-quarters of the world had turned into radiation zones, the rest lay in ruins."

Jake swallowed hard. He never expected the world as he knew it to end like that. He always thought that the weapons ensured that a war wouldn't happen. They were supposed to be a deterrent. He had almost come to terms with the fact that most of the people he knew were long dead. Finch's recounting of events rubber-stamped it.

"A lot to take in, Captain Phillips?" Finch said.

"You can say that again. So where are we, and what's left?"

"We're in North America, and our eight strongholds are all that's left for hundreds of miles. At the moment, we're in the chrysalis stage."

Jake shrugged. "The chrysalis stage?"

Finch slammed his glass on the table. "Don't you know anything about butterflies?"

He seemed a few spoons short of a full set. Jake didn't want to anger Finch and end up back in the forest. "I'm sorry. You said that eight strongholds are all that's left. What about the psychopaths I met in the forest?"

"There are only cows in this world," Finch said while wiping his hand with the bottom of his sweater.

Jake didn't have the faintest idea what he was talking about. He waited for Finch to continue.

"It's an acronym, Captain. I assume you know what an acronym is?"

"Uh-huh."

"Citizens, Outlaws and Wastelanders. Citizens live in the strongholds and are the remnants of the civilized world. Outlaws live in the hills and mountains. They threaten our rebuilding efforts through thievery and murder. Wastelanders are survivors from the edges of the radiation zone. They quickly evolved to be aggressive and generally hunt in small groups, but have low intelligence. In the last few years, they've started coming north in small numbers."

"Why do you think they're heading north?" Jake said.

"My best guess is that they've run out of local food sources and are searching for more. Unfortunately, when they see our strongholds, they invariably attack. Thankfully, they're not clever enough to coordinate themselves, and we can deal with the small groups."

Jake sat back and puffed his cheeks. He still didn't have any answers to his personal situation, but the bigger picture was clear. Finch kept referring to the strongholds as a collective group, which meant he could be close with Epsilon.

"How are the strongholds organized?" Jake said.

"We all produce different goods and trade through a neutral party. He decides the cost of produce, goods and materials based on output. If the clothes and shoes from Zeta are in demand, he drops their value. If Sigma can't produce enough building material, he ups their value so they can keep supplying their town with our crops. Epsilon makes weapons and metal objects, Theta has a chemical plant, Omicron produces vehicles, Lambda makes energy and electricity solutions, Kappa makes alcohol, tobacco and has a fish farm. That's how our world turns. It's not important now."

"Who's the neutral party? Sounds like a big job."

Finch's eyes narrowed slightly. "He's called the Trader. The strongholds started out as pockets of survivors. As they grew and got in touch, they all agreed to produce different things to supply each other. It avoided any stronghold spreading themselves too thinly, and guaranteed a regular supply of items needed to start forming a civilized society again."

Jake got the impression that he didn't like the arrangement, but decided against questioning that part. Every society had their own problems, and one built under such dire circumstance could easily be excused for early teething problems.

"But the strongholds couldn't agree on a trade price?"

"Exactly. This was before my time, but to settle matters, the eight strongholds signed a treaty, giving a *neutral* person the power of our economy. They survey the state of each town, check their produce levels and ensure a balance is maintained. We're on our fifth Trader at the moment. You'll meet him soon enough."

"What about your population clocks? A guard outside told me the numbers on your mansion—"

"Manor."

"Sorry, manor, is Omega's. A newspaper in Epsilon mentioned that if they couldn't find a way to increase trade, they'd have to cut theirs down."

Finch laughed. "They're fools. We all have population limits, set by the Trader, based on how many people we can accommodate. Resources are limited, and we don't want strongholds packed with the starving and diseased. Omega is currently set at six thousand. It used to be two thousand until I expanded and rebuilt our defenses."

"Do you turn people away? Is that how Outlaws are created?"

Finch emptied his glass while maintaining eye contact. He exhaled, waved the boy over, and pointed to the tray.

"It's dangerous to make assumptions in this world, Captain. I've never had to turn people away. If other strongholds can't find ways of expanding, I suppose they might; you'll have to ask them. Today our clock reduces by one after a murder in the forest."

"Nobody beats the clock," Ross said from behind him.

Jake turned to him. "Meaning?"

Finch snapped his fingers. "It's a turn of phrase. Everybody dies. Citizens of Omega are given a stamped set of dog tags. That's their clock identification number. Life expectancy nowadays is not what you're accustomed to. We still don't have the same kind of medical treatments, and the dangers outside the walls are growing."

Jake wondered what would happen if Omega had a rush of births, but decided against asking. Irritation rose in Finch's voice when he went into detail. He decided to change the subject and would find out more about how things worked through some of the people around Omega, if they allowed him to stay.

"Do you know how my ship ended up in Epsilon? Or what happened to the rest of my crew?"

"All I know is that it grounded forty years ago near Epsilon. When they investigated, they found you in stasis and the rest of the ship empty. They were one of the smallest strongholds, still are, and wanted to boost their economy by bringing in your ship. They traded with Omicron for assistance to drag it inside their walls. You were popular for a few years."

Ninety years in space and forty on the ground. Endeavor could've cruised orbit on autopilot until a mechanical defect initiated an emergency landing. It still didn't answer why nobody was at the controls, or what happened to the crew after landing. If they were still alive and out of stasis, most would be in their late sixties. Somebody would've come back for Jake.

The only way to find out would be to access the mainframe in the hull. Jake didn't want to go back to Epsilon just yet. He would after establishing his own safety, and Omega might be the answer.

"If I were you, I'd forget about your colleagues," Finch said. "We would know if one entered a stronghold. The chances are they were killed by Outlaws."

Jake nodded in agreement. "Looks like I'm stuck here. Do you have a place on your team for me?"

"It's my turn to ask you a question first. How did you wake up?"

"I don't know."

He considered why he hadn't asked himself the same question. Somebody either manually did it, which meant knowledge of his ship's operating system, or the energy cell had drained to five percent, triggering an automatic procedure. The second explanation seemed the most likely, meaning Epsilon couldn't put him back even if they wanted to.

"Wouldn't you say the timing was convenient?" Finch said.

Jake shook his head. "Convenient how? I'm finding it just the opposite."

"Things are happening, Captain. Toads are moving in the shadows. They want to shoot out their greasy tongues and eat us."

Finch's odd metaphor suggested that Jake was part of a movement against the strongholds. Or at least, that's what he thought. "You're saying that I'm part of a plan against you? I can assure you that I'm not."

"So you say."

Finch picked up the magnifying glass and focused on the dead cabbage white butterfly again.

"Where do we go from here?" Jake said.

"I've explained the metamorphosis of our world, and how we are in the chrysalis stage. We are still feeding and growing in safety before expanding to be a glorious lepidoptera. Everything has a price, a trade value, including you."

Jake's pulse quickened. Finch intended to use him as leverage for something. "I can be a useful part of your town. Give me a chance."

"I've done you the courtesy of explaining the situation. Now you have to accept our way of life." Finch dismissively waved his left hand. "Guards. Take him to the cells and call for the Trader."

Ross moved to Jake's side and pointed a pistol at his head. The two guards grabbed an arm each. Finch picked up a pin from his table and stabbed it through the butterfly's body.

Chapter Six

Skye marched up the white stone steps of Governor Finch's mansion and balled her fists. If Ross thought she would listen and stay behind at the tower while he filled Finch's head with nonsense, he had another think coming. She had no doubt that he already concocted a self-promoting story about the attack.

It was up to her to make sure Finch knew the truth. The return of Sky Man couldn't be passed off as a minor incident. Nobody in Omega would want to be part of his version of carnage. The attack on west tower had to be him testing their defenses for a larger scale invasion. She didn't care what Ross said about it; they needed to take the warning signs seriously and be ready.

She paused outside the Venetian doors at the front of Finch's mansion and made sure things were straight in her head. Ross would offer a stiff counterargument or say whatever he thought would please the governor. She had to be compelling and put facts and logic ahead of Ross' hot air.

Finch recovered his doors from a salvage mission to an abandoned old city in the far north. He disappeared on his scavenging trips every week since Skye arrived at Omega. His pet project was turning the once simple-looking structure into a palace and fortress where he could lead the stronghold and display the latest total on the population clock. It provided a constant reminder of the numbers the guard were responsible for, and the ongoing success of his expanding operation.

Two chrome gargoyle heads were screwed to the door. Iron rings hung from their mouths, acting as knockers. They frightened Skye as a child and reminded her of the twisted screaming faces during the attack on her settlement.

She grabbed the ring to knock. The door clicked open. She knew her way around the place after living here as a child and decided to proceed to his study. He wouldn't mind, and she didn't want to give Ross too long to spin his web of lies.

Her boots squeaked across the shiny tiled hallway. Finch's housekeeper, in her smart white dress, descended the staircase and rubbed a duster along the ornate wooden banister.

Skye cleared her throat; most people did before speaking in Finch's mansion. Mary glanced over. "Is Governor Finch around?"

"Skye, how lovely to see you. Will you be staying for lunch? We're having your favorite, pea and ham soup."

She returned Mary's warm smile. The offer reminded her that she hadn't eaten for hours. "That would be lovely. Thank you."

"The governor's in his study with Captain Ross. Did he bring in Captain Phillips?"

"I'm sure he's told the governor that he did. Sam and I found him outside the wall in the middle of an ambush."

Mary placed her hands on her hips and looked up. "Let me see. I first saw him in 2176 … or was it 2177. Just over a year after they brought in the ship. We were all so excited."

"I can imagine. Doesn't seem that popular nowadays."

Mary sighed. "Things change. I've seen enough of that to last me a lifetime."

She squirted wax on the twisted spindles and continued to polish.

None of Skye's generation were particularly interested in Phillips, although she enjoyed visiting Endeavor Three as a child, and viewed it as a living capsule of a former world that would never come back.

She continued past an antique mahogany bookshelf stuffed with tatty paperbacks, and reached two varnished wooden doors with brass handles. The one on the left led to the dining room and kitchens. The food here was a step above the stew served at the mess hall, and the smell of freshly baking bread seeped through the gap under the door. Mary's offer didn't need repeating a second time.

Skye opened the door on the right and walked along the bright naturally lit corridor toward the study.

Paintings hung on the wall at regular intervals. All of a better quality than the ones that hung in Ross' office. The one of an old sailing ship, with is sails bulging with wind, was always her favorite. One day she planned to visit the coast and spend hours watching the ocean.

She knocked on the closed study door.

"Come in," Finch shouted.

The sweet strong odor of cigar smoke hit her as soon as she walked into the office. Finch and Ross sat opposite each other on brown leather chairs. A thin gray cloud lingered over both of them.

Ross turned his head and scowled. "What the hell are you doing here?"

Finch leaned forward and flicked ash into a tray on the glass coffee table between them.

"Didn't I tell you?" Ross said. "She can't follow simple orders."

Skye rolled her eyes. "I think the governor deserves to know the facts about today. I'm here to provide a firsthand account."

Finch raised his hand. "Enough. You're both officers of Omega, and I don't expect you to argue in my office."

"Sorry, Governor," Ross said.

"Skye, what are you doing here?" Finch said. "Captain Ross told me that he left you in charge while he reported on the attack and brought Phillips to me."

"I left Sam in charge. He's one of the good guys."

Finch dusted ash off his trousers, stood, and approached to within inches of her face. His steely bloodshot eyes bored right into her. This was not a man to disobey. She'd seen him give plenty of dressing downs during her time living at the mansion and didn't want to be on the end of his next.

Skye edged back. "I wanted to tell you about the attack. New information has come to light that I think you should know about."

"You thought disobeying Captain Ross and coming to me directly would be the best way of doing that?"

She glanced over Finch's shoulder at Ross. He gave her a smug grin and relaxed back in his chair.

"You need to hear this, Governor. I'm serious."

"Captain Ross says you claim the attackers were working for this … Sky Man? Haven't we been down this road before?"

She traveled the previous road as a frightened girl. This information now came from Omega's most experienced tracker. "I overheard two wastelanders talking in the forest before a third discovered me. Are we supposed to think that the attack immediately after was a coincidence?"

"Men you allegedly killed," Ross said, "making it impossible to question them. It's all very convenient."

"I know what I heard. Whoever Sky Man is, they were his men."

Finch walked to his desk, pulled another cigar from a wooden box, and clipped off the end with a penknife. She knew he could get slightly strange with his butterfly obsession, but surely he would see some truth in her words.

He lit the cigar and sucked until he produced a bright red glowing tip.

Skye's eyes stung from the smoke, but she resisted the temptation to rub them. "Perhaps Phillips saw something? He was out in the forest too."

"We won't be hearing from him anytime soon," Ross said.

"Where is he?"

Finch locked his jaw and puffed out a smoke ring. "He's detained in our holding cells for his own safety. I've requested Trader come to Omega immediately."

"You locked him up? He helped us, Alexander … he's not working with the wastelanders."

Ross raised his eyebrows. Skye immediately regretted using Finch's first name in front of another citizen.

Finch frowned at her and shook his head. "I allow you a lot of leeway because of who you are, but you're still an enlisted officer in my defense force. You don't get special treatment, nor do you question my orders. Phillips is not our prisoner; he's the property of Epsilon and belongs in his box."

"Who knows what Epsilon are going to say about his arrival?" Ross added with self-righteous delight in his eyes. "I'm sure they won't be happy their cash cow has fallen on our doorstep."

Skye imagined pistol-whipping the smarmy look off his face and smiled.

"Do you find Phillips amusing?" Finch said.

"Not at all. You're right," Skye said. It was pointless trying to carry on the conversation with Ross in the room. Every time she tried a reasonable tack, he jumped straight in and sent the conversation down a rat hole.

"I was just sending Captain Ross back to bring you here," Finch said. "It seems in your haste to be heard, you have saved some time."

Ross stood and straightened his jacket. "Are we finished, Governor?"

"That will be all, Captain Ross. Thank you for your continued support and service."

She cringed after Ross gave Finch a limp salute. He turned on his heels and walked toward the door, giving Skye a look of disgust as he passed.

The door slammed behind her. Finch's stern expression softened, and he gestured her to the leather armchair. "What am I going to do with you? Maybe it was a mistake allowing you to enlist."

"Alexander," Skye said, willing to be more informal and plead to the better side of his nature. "I know what I heard. You have to believe me. Somebody coordinated that wastelander attack. They've never attacked here in numbers before."

He sat opposite and crossed his legs. "But you successfully repelled the attack. I don't think we've anything to worry about."

"What if they come in larger numbers? Should we think about demolishing the steps?"

"I trust you, so I will proceed on the basis that it may happen again. I don't know who the wastelanders follow or why they grouped together, but I have ordered more men to each of our towers. I can't do much more than that, I'm afraid. Once the Trader arrives, I'll talk to him about acquiring more weapons."

Skye sighed with relief. She hoped that some of the previous conversation was for the benefit of Ross' ego. "Thank you. You won't regret—"

"But," he interrupted, "I won't have you undermining the authority of Captain Ross. You don't have to like him, but you will listen to his orders. Whenever you act against his orders, you disobey my office. Do you understand?"

Skye gave him a resigned nod and bowed her head. He acted like a father to her after her arrival in Omega. She hated disappointing him, although she got what she wanted out of her meeting. Extra forces around the wall and more weapons from Epsilon. Hopefully the new shipment would be better than the last pile of junk.

Finch stood and rubbed his hands together. "That's settled. How about we grab some lunch?"

* * *

Skye ripped a piece of bread off a crusty loaf and dunked it into a steaming bowl of soup. The smokiness of the ham and pepper seasoning immediately hit her taste buds. Mary knew how to cook and never failed to hit the mark.

Finch watched her and smiled. "Don't they feed you on the wall?"

"You should take a trip down there and try it. It's pigswill compared to what you eat."

"You're always welcome at my table. I miss having you around the place. It's not the same talking to the paintings and statues, although they don't answer me back."

She rolled her eyes in mock offense. "So, what's the favor you want?"

"I need you to lead a convoy out to Zeta. Three casualties require further treatment. The governor has agreed to treat our boys in their medical center."

"You want me to babysit a convoy? I'd prefer to stay here in case of another attack. Why not send a junior rank?"

Skye dunked another chunk of bread in the soup and savored the taste. She appreciated Finch's offer to dine more regularly, but didn't want to be seen as receiving special treatment. She'd worked hard since joining the force to avoid any of those accusations.

Finch pushed his bowl away without touching a drop. "I'm sending you because you're the only one I can really trust. You'll be delivering special cargo. A trade I've arranged with some friends in Zeta. I don't want anyone else involved."

She rested her spoon in her bowl and looked up. "You've cut a deal without telling Trader?"

"I'll be honest with you. He doesn't know and wouldn't approve if he did. I'm keeping this one off the books, but I can assure you it will lead to a long-term improvement."

Finch stood and walked to a drinks cabinet. He unscrewed a bottle of whiskey and poured himself a generous measure.

"Unsanctioned trades?" Skye said, wondering why he would take such a risk. "You know I'll help, but we're both aware of the consequences if people find out?"

"They won't," Finch said. He swallowed the whiskey in a single gulp and deeply exhaled. "You know how I feel about the Trader. He doesn't give Omega a fair deal, and today's attack shows how vulnerable we are. A few of us are working together to strengthen all of the strongholds. He wants to line his own pockets. I'm thinking about the people. Will you help me?"

Skye thought for a moment. Finch's intentions seemed noble, but he asked her to take part in an operation against the rules of the stronghold treaty. She knew it was a bad idea, yet her history with him obliged her to go along with his scheme.

"You realize what you're asking me to do?" she said.

"I wouldn't ask anyone else."

"I'll do it, this one time."

"I knew I could count on you. There's just one more thing ..."

"Which is?"

"After you've delivered the goods to my friend in Zeta, he has another job for you. I've told him that you are my best tracker and sniper. They're having a problem with outlaws from the mountains to the west of the stronghold. The leader has them organized, and the attacks are getting worse. Zeta needs him dealt with."

Sky frowned. "Dealt with?"

"I would like for you to take care of him. This man and what he stands for is a threat to all of us. I told my friend you could get the job done. Without leadership they will scatter like common thieves. It would mean a lot to me, and all of our futures, if you could finish the job that Zeta can't."

Killing wastelanders was one thing. They were psychopathic monsters with no morals. Outlaws who lived around the edges of the strongholds were a minor problem; at worst they were imprisoned. The odd murderer might be hanged, but that hadn't happened for years. Finch wasn't talking about the pursuit of justice; he wanted an assassination.

"Shouldn't he be brought to trial? Zeta can prosecute him under their laws."

"Zeta have tried and failed to capture him. He's dangerous, Skye. If you don't want to do it, I can find someone else, but I promise you this is the only way."

Skye no longer felt hungry and pushed her bowl away. "I'll speak with your man in Zeta and get the lowdown on the outlaw."

Finch smiled. "What would I ever do without you?"

* * *

Skye sat in the passenger seat of the SUV, ready to leave Omega for the strange mission. She didn't feel right about it, but she trusted Finch's judgment.

Six members of the force carried their three casualties on stretchers and placed them on the back of a covered truck. Four more heaved on a securely strapped metal container carrying Finch's special cargo. A second SUV with three guards brought up the rear of their small convoy.

Skye briefed the drivers that they would move at pace and only stop for blockages in the road. They happened more often in the last few months and were usually a thinly veiled warning sign of a wastelander ambush. A smarter enemy would change tactics, but they never learned.

She grabbed the handheld radio off the dashboard and gave the order to move out. Her driver started the SUV's low rumbling engine. It often amazed Skye that no matter how much they lost during World War Three, society still managed to pick up the broken pieces and start over. The SUV, built in the factories out in Omicron stronghold, was a testament to the human ability to survive and flourish, no matter how bad things got.

The siren began to intermittently bleep, signaling an arrival. The two large iron main gates cranked open.

A hard-top SUV with tinted windows sped through the gap, closely followed by five more and two trucks. The lead vehicle stopped alongside her, and its passenger window lowered.

The weather-beaten face of an old man wearing sunglasses peered out. He flicked a cigarette end out of his window and smoothed back his shaggy gray hair. "You're leaving just as I've got here, Skye. Where are you heading on this mighty fine day?"

Skye tried to act as naturally as possible. "We were attacked this morning. I'm taking three casualties to Zeta."

The old man removed his glasses and stared at her with his opaque blue eyes. "Finch shouldn't be giving you the boring jobs. When are you gonna come work for me and have a real adventure?"

She forced a smile. "You would be so lucky."

"Do you know why he's called me here? Ross told me it was urgent."

"I found Captain Phillips outside our wall this morning. I'm guessing they want you to return him to Epsilon."

His eyes widened slightly, not by much, but enough for Skye to notice. Conscious of the fact that she had contraband in her convoy, she gestured the driver to move forward. "These men aren't going to heal themselves. I'll see you again sometime."

The old man nodded and closed his window.

Skye breathed a sigh of relief. It was just her luck that Trader arrived at the moment her vehicles lined up to leave. Thankfully he didn't inspect the truck, and the convoy headed for the gates.

Chapter Seven

Jake estimated that an hour had passed since the guards cuffed him and locked him up. Omega's cells consisted of three six-by-eight empty spaces built out of concrete blocks with a rusty sheet-metal roof and barred entrances. They faced a small pigpen and a rotting shed filled with the noise of clucking chickens.

A pungent mix of dried urine and animal dung invaded his nostrils. That was nothing compared to the bad taste Finch left in his mouth. His only interest in Jake seemed to be what he could get in return for him. He guessed that when the Trader showed up, he would broker a deal between Finch and Epsilon for Jake's return to his former captors.

He leaned in the corner of the middle cell and rubbed his hand against the dry crumbly cement, which oozed out of the gaps between the blocks. Jake doubted the shoddy construction housed long-term residents. One hefty shove would probably bring the whole thing down on top of him. Not the smartest escape plan in the world. He would just have to wait for a better opportunity to present itself.

The time for reflection about his family, friends and the state of the world would have to remain on ice until he dug himself out of his current hole. He needed to remain focused. In his experience, people who saw a glass half full rather than empty invariably got a better result. It served him well throughout his life. When he struggled with school, he knuckled down and put in extra hours. He captained the academy football team through support and encouragement, and quickly made a name for himself in the Fleet by thinking on his feet and taking the initiative.

Footsteps squashed through the mud outside.

The same two guards appeared. The friendlier one from before twisted a metal key in the lock and creaked the door open.

"Governor Finch wants to meet you by the Trader's convoy."

That explained the intermittent siren half an hour ago. Jake expected gunfire to crackle along the walls but instead heard the rumble of vehicles.

The guard gently held his arm and pushed him forward.

"Can you tell me anything about the Trader?" Jake said.

"He's a good man from what I can tell. Governor Finch gets annoyed with the value he places on our produce, but I guess it's the same for everyone."

"Do you know what they've got planned for me?"

"They've been arguing about it for the last fifteen minutes. Please don't drop me in the shit by talking. I don't want to follow you into that cell or lose my tags."

"I thought you had those tags for life?" Jake asked.

The guard grunted. "If Finch makes you an outlaw, any citizen is entitled to kill you on the spot. If you make it out of the gates, what life do you have?"

"Doesn't sound like the green shoots of Utopia he described?"

"My advice is don't scratch the surface, Captain, you won't like what you see beneath, and it might get you killed."

"I thought you said Finch was all right?"

"He is if you toe the line. You're only a number as long as he allows it."

He gripped Jake's arm a little tighter. A clear signal to stop talking as they passed the humming base of a wind turbine and joined the main paved road that ran through the stronghold.

Eight vehicles lined the road between the shabby bungalows. Three gun-metal-colored SUVs at the front, two green five-ton trucks with chunky wheels in the center, and three more SUVs at the rear. All had a basic angular design, and their exhaust pipes belched out thin black, gritty gasoline-smelling smoke that drifted away on the breeze.

Twenty men and women, dressed in dark brown cargo pants and matching long-sleeve shirts, stood at the side of the convoy chatting amongst themselves. Each had a rifle over their shoulder and a pistol in a plastic thigh holster. One spotted Jake and nudged a couple of the others. They all turned and stared. He returned a nod.

Finch and a man with a gray ponytail and goatee, dressed like the rest of the convoy crew, walked between the front two vehicles. He stopped a yard short of Jake, raised his sunglasses and smiled.

"Now will you agree to make the trade?" Finch said from behind him.

The man ignored him and faced Jake. "Nice to meet you, Captain Phillips. I'm the Trader. Just call me Trader, it's less formal," he said and extended his hand. "You must be terribly confused."

Any sign of friendship was welcome. Jake gave the man's hand a firm shake. "You can say that again. You wouldn't believe the day I've had."

Trader sighed and replaced his glasses. "Unfortunately, I would. This is the world we live in. But it won't be like this forever."

He had a disarming upbeat warmth although Jake kept his guard up. Trader's next actions would be a better publication of his real thoughts.

"Do we have a deal or not?" Finch asked.

Trader spun to face him. "I'll take him to Epsilon after we've visited both bunkers. I'll give you a twenty percent cut of our finds and make sure Epsilon gives you thirty of their best rifles."

It seemed he was no better than Finch, apart from one subtle difference. Rather than being overt about his callous functionality, he preferred the wolf in sheep's clothing approach.

"Which bunker are you visiting first?" Finch said.

"Does it matter?"

Finch stepped closer to him. A distance Jake felt would invade Trader's personal space, although the older man stood his ground.

"You probably watch a butterfly thinking it's aimlessly fluttering around," Finch said while twirling his finger. "The reality is that they follow strict flightpaths. I believe you are the same, Trader. What is your flightpath?"

Trader shook his head. "You really need to loosen up, Finch. If it really bothers you, I'm going west, refueling at Sigma, and heading east. I'll deliver Captain Phillips in two days."

"Thank you. I'll have the guards open the gates."

Finch turned and walked away. Jake found the whole exchange odd, but it left him in no doubts about his fate. He just hoped the leader of Epsilon would see sense when he explained that stasis was no longer possible, due to the energy cell availability.

Trader waved the Omega guards over. "Take off the cuffs."

The younger one felt for the keys on his belt. "Are you sure?"

"Are you telling me how to do my job, boy?"

"No, sir."

He released both cuffs and took a step back.

Trader turned to his team. "Saddle up, guys. We're heading west."

They moved for their respective vehicles. Trader headed for the front SUV, leaving Jake standing by the side of the road. As much as Jake wanted to escape everything, being with this man appealed a lot more than staying in Omega.

"Forgetting someone?" he said.

"You're riding shotgun with me," Trader said. "Move your ass, or I'll leave you here."

Jake headed immediately for the passenger door.

* * *

Trader spread an old faded map of Oregon over the steering wheel. He overlaid a transparent piece of plastic with eight blue crosses drawn in a rough circle and two red ones either side of it. He tilted them toward Jake.

"Do you recognize this?"

Jake nodded. "Oregon. Are those eight crosses the strongholds?"

"Thought you'd pick it up quickly. Do you know the locations of the two red ones?"

Jake squinted at the map, but the locations didn't ring any bells. One was located in the middle of a national park, the other just south of a small town.

"Can't say I do. Should I?"

"These are two of your Fleet's bunkers. I located them a few years ago, but we can't get through the blast-proof doors. There's a protected keypad in the entry tunnel. Do you know the access code?"

Jake checked the map again. He remembered that a system of lockdown facilities were set up around the country, in case of nuclear war. Some were designed to last for centuries and were packed with supplies. The tantalizing prospect also existed that he might actually find a group of his colleagues in hibernation. Collectively they wouldn't bow to any mini-dictators, their clocks or threats. The access codes were issued to captain and above. As long as they hadn't changed after the war, Jake could get in.

"If I open the blast doors, what's in it for me?"

A broad grin stretched across Trader's face. "Didn't take you long to get used to this world. Let's get one thing straight. I'm not taking you back to Epsilon. Consider yourself a free man. Open the glove box."

The comment took Jake by surprise, but he didn't question it. He clicked open the latch, the compartment fell open, and he stared at the contents.

"It's yours. Go on."

Jake took out a holstered gun attached to a webbing belt. He drew it and inspected the weapon from different angles. The mechanism looked fairly standard for a semiautomatic. He released the magazine out of the grip, checked it contained rounds, and slid it back home. It locked in place with a light click, and he put one in the chamber.

Omega's siren warbled intermittently. Trader crunched the SUV into gear, looped around a parallel street, and headed for the stronghold's main entrance. Jake looked in the rearview mirror. The rest of the convoy followed, splashing through the water-filled potholes that peppered the road.

"If I'm a free man, which I assume is conditional on me opening the bunkers, can I go my own way?"

"You can go your own way, Jake. May I call you Jake?"

"Sure. I would ask how you know my first name, but that's kind of a stupid question."

"It is. As I was saying, it's a dangerous world out there. Trouble is coming. Wastelanders are appearing more frequently, and we don't know why. Maybe because supplies outside of the strongholds are limited. You would be making a mistake if you think running would improve your situation."

"What are you suggesting?"

The stiff suspension made every loose fitting of the sparse black plastic interior rattle as the SUV bumped along the paved road. The iron front gates opened, presumably from a winding mechanism in the stone gatehouse. Two men in royal blue jackets stood on the rampart on either side and waved them out.

"I'm suggesting that you join my team. I'll smooth things over with Finch and Epsilon. I can show you how this world works. How I keep things in check. You can be a part of improving it."

"Why me?"

"Because you're professionally trained and pure. You haven't been raised to hold the same prejudices and hang-ups that exist today. In order to maintain harmony and parity between the strongholds, I have to take a step back and take a high-level view. It doesn't make me popular, but it avoids our society making the same mistakes that got us here in the first place."

"You mean the mistakes my generation made?"

Trader smiled and shook his head. "I doubt anyone holds you responsible for political decisions on a global scale. If we treat the eight strongholds as a microcosm of our previously failed civilization and ensure limited arms, equal trade and sensible expansion programs, we've got a chance."

Jake gazed out of the window and considered Trader's proposal. He appeared genuine, and although a lot of unanswered questions remained about his world, the choice of going back into the wild and fighting wastelanders, returning to Epsilon, or living under Finch's control were far less appealing. He decided to go along with the offer for the time being. The bunkers might provide an alternative option.

"You've got yourself a deal."

"Excellent. You've made the right choice. Mind if I smoke?"

"That's a rhetorical question, right?"

"You're working me out quickly."

A mile outside Omega, the dirt road changed into a former highway. Weeds and trees, growing through cracks in the asphalt, reclaimed the outside lanes, almost fully concealing a dark red rusting barrier in the median strip. Two tracks ran the length of the inside lane. Constant usage must have kept nature from reclaiming the whole road.

Trader pulled onto the moss and weed covered shoulder. A single SUV roared past. He wound his window down, pulled a plain white box out of his trousers, flipped it open, and offered a cigarette to Jake.

"No, thanks. I'm not about to start after avoiding them for 157 years. Where's that vehicle heading?"

He lit a cigarette and blew smoke out of his window.

"It's our forlorn hope. I always send a vehicle a few hundred yards ahead. If there's wastelanders in the area, it will flush them out. They usually attack on sight, so it avoids them hitting the main convoy. We're always quickly on top of them."

Jake remembered the name *forlorn hope* from when he studied historical military tactics at the academy. He thought that those who were ignorant of the past would make the same blunders. Trader was in tune with the idea, and Jake wondered where the man acquired his knowledge.

"Where did you read about the forlorn hope?"

"I took a Bernard Cornwall book out of Theta library, and it seemed to fit with our lead vehicle's situation. Leading part of an operation and greater risk of becoming a casualty. Our tactics are evolving to deal with the increasing threat. Fifteen years ago, I could drive this road with little fear. Now we run the gauntlet on a daily basis."

The lead vehicle disappeared through a dusty haze. He took two more drags of his cigarette and flicked it into the weeds. "Better get going."

Trader held his arm out of the window and waved the vehicles forward. He pulled in front of the procession and punched the accelerator. Cool wind rushed through the gap in his window, clearing the stench of tobacco smoke.

"How did the wastelanders evolve? I'm surprised they're not all dead?" Jake said.

"Trader four, my old boss, told me radiation is energy. Populations in the heavily concentrated areas died. The energy still passed through the molecules of people on the edge of the zones, ionizing or reducing them, thus altering their chemistry. The change affected DNA, which is what caused the mutations. Their offspring are much worse."

"Everyone in those areas turned like that?"

"I doubt it, but you can imagine how they quickly dominated a landscape."

Jake couldn't fathom whether the technical detail provided a solid explanation or if the theory evolved through the sands of time. Whatever the cause, he'd witnessed their aggressive and uncharacteristic human behavior first hand.

A continuous horn blast sounded in front.

Trader drew his pistol from out of his holster.

Jake tensed and peered through the windshield. They approached two faint red glows through the dust. The lead vehicle's taillights. Its horn continued to wail.

Trader stopped. An SUV pulled alongside their vehicle. The five-ton trucks' air brakes hissed.

The lead vehicle's white reverse light flicked on, and it shot backward with a high-pitched whine.

"Let's roll," Trader said and kicked his door open.

Jake jumped out and ran to join him at the lead vehicle driver's window. A woman wound it down. "The road's blocked by a tree trunk."

"Fallen or placed?" Trader said.

"Placed. It's been chopped at the top and bottom."

Trader looked along the dust-shrouded road. "They're learning. We need to be careful with this one."

Boots thudded along the road surface. Ten of his team surrounded him and aimed either side of the highway.

"We've got a trunk ahead that needs moving," Trader said. "It looks like a trap. Four of you clear it; the other six organize yourselves in all-round defense. Jake and I will patrol between you."

"Is Rip Van Winkle part of the team?" a woman with short blond hair said.

"His name's Jake. Drop the childish nicknames. He's military trained and will benefit our team. Now let's move."

The team shouldered their rifles and advanced at a slow pace. Dust stung Jake's eyes and impaired his vision. They had fifty yards of visibility in all directions.

"Rip Van Winkle?" he said.

"Most were taken to see you as a child. I've heard a few others."

"What's with all the dust? I don't remember Oregon being like this?"

"The levels built up because of the decaying towns and cities. It comes in waves. This should be hitting Omega in half an hour."

Four of the team grabbed one end of the trunk and heaved it to the side of the road. The other six formed a wide circle around them, each covering an arc of fire to their front.

Trader stopped twenty yards short of them and put his finger to his lips.

Something rustled in the undergrowth next to the shoulder.

He swung his pistol around. A scream pierced the air.

Footsteps pounded along the road ahead. An axe spun over the team clearing the log and skidded along the surface past Jake.

Two wastelanders charged out of the undergrowth at Trader. He fired at both. One collapsed, the other continued forward, clutching the side of his stomach. Jake pumped two rounds into his torso. The force of them checked him, and he collapsed backward, five yards from their position.

Rifles cracked to Jake's left.

The wastelanders were trying a badly coordinated pincer movement. Trader edged to Jake's side, and they both aimed at the still bushes and shrubs that lined the highway.

One of his team sprinted over. "We've taken two down ahead. All clear back here?"

"For the moment. Clear that damned log. If others are in the area, they'll be attracted by the shots."

He nodded and returned forward. Jake glanced down at the closest wastelander in his dirty black leather clothing. He had a golf-ball-sized growth above his left eye and boils on his neck.

For the next minute, Jake and Trader stood in silence, sweeping their weapons across the side of the road.

"All clear," a man called from ahead.

"Move out!" Trader shouted.

The group collectively returned to their vehicles. Jake slammed the SUV door and clicked down the lock.

Chapter Eight

Skye's convoy sped through the decaying landscape along a weed-infested road. She cupped her hand over her eyes, protecting them from the dust, and gazed at the abandoned ruins of a small town. The shell of a large house on the outskirts, with two rusting vehicle skeletons in the drive, signaled they were five minutes from Zeta. Finch once told her that the place was Gothic revival style, but that didn't mean much. She used features like this ruined house as distance markers between the strongholds.

Wastelanders had once used a row of five wooden shops by the side of the road to stage an ambush. She swept her rifle along broken dirty windows and looked for any signs of movement around the collapsed shelves inside. They always chose a hiding place to spring an attack, but never in a large group like this morning.

The SUV crashed through a gouge in the crumbling asphalt. Skye grabbed the steel roll bar to steady herself and let her weapon hang loose.

"How long are we staying for?" the driver said.

"I'm not sure yet. You might have to go back without me."

Skye's thoughts turned to Finch's second request. Killing an outlaw. She had never shot anyone in cold blood before and started to have second thoughts. Completing the mission would depend on what his contact told her about the man and his crimes against society. Putting a bullet in someone's head for stealing food wasn't an option.

A gust of wind blew across the vehicle, coating her in more grainy dust. The analogue dashboard clock clicked past three o'clock. They did well to reach this far in sixty minutes.

The walls of Zeta loomed in the distance, built on a natural plateau with excellent views for miles around, when conditions allowed.

Skye could never take her eyes off the old gas station that lay half a mile from the gates. Eroding remnants of six fuel pumps protruded from the cracked forecourt. Two still had faded black rubber hoses attached. Six concrete columns surrounded them, the supports for holding up the roof, which slumped in the middle and rested on top of a derelict brick building.

It was hard to imagine how easily accessible resources were to people before the war. Driving around in safety, shopping in stores and having access to friends and goods through a computer seemed an abstract idea. Skye liked to look on the bright side. She lived in the same space but had a different set of challenges.

One day the planet would be connected again, but they had to make it safe first. The emergence of Phillips might push forward the development, and Skye looked forward to speaking with him again, if Epsilon didn't put him back to sleep. In her opinion, they couldn't afford to let a source from the old world go untapped.

The SUV hit the smooth paved road and approached the gates to Zeta. The area surrounding the stronghold still had scorch marks from their regular burns. Zeta liked a clear space outside the wall, to avoid any nasty surprises. A repainted old sign that gently rocked in the breeze read *Welcome to Zeta.*

It didn't feel like four years since her last visit. She had several reasons for avoiding the place. Most of all, the officers rubbed her the wrong way. They were always looking down their noses at their guards and citizens. Omega wasn't perfect, but it was nothing compared to the oppression that resided here.

Zeta produced uniforms that clearly set the officers apart. Dark blue forage caps, stiff navy jackets and trousers, and boots that gave off a metal click when they walked along the paving. A citizen's heart must've sunk when they heard that sound approach. Skye felt sure the governor selected the most brutish people to commission. He ruled the place with an iron fist. She could never fit into his way of thinking.

The medical center provided a saving grace. Zeta's strict discipline helped run the place with precision, and it quickly boosted their population clock when their reputation for disease-free care spread around the other strongholds.

The thick wooden gates between the high granite walls opened. Two guards walked out of the small gap and stood either side of the road. One lifted a handheld radio to his mouth.

Skye switched to the Zeta channel.

The radio squelched. "… confirm who you are?"

"Zeta guard, this is Lieutenant Skye Reed from Omega. I have three casualties for the medical center. Over."

"We've been expecting you. Drive in and park on the right."

"Copy that, Reed out."

The gates fully opened. Several storage trucks moved out in the opposite direction, no doubt delivering clothing under the instructions of Trader.

Skye's convoy drove through the gates and parked in a cobbled yard next to the guardhouse. Skye jumped out of the SUV and went to sign in. Zeta kept a written record of every coming and going from the stronghold. They liked to make sure visitors didn't linger and take advantage of their resources.

Two men pushed open a tall sliding door on the side of the block-built textile factory. A woman wheeled out a dumpster full of waste material. Skye peered inside at the busily whirring rollers on the mechanical hemp-spinning machine.

Although the internal area of Zeta covered three times the size of Omega, fifty brick-clad apartment blocks packed tightly around the factory. Beyond that, they harvested hemp. The real key to the stronghold's success.

Skye entered the guardhouse and stood in front of the counter. An officer flipped open a hardback folder, thumbed to today's page, and passed her a pen. "Sign here, please."

"No problem. Have you seen any wastelanders in groups recently?"

"One attacked a patrol vehicle yesterday. Why do you ask?"

"A group carried out a coordinated assault on Omega today. Thought I'd better warn you."

She wrote about the three casualties being delivered, and put a vague description about goods to be delivered after seeing a similar wording a few lines above.

He gave her a false smile and snapped the folder shut. "We'll keep a lookout for wastelanders. You're free to get on with your business. Please leave by sundown."

A bearded officer stood by her SUV with a clipboard tucked under his arm. "Are you Lieutenant Reed?"

"Call me Skye. Is there a problem?"

"Governor Harrison wants to see you. Come this way."

"Can we drop the casualties off at the medical center first?"

"My team will see to that. We can't leave him waiting."

Skye reluctantly nodded and followed him past the factory toward the headquarters, a drab steel building with eight plastic windows.

The Zeta officer held open the entrance door and led Skye past a sparse reception area with a tatty calendar on the wall. They stopped outside a blue door with *Governor* stenciled on it in black lettering.

The officer knocked three times and stood to attention. Skye followed suit, hoping to avoid any unwanted scrutiny.

Footsteps pounded inside, and the door swung open. The instantly recognizable figure of Harrison stood in the entrance, dressed in his officer's jacket with light blue epaulets. He beckoned her into his office. "Lieutenant Reed, I haven't seen you for years."

"Hello, Governor. I've been busy around Omega. You know how things are."

He sat behind his desk and studied a piece of paper. "It says here that you've got three casualties. Is there anything else you need to tell me?"

Knowing Harrison deeper than his mask of civility, Skye decided to tell him about the shipment. The chances were that he already had his men look in the back of the truck while she visited the guardhouse.

"I've got a delivery for Foreman Rhodes."

"A sanctioned trade?"

"No. It's just an exchange of goods outside the system. No reason why we can't help each other, right?

He sucked on the end of a pencil and stared at her. Skye cursed Finch inside for putting her into this position.

"What do you have in the container?"

"Knowing Governor Finch, it's probably items scavenged from one of the old cities. I'm not trying to hide anything."

Harrison groaned and sat back. "Tell Finch he needs to speak to me personally in the future. I like to run a tight ship, which doesn't include having bric-a-brac passed around citizens."

"I understand, Governor. I'll be sure to tell him when I return to Omega."

"Make sure you do. Between talking about butterflies and searching for junk, I'm sure Finch has a brain in there somewhere."

"Can I make the delivery to Foreman Rhodes? I'd like to get back by last light."

"I'm coming with you. Rhodes has some questions to answer."

Skye nodded.

* * *

A worker directed Skye and Harrison to the far end of the factory. Rhodes, a middle-aged man dressed in navy coveralls, stood by a large open door that led to the hemp fields outside. He looked surprised to see them both and walked across the smooth stone floor to meet them.

"Can I help you?" he said and nervously fidgeted with his cuff.

Harrison jabbed a finger into his chest. "Lieutenant Reed tells me you've got a delivery from Finch. Why didn't you tell me about it?"

"It's nothing, Governor. Just some old tools we're exchanging. He sends me the surplus from Omega. I send him our broken ones."

"Why does he accept the trade?"

"I don't know. We usually throw them away. I've managed to get us a return."

Harrison took a step back and smiled. "I bet the selfish idiot uses them in his garden. Bring me some items from the container so I can inspect them."

"Yes, Governor. I'll do it when I finish my shift."

"Make sure you do. If I find out you're lying …"

A machine rattled behind Rhodes. He glanced over his shoulder and back at Harrison. "Would you like me to give Lieutenant Reed a tour of the factory?"

Harrison sighed. "If you must. I'm sure, like me, she's got better things to be doing."

"I don't mind," Skye said to the governor. "Beats patrolling the Omega rampart."

"Forgive me if I don't stay for the whole show?"

"I won't be offended, Governor," Rhodes said. "You know this place back to front."

"No need to kiss my ass, Rhodes. Get on with it."

Rhodes led them to a large container with a pulley system on the side of it. "From the hemp fields you saw on the way up, we move the harvest to here. This is where we process the plants. We separate the woody core from the bast fiber with a hammermill."

"Interesting," Skye said, but felt the opposite.

Harrison wasn't even listening. He followed four yards behind them and fiddled with his radio. A spinning machine started to clatter on the far side of the factory.

Rhodes raised his voice. "The bast fiber is then cleaned and carded to the desired core content and fineness. Isn't that right, Governor?"

Harrison looked up. "What?"

"I was telling Lieutenant Reed about the cleaning and carding."

"Right. Cleaning and carding. Carry on."

"We carry out a chemical removal of the natural binders to produce weavable fiber."

Harrison covered his mouth and yawned. "I'll leave you in the capable hands of Foreman Rhodes. Make sure you tell Finch what I told you."

"I will, Governor. Nice to meet you again."

He narrowed his eyes and turned to Rhodes. "And you. Don't forget to bring me a selection of those tools. I need to decide if I can distribute them more efficiently."

"Yes, sir. I'll do it tonight."

Harrison gave Rhodes an extended glare before leaving by the open factory door.

Skye watched him leave and let out a deep breath. Acting was never her strongest quality, and now she was firmly part of whatever Finch and Rhodes had going on.

"Thought the old coot was never going to leave," Rhodes said, changing his tune from nervous to confident. "Best way to get rid of him is to start explaining just what we real citizens are doing. All he's bothered about is running his damned group of bullies."

"I don't appreciate you or Finch compromising me like this. I only agreed to do it as a one-off favor."

Rhodes smiled. "It's really no big deal. Be comforted by the fact that you're helping the people who deserve it the most."

"Finch said the same thing. I doubt it will help at my court-martial."

"It won't come to that. Trust me."

Rhodes appeared and sounded more genuine than all of the officials in Zeta. She gazed out to the hemp fields. Rows of men and women, with baskets hung around their necks, stooped and collected the latest harvest. All were dressed in nothing more than glorified rags. A telling sign from a place that regularly sent clothes to the other seven strongholds.

If the delivery helped the workers, it at least provided a justification against the risk involved in carrying it out. This place was probably heading for a revolution.

Rhodes gestured his head to a dark corner of the factory. Skye followed him, and they stood behind a stack of compressed hemp.

"Let's get down to serious business," Rhodes said. "Finch tells me you're one heck of a tracker. Did he mention what the outlaws are doing to my workers?"

"He said you were having a problem but didn't go into specifics. Before you continue, it's only fair to tell you that I haven't made my mind up yet."

Rhodes nodded and glanced in both directions. "We have fields spread outside the city walls. I found a perfect spot a mile west, and we send workers out every day."

"The outlaws are attacking Zeta workers? What for?"

"We send out a supply of food so they don't have to come back for lunch. At first the outlaws raided us for food. The attacks have gotten worse lately. Some of the things they've done to those poor girls …"

He closed his eyes and bowed his head. Skye hadn't heard of this type of behavior before, apart from a few old stories about wastelanders. The thought of it disgusted her.

"Do they take the women?" she asked.

"Yes, and murder our men. It's spiraling out of control, and we need to stop it."

"Why won't Harrison do anything? Doesn't it put pressure on your workforce and clock?"

"Some of the workers aren't officially on the clock. He calls it his expendable resource pool and doesn't bother sending out guards. They have to use their farming tools to defend themselves."

"That's illegal. Does Trader know about it?"

"What do you think? We're not exactly above the law ourselves."

"Tell me about their leader. How do you know he's responsible?"

"It started getting worse after he showed up. It's always the same story. A man with a graying black beard, directing a band of outlaws. They attack any individual who strays from the group."

The thought of being one of his victims sent a chill down her spine. Nobody deserved to be subjected to that kind of abuse. "Can you give me a description and possible location?"

"Finch told me you were the right woman for the job and would understand. I've already prepared the details."

He handed her a rolled piece of paper. Skye stuffed it into the thigh pocket of her cargo pants. She still didn't like the idea of killing a man in cold blood, but this outlaw deserved everything that was coming to him. If Zeta wouldn't make him pay, she would.

"Consider it done, Rhodes."

Chapter Nine

Trader led the convoy toward the first bunker. Jake had visited three installations before, but not this one. From a distance the layout looked familiar. A large flat area, roughly three square miles, surrounded by a chain-link fence, a building by the gate and one over the top of the bunker's entrance. The loading doors were obscured by a grass mound three hundred yards from the building and could only be opened internally. All pretty unexceptional to a casual observer. It was designed to be that way.

"Sure you remember the code? That chamber hasn't fried your brain?" Trader said.

"You just get me there. I'll open the loading doors if the bunker has power."

Jake couldn't forget *072069*, the date man first stepped foot on the moon. Fingerprint recognition was also required for access. Keeping the code to himself would provide his ongoing usefulness. A finger would be easy to snip off a dead body.

"Good. We'll load up, and I'll make my other delivery to Sigma. That's where we stay between trades. I think you'll like it."

"If it's anything like Omega, I doubt it."

Trader laughed. "There's only a couple like Finch. Sigma is probably the closest thing to the world you remember, and they don't have a butterfly-obsessed leader."

"What are you hoping to find here?"

"I'm hoping you can find me things. Weapons, technology, supplies, tools, anything that can make our society stronger."

Jake cast his mind back to the first time he toured one of the underground facilities. He walked around the cavernous cryo-warehouses filled with vats of water, equipment and freeze-dried food. Corridors led to smaller storage units stocked with frozen produce like milk, meat, eggs and vegetables. It also had an airtight armory housing rifles, machine guns and guided weapons. The duplex living quarters had stasis pods on the lower floor, and an operations room, kitchen, bedrooms and a social area on the upper level. All areas were controlled by a sophisticated management system in the operations room, which monitored each part and isolated any individual problems. The techs called it compartmentalization.

"There's more than two of these places," Jake said. "I know locations in Wyoming."

"It's enough for now. We've got plenty of time on our hands, and it'll tell us if it's worth finding more."

The chain-link fence undulated in height around the facility's perimeter where some of the supports had collapsed. On the standing sections, rusty chain-link curled up from the ground where the fastenings rusted away and the fence pinged free.

An early evening breeze sent a ripple across the waist-high grass inside the facility. The front gate, also chain-link with a steel frame, loosely hung from its bottom hinge. Trader aimed the SUV at it and accelerated. Jake braced himself. The front bull-bar crashed against it, and it flew to the left with a metallic rattle.

He skidded to a stop outside the ivy-covered topside building. The other seven vehicles followed, flattening the plants that sprang from the cracks in the concrete paving, and came to a halt in an extended line.

The setting sun shined directly through the windshield, warming Jake's face.

Trader opened the SUV's rear door and passed Jake a black handheld spotlight that looked like a police speed gun. "You'll be needing this."

Jake clicked it on and off. "Bunkers were designed to last a thousand years. Unless it's been sabotaged or suffered a chronic system failure, we should be okay once we're in."

"We'll see about that," Trader said and turned to his assembled team. "Tess and Pete, come with us and secure the area. The rest of you keep watch until we confirm entry and removable contents."

A tall, stocky man with red hair organized the team around the building. Two split off and joined Jake and Trader.

Only a few faded light blue patches of paint were left on the rusty door. Trader shoved the handle down and shouldered it open.

Jake peered inside the gloomy entrance. Thin light radiated through the dirt-stained window, illuminating a workstation in the corner. Mold spores freckled the leather swivel chair and gray laminate desk. The cracked monitor screen and keyboard had dust smeared away from their surfaces. They would be far too eroded to use; besides, the topside building took its power from conventional sources.

"This way," Trader said and flicked on his spotlight.

Jake did the same and followed him through the office along a dark corridor. Floorboards creaked beneath his feet, and he ducked under a cobweb. The configuration matched the bunker he previously visited one hundred and thirty-five years ago. In the room at the end of the corridor, Trader shone his beam at the circular steel hatch. The floor tiles that used to cover it were piled in the far left corner.

He waved Tess and Pete forward. They both grabbed each side of the hatch wheel and twisted. Metal threads screeched against each other as they rotated it open. Not quite as bad as fingernails along a chalkboard, but close. Pete grabbed the raising handle, grunted and pulled it open. It dropped backward with a hollow thud, sending a puff of dust into the dank air.

Jake shone his spotlight down the vertical shaft. A metal ladder was attached to a smooth concrete wall and descended two hundred feet. Staff usually entered through the loading doors after using the topside intercom. This hatch was designed as an emergency or reconnaissance exit after bunker lockdown.

"How did you know it was here?" Jake said.

"People have known for years," Trader said. "You'll see when you get to the bottom."

Jake attached the spotlight to his webbing belt so the light shone by his feet. "Here goes."

The ladder felt chilly against his hands, and the temperature dropped as he descended, sending a shiver down his spine. Jake gripped each rung tightly and maintained three points of contact. His spotlight flashed around the wall below with each step down.

He looked up and squinted at Trader's spotlight, stabbing through the dark and dazzling his eyes. The hole at the top gradually reduced in size, and the clinking echo of hands and boots against metal increased.

Jake felt vibrations through the ladder and the sound of rifles scraping against the side of the shaft. The others climbing down. He looked between his legs to where his spotlight's ray hit the ground twenty feet below. He increased his speed of descent, and his boots landed on the solid surface.

Jake shone his spotlight along a sparse, musty smelling, forty-yard tunnel and moved his beam around the blast door at the end. A metal guard surrounded the entry panel on the left wall.

Trader wheezed down the last few rungs and let out a deep breath. "Shouldn't have started smoking. Bad for my health."

"Driving between strongholds under the constant threat of attack isn't good for it either," Jake said.

"True enough. But what we find here might help."

Pete and Tess quickly followed. She dusted herself down and clicked on a head torch. Jake walked along the tunnel toward the blast door. Dew covered the walls and dripped from the roof. Dark lines formed in the concrete where it had cracked and decayed; patches of mold surrounded them. The internal bunker walls were twice as thick as the entry tunnel's. He hoped the rot hadn't set in too deep.

The blast door had scratches and small dents around the edges, and two black explosion marks against the bottom of it. Probably feeble attempts to get in with tools and a couple of grenades.

Jake pointed to the minor damage. "This your work, Trader?"

He shrugged. "Had to at least try, didn't we?"

"And destroy the panel in the process? Not the smartest move."

"It's still intact. Do your work."

Trader creaked the protective shield to one side and revealed a silver box. A weak blue light illuminated around the edge of each circular key and the black thumb screen to the left of it.

Jake protected the keypad with his body, keeping it out of sight, and keyed in the code. A green LED winked continuously. He pressed his thumb against the pad. Nothing happened.

"Do we have a problem?" Trader said.

Jake felt conscious that he had his back to three armed people, who had rescued him from Omega and expected him to open the bunker. He already witnessed how brutal this new world could be.

"Give me a second," Jake said.

He licked his finger and smudged it across the thumb screen before keying in the code again. Taking a deep breath, he pressed his thumb firmly on the pad again.

The winking light turned solid green.

A boom echoed along the tunnel after the heavy bolts of the triple lock system snapped back into the door. It yawned open, and a blast of warm air rushed out. Jake's pulse raced at the thought of touching his own reality again.

Only five of the hundred ceiling lights in the cryo-warehouse were on, casting a faint radiance over the fifty rows of tall metal shelves below. At the far end, elevated above the infrastructure, monitors glowed from behind the control room's observation window.

Rapid footsteps slapped against the warehouse surface. A man wailed.

Jake drew his gun.

Trader and his two-man team advanced. He held his arm out to stop them.

"This is Captain Jake Phillips of Endeavor Three. Identify yourself."

The sound of a slamming door reverberated around the warehouse.

"He must be one of yours," Pete said. "We would've known if somebody came out here."

"If the wastelanders didn't get them first," Jake said.

"Doesn't mean to say that someone hasn't come in," Trader said.

"Not likely. Unless it's one of the other captains from my bomber."

The idea of it excited Jake, but he wanted to maintain his composure and not let his thoughts run wild. They had stasis pods in here too, and the occupant might be another Rip Van Winkel. The nickname amused rather than offended him. People who couldn't take a joke or nickname usually suffered in the Fleet. Rightly or wrongly, it was just the way things worked.

"Do you know the layout?" Tess said.

Jake nodded. "Follow me. He's probably gone to the living quarters."

He crept forward and swept his gun across the warehouse. Shelves towered over him at either side. Two sacks of grain had burst across the floor. Empty packets of freeze-dried food littered the lower shelves. Supplies were being used, and plenty of them.

Pete and Tess prowled along between two aisles. Jake edged around a small lift truck with a half-full crate of sugar balanced on its forks and moved along the side of the facility.

The ceiling lights flickered off.

Jake crouched against the shelves. He heard the others shuffling to cover.

Trader raised his spotlight. Through the gaps in the shelves, Tess' head torch shone down in front of her. She adjusted the beam to her front.

"Pete, where are you?" Trader said.

"One row across."

"Get over here. We need to stick together."

Pete ran toward the end of the aisle. A quicker route to get to Trader's position, rather than doubling back. Jake heard a twang, like a guitar string snapping.

"Get down!" he shouted.

He dove behind the truck. Trader skidded across the floor next to him.

A deafening blast ripped through the air, accompanied with a blinding flash of light. The shelves rattled. A sack split above him and dried peas rained on his head.

Pete cried in anguish.

A high-pitched tone whistled in Jake's ears. He sprang to his feet, grabbed Trader's arm, and hauled him up.

"What the hell?" Trader said.

"Trip wire. Looks like he's booby-trapped the place."

Jake shone his spotlight three feet in front, and slowly moved around to Pete. Tess knelt over him and sliced open the right leg of his cargo pants with a knife.

Pete screwed his face up and tried to lean up to look at his leg. Trader focused his light on a bloodied gouge in his calf.

"We'll get you out of here. Don't worry about that," Trader said.

Pete hissed through clenched teeth. "How bad is it?"

"You'll live. Straight back to Sigma when we've finished here."

"I'll get the others," Tess said.

Jake decided to take the lead. They needed to be assertive. If the occupant had rigged trip wires across the warehouse, he'd have a gun trained on it too, turning the place into a killing ground.

"We need to move," Jake said. "Tess, help Pete back to the tunnel and take care of him. If you can't stop the bleeding, tourniquet his leg. Trader, let's go."

Tess looked at Trader.

"Do it," Trader said.

"Double back and make our way around the edge," Jake said. "Take it nice and easy and get to the upper level. He must've hit the lights in the control room."

They were probably facing a military man. If they came back later, the defenses might be stronger.

Both he and Trader held their guns in their right hands and spotlights in the other. Jake retraced their steps and moved to the left edge of the warehouse. His light punched through the dusty darkness and searched the ground ahead of them.

In an ideal world he wouldn't advertise his position like this, but with the threat of trip wires and other potential dangers, they needed to carefully survey their route.

Jake stopped and crouched before reaching level with the light from Tess' head torch. He could see her applying downward pressure to Pete's shrapnel wound through a gap in the shelves. Pete held his hand over his mouth, trying to stifle his moans.

Something glinted ahead. Jake edged forward and identified another wire, a foot off the ground. He followed its line from a vent on the warehouse wall, across to the shelving units. Three grenades were taped to the leg of a unit. The wire attached to the pin of the middle grenade.

Trader crawled alongside him. "We can always come back."

"No. He'll be expecting that. If you send in a larger group, you'll pick up more casualties."

Jake stepped over the wire and checked for a secondary trap.

A burst of automatic gunfire rattled overhead. Rounds smacked into the wall above Jake. He rolled to his side. A muzzle flashed in the control room as another burst peppered the shelves close to Tess and Pete. One of the rounds ricocheted off the metal frame and whizzed through the air. The control room window's shattered glass showered the warehouse floor.

Jake carried out a quick search of the space between himself and the door to the upper level. Without seeing any signs of a trap, he flicked off his spotlight, jumped to his feet, and sprinted for the door.

He reached it in seconds and dragged it open. Blue light bathed the far end of the corridor, the area with huge cryo-units that contained frozen meat, dairy and vegetables. Jake's stomach growled, reminding him that he hadn't eaten for the last one hundred and thirty years, or ten hours if he wanted to be picky. That could wait.

Vinyl-covered stairs to his right led to the upper level. He aimed high and climbed, treading as softly as possible.

Three single shots echoed from the warehouse. A burst of automatic fire replied. Trader keeping the hostile occupant busy. At least he had the sense to realize Jake's play.

Jake reached the top and craned his neck around the corner. The monitors from the control room cast light from its open entrance into the gloomy corridor. Another burst of gunfire rattled. Shell cases clinked and rolled on the tiled floor.

He crept toward the entrance and listened. A man mumbled something, fired again. Jake heard the click and metallic slide of a magazine release. He seized the opportunity, swung around the door, and aimed at a skinny figure ducking below the window.

"Freeze. You've got three seconds to drop your rifle."

The man ignored him and fumbled with the magazine. A graying beard reached down past his chest. Stains covered his sky blue Fleet T-shirt and filthy white underpants. Red, green and blue lights flashed on the console behind him.

"Two."

He shot a wild glance at Jake through his red-rimmed eyes. The room stank of stale body odor.

"One."

The man dropped his magazine and rifle, and raised his shaking hands.

"Hit the lights," Jake said.

"Excuse me?" he said in a low voice.

"I'm Captain Jake Phillips from Endeavor Three. Hit the lights. Now."

"You're one of us? Do you hear the voices?"

The man had clearly lost his marbles, but Jake knew that people in these types of situations needed firm direction. "I won't ask you again. Turn on the facility lights. I'm not going to hurt you."

He pointed at a monitor showing a view outside from the loading doors. "Crazy people attack them. It's not safe."

Jake stepped forward. The man scampered to the console. They were roughly the same height, just over six foot, but his stick-thin frame probably weighed about one hundred pounds. Half of Jake's fighting weight.

He pressed a series of buttons, and all one hundred lights flicked on in sequence across the warehouse. Fluorescent lights blinked on in the corridor and the control room. Deep wrinkles lined the man's face, and his fingernails were chewed down to the quick.

Jake edged to the window. A trail of blood led from Tess and Pete's position toward the tunnel. Trader hunched behind a metal crate by the wall.

"Get up here and bring some rope or ties," Jake called down.

Trader raised his hand in acknowledgment and searched the shelves.

"What do the voices tell you?" the man said.

Jake jerked his gun at a black ergonomic chair next to the console. "Take a seat."

The man flopped down and licked his lips. Jake slid the magazine and rifle away with his foot.

"Please don't take me outside," the man said. He locked his fingers together and shook his hands. "I'm begging you. From one officer to another."

"What unit are you with, and how long have you been down here?"

He looked confused and scratched his long greasy thinning hair. "I've always been here. He commands it."

Jake shook his head and sighed. This man needed help.

Trader banged up the stairs, entered the control room, and froze. He and the man stared at each other.

Jake took the small drum of orange plastic rope off Trader. "Can we take him to Sigma for treatment?"

"He tried to kill us, Jake. They won't accept someone like this on their clock."

"We don't have to tell them. He's lost his mind and needs help."

"It's not as simple as that."

"I've been meaning to ask you how these clocks work."

"He can't come with us. The world has changed, and you need to start getting used to it."

The man leaned forward. "Who is *he*? The cat's mother?"

Jake ignored him. "Just this once, for me. If they can nurse him back to health, who knows what information he might have?"

Trader rubbed his chin. "I could try to sell him like that. Just don't blame me if they refuse him entry."

"It's a deal."

This person was probably a man from Jake's world. Stasis and his solitary life in the bunker had affected his mind. Jake couldn't leave him here to rot in madness.

Jake lifted the man from his chair and pulled his arms behind his back. He tried to breathe through his mouth to avoid the stench.

"Please don't take me away," the man said.

He didn't have the strength to fight back as Jake bound his wrists. "This is for your own safety. We're taking you to get help. Relax and you won't get into any trouble."

Trader cupped his nose. "He's not riding with us."

"Put him in the back of one of the trucks."

Jake finished securing the man and scanned the console. The blast door button had a protected lock over the top of it. He popped it up and depressed the button below. A distant rumble echoed from the other side of the warehouse.

* * *

While Trader frog-marched the man up the long concrete ramp that led to the surface, and brought his men and vehicles down the ramp to collect supplies, Pete and Jake searched the facility.

He could see through the cryo-units' frosted windows that they were all empty of frozen food. Jake moved along to the armory and thumbed the pad outside. Oxygen hissed into the room from vents near the ceiling before the door slid open.

Only a single rifle was missing from the racks, and it lay on the control room floor. Trader would have his bounty of fifty rifles, forty pistols, thousands of rounds, ten guided weapons and a hundred missiles.

Jake shuddered when he thought of someone like Finch getting his greasy paws on an arsenal like this. He hoped Trader was the man of principle he claimed and supplied them responsibly.

Trader talked about learning from mistakes from the past. Building up forces and weapons capability had often been a precursor to war. Jake was aware that it took him less than twenty-four hours in his new world to boost their fighting capabilities. He decided to forget the other locations he knew about in Wyoming.

Vehicle engines revved in the warehouse and doors slammed. Jake returned upstairs to explore the living quarters.

Nearly all sixty beds in the long barrack room were neatly made with folded gray blankets, apart from one scruffy bunk in the corner. Empty cans, cartons and bottles piled around it. The man lived a tramp's existence, probably for a few decades, judging by the state of him.

Jake decided against going through the metal lockers by each bed. They would contain people's personal effects and clothing. It didn't feel right. If men and women weren't here, there was a chance they could still be in stasis, his next destination.

He descended a flight of stairs at the far end. The room below matched the dimensions of the one above. Silver stasis pods lined the walls on either side. These were in a standing up position, unlike the horizontal ones on Endeavor.

Red alarm lights flashed over every one. Jake checked the first on the right. The vital signs of the occupant were nonexistent on the status bar, and condensation covered the plastic lid. He pulled his cuff over his hand and wiped it.

The body inside, in a dark blue Fleet uniform, was in an advanced state of decomposition, almost a skeleton apart from the black skin that clung to the face. Jake checked the next two and found the same thing. Condensation covered the rest, but he didn't need to check. All but one of the pods were now rectangular coffins.

A monitor in the middle of the room reported the alarm history. He scrolled through to the start of the reported issues. The system suffered a chemical supply failure thirty years ago.

The man outside was probably on watch when it happened. There always had to be one person awake. He attempted ten system reboots. Clearly not a technical expert, as it was a supply rather than software issue.

Jake imagined the despair he would feel in the same situation. The world outside had gone, and he was responsible for maintaining the bunker's life. Everybody died on his watch, no wonder he went crazy.

He returned to the warehouse, feeling deep sadness at what occurred in the bunker. Jake consoled himself that their hope for the future was silently snatched away, unlike the victims of the war.

Trader's team were busy filling the trucks. He turned to Jake and smiled. "This is beyond our wildest dreams."

Chapter Ten

Skye stopped halfway up a scree slope and knelt next to a tree. The sketched map Rhodes gave her proved more useful than she initially thought. The basic drawing called out all of the main landmarks from the road as she headed east into new, more mountainous territory.

According to an outlaw Rhodes captured last week, the raiders were camped near a cave system shrouded by an alpine forest. She stood at the edge of the forest and would use her tracking skills from here to stalk her prey.

The dust storm had passed, and the setting sun cast long shadows on the ground. She needed to move if she wanted to take advantage of the remaining natural light. Approaching her target under the cover of darkness had its advantages, but not for this task. Skye needed to scan the ground for clues and wanted to get a clean shot from a distance to enable a safe escape.

She unstrapped her pack, drank some water, and unrolled the pieces of paper that Rhodes gave her for a final examination. The drawing of her target looked pretty generic, a bearded man, although he was missing his left eyebrow. Skye hoped it wasn't an oversight by the amateur artist.

The captive named him as James Ryder. Other than being a thorn in Zeta's side, his history was unknown. He hated the strongholds and their way of life, and made it his personal crusade to disrupt their activities. She hoped, like other leaders of their world, he would take advantage of his position and be easily identifiable through clothing or living arrangements.

Nothing about his description sounded unusual for an outlaw. Most Skye encountered in the land around Omega were bitter about the strongholds. They made the choice not to conform. Nobody forced them to do it. Issues only arose when they attacked society's way of life, and Ryder took it to a new disgusting level.

Outlaws didn't want to understand that things were harsh, and a system was needed to ensure future survival and development. Their notional idea of freedom only meant severely limited resources and an increased danger to their lives. It led them to attack the very thing that provided a realistic way forward.

Skye strapped on her pack, shouldered her rifle, and crept through the trees, scanning for any signs of movement or unnatural disturbance on the loose stony ground.

The air cooled as she climbed higher and the sun continued to dip. If Ryder wasn't in his camp and the outlaws moved into the caves, things would become difficult. A clear sky meant it would be cold tonight, and waiting for her target to emerge would mean an uncomfortable night. Skye came prepared with a fleece and some food in her pack. She didn't have a time constraint on her mission and wanted to complete it and get back to Omega.

The ground between tree trunks became increasingly rocky, and no clear route led to the top of the hill. She could understand why the outlaws chose to hide out in this wild terrain.

Light footsteps pattered across a rock ahead. Skye crouched behind a boulder and focused on a small cluster of pines. A sentry positioned on the outskirts of their camp might sound an alarm. Her mission wasn't to kill her way to Ryder. If her location was compromised, she would have to come back again.

She leaned down and pulled a dagger from her boot. Silent protection if an outlaw attacked. A gunshot would likely bring most of the outlaws to her position. Being captured was her worst nightmare, after hearing Rhodes' story.

A small wild dog shuffled out from the dry scrub a few yards away.

Skye moved to her left, hoping to avoid its attention. Her experience found them to be jittery animals, prone to barking and running if threatened.

Her foot slipped on a loose stone. It rolled away and bounced down the hill, pinging off larger rocks. The dog snapped its head in her direction.

Skye winced. It let out five loud barks and bolted away. In the silent alpine forest, that would be heard from a reasonable distance. Animal noises were common occurrences on this type of ground, but they were also a sign of human presence. She moved to her left and found some cover.

Skye waited for five minutes behind the trunk. Nobody came to investigate. With natural light fading, pulling away her chances of striking from a decent range, Skye continued forward until seeing the edge of a natural plateau ahead, with a rock face stretching above it. It matched Rhodes' description. She dropped to the prone firing position and leopard-crawled between two trunks.

A breath of wind blew through the pines, carrying a voice. Skye darted behind a jagged rock and peered over it.

Two men, dressed in filthy old Omega jackets, casually made their way down from the plateau. One carried a steel hunting knife.

"Where's that damn dog?" Knife said.

"He'll be around here somewhere."

"Explains the missing supplies."

The other man grunted.

They continued past Skye's position. She moved further around the rock to avoid being seen. It would just be a case of waiting for them to return to camp and continuing with her objective. Neither of the men seemed suspicious of the animal being disturbed.

Skye kept as still as possible and listened. Faint chatter carried on the breeze. Not from the men below, but from above. It had to be the camp.

Five minutes later they trudged back up the hill and chatted to each other while looking straight ahead. This time they passed within twenty yards, picking a line through the rocks to avoid climbing.

"We ain't finished checking the perimeter."

"Ryder won't know the difference, come on."

"You never catch those damned things."

"You can talk."

They continued forward. Skye leaned over the rock. The man with the knife reached the top of the plateau, tucked his hunting knife in his belt, and looked directly back at her position. Skye immediately ducked down.

"Put your hands in the air. No fast movements," a male voice said behind her.

Skye looked over her shoulder. A pistol was aimed at her head.

A young man with greasy brown hair smiled. "One of the oldest tricks in the book. You Zeta people are so predictable."

Skye raised her hands. "I'm from Omega. I only came to observe."

He laughed and shook his head. "Do you think we haven't got watchers all over this place? I'll give you some credit. You got closer than most others."

The two other men bounded down the hill and stood on top of the rock.

Knife looked down at Skye. "I never like playing the stupid one, but it works."

She shrugged. The thought of what they might do to her gave Skye the biggest concerns. "Let me go. I won't say a word or return. I promise."

"Our orders are to bring in any intruders alive. Unless they cause problems. Do you have any other weapons besides the rifle?"

Skye reached into her boot, slipped out the dagger, and threw it to the ground. Striking out would probably mean a swift end. If they took her to see Ryder, that would be the time to fight. If she was going out, at least she'd bring him down too.

The man holding the pistol leaned over her. "Sorry about this."

"Sorry about wha—"

She felt a sharp blow against the side of her head. The forest blurred and her shoulder hit the ground.

* * *

Skye felt dull pain above her left ear. She shivered and opened her eyes. The cool air set about her skin, causing goose bumps to rise on her arms. Flickering torches attached to rocky walls lit up a cavernous area around her, highlighting stalactites. A drop of water fell and landed in a pool on the ground. The impact echoed around the cave. The sound of chatting came from the next chamber.

Her wrists were bound with thick rope. She struggled to wriggle her hands free, but they'd done a good job. At least they hadn't tied her ankles. Skye gingerly rose to her feet and leaned against the cold stone wall.

A man appeared in the entrance. "Nice to see you're awake."

He moved along the ledge toward her and ducked under two torches. Skye squinted into the gloom and tried to judge his intent. An orange glow from a tobacco pipe lit up his face. Bearded with a missing left eyebrow. The outlaw, James Ryder.

"What are you going to do to me?" Skye said.

"Strange question. I think what you were going to do to me was more of the issue. Wouldn't you say?"

Skye decided to stick with her original story. "Nothing. I came to observe."

"Sure you did. You got a heck of a lot closer than any of the others before you."

"Lucky me."

"My man tells me you came alone. Why?"

With her tracking skills and aim with a sniper rifle, Skye thought she didn't need anyone else. Ryder's men had proved her wrong.

"Who says I'm alone?"

Ryder puffed twice on his pipe and laughed. "I do. I'm sure you're the best they've got, but it takes more than that to get the better of us. What was in it for you, a promotion?"

"None of your business. Kill me if you want, but if any of your men get even the slightest thought of *interfering* with me …"

Ryder raised his eyebrow. "Is that what they told you? My men are good people. We have women and children here. Don't judge us because we're not part of your tyrannical system."

"I was told your gang killed people. Attacked and captured women. You've been doing it to Zeta for months. They don't sound like model citizens to me, Ryder."

"So you figure because we don't have shiny tags around our necks, that makes us monsters? Most of the people here are only here because of the flaws in your precious strongholds. If you don't fit into their perfect little pigeon holes, you're cast out as a criminal."

"Are you claiming that you and your people have never broken a law?"

He sat on a rock next to her and pulled a knife out of his belt. "Your laws are not our laws. We're free people, not sheep following the will of a lost shepherd."

"Laws and systems are there to govern and ensure the safety of citizens. Without them it would be anarchy. Our very survival depends on it."

Ryder leaned forward, slipped his knife between Skye's hands, and sawed through the rope with the serrated edge. Skye gently caressed the red marks on her sore wrists.

"Is it enough just to survive?" Ryder said. "Humans have always been defined by our ability to adapt, grow and learn as a species. Putting a leash that tight around your neck stiffens everything. The strongholds are blind to the fact they are stuck in a bubble. Honestly, I really thought the daughter of Thomas Reed would be more open-minded."

Skye tilted her head to the side. How could he possibly know that?

"So you are Tom's girl. You look just like him, and I heard you settled in Omega."

"You knew my parents?"

"Friends of mine, for my part anyway."

"That's impossible. How …"

"Did fine upstanding citizens like your parents get to be friendly with a filthy outlaw? That's what you're wondering, right? I had tags just like you. Hell, I ran a whole section of the Omega wall. Just couldn't keep my mouth shut."

"You're from Omega?"

"Sigma till I was about eighteen. They transferred me to Omega after they had a clock increase and needed more guards. When Finch's coup went off, fifteen or so years back, he offloaded me. If you question that guy, there's only one way you're going."

"I know Finch. He's not like that."

"Are you seriously telling me you've been living there all these years and people haven't disappeared? Talk to some of my people. They'll tell you about the man beneath the mask."

Skye shook her head. "You just have a different idea of freedom."

"The system is all he cares about. If you don't blindly follow, which I assume you do, you're an outlaw in his eyes."

She didn't expect a rational conversation with this man. Ryder seemed reasonable, although deluded with his views of the world. If her parents considered him a friend once, she struggled to believe he could be all the things Finch and Rhodes described him to be. That meant someone was lying to her.

"Why didn't my parents take you in after you lost your tags?"

"I suspect if I asked Tom, he would have, but I never did. I'm happy being free. He was a good man, and we shared a lot of the same views. He felt we should work to change the system from the inside."

"Did you lose touch with him after that?"

"He helped us out with supplies when times were tough. Your mother too, with the sweetest apple pie I ever tasted. They were the real good guys in this whole damned mess."

One of the few memories that always came back was her mother serving a large slice of steaming apple pie. The hint of cinnamon, buttery pastry and thick cream were almost real enough to smell in her mind. Ten years had done nothing to stop the craving.

"You'll have to forgive me for being more than a little confused, Ryder."

"I'm sure you expected me to be an ogre. Sorry if I've disappointed you."

"Let me go back to Omega. I'll investigate your claims. This isn't the first piece of corruption I've discovered today."

Ryder smiled. "I wouldn't let Tom's kid risk herself at my expense. You're staying here until we move on."

"Why? I can see you're not a murderer. I won't say a word."

"It's only for a day or two. Once they work out you've failed, Finch'll send a bigger crew. We'll be gone and you can rejoin them."

Rapid footsteps echoed through the cave. Ryder reached for his pistol and turned to the gap between the two chambers. A man ran through, rested his hand on the wall, and took a few deep breaths. He swallowed and looked up. "We've got company."

Ryder turned to Skye and narrowed his eyes. "How many did you bring?"

"I came alone and wasn't followed."

The man shuffled along the ledge and grabbed his shoulder. "It's wastelanders."

"Let me help you," Skye said. "I fought off a group this morning."

Ryder tapped his pipe on the ground and scraped his foot on the glowing embers. "Wait here until we've seen them off."

"I'm serious. They'll kill me as quickly as they'd kill you. Give me my rifle. It'll increase your chances."

He thought for a moment and nodded. "This way."

Ryder led her through the gap into a larger chamber. Women and children huddled together on rags stretched over the ground. Old wooden boxes filled with food and tools sat scattered around them.

Skye noticed her rifle balanced on top of one of them. She didn't hesitate to ask Ryder and rushed over. A young woman of a similar age had her arm around a small boy, who buried his face in her armpit. She glanced up at Skye with fear in her eyes. Skye gave her a reassuring nod and rejoined Ryder, who stood by the next entrance.

"There's three chambers to this cave system. We defend from outside and inside the front one. If anyone gets through, God help us."

She followed him to the front chamber. A rough, thirty-yard-wide, circular space. A single torch on the right-hand wall provided gloomy light. The shadow of flames licked along the roof.

Twenty of Ryder's group knelt in the middle and aimed their weapons at the elevated six-foot-wide entrance. Skye crouched next to a man holding a shotgun with a box of shells by his side. She stared at the dark entrance. Wastelanders screamed outside. A usual battle cry when they spotted a potential victim.

Two gunshots split the air.

Six of Ryder's men darted through the entrance and joined the rest in the middle of the chamber. One ran straight to him. "They're nearly here. We had no chance holding them off at the ledge. There's too many."

"How many?" Ryder said.

"Maybe fifty? It's too dark. They killed Andrey."

The screams stopped. Somebody grunted outside. Feet scraped against scree. A stone rolled through the entrance and bounced down the rocks and landed in the chamber.

A figure shot through the gap and roared.

Chapter Eleven

Trader's team secured the man from the bunker in the back of one of the trucks, away from the weapons, food and radios they took. Jake closed the loading doors and exited back through the shaft. They could visit at least another thirty times and still wouldn't have room for everything. Being the only one who could get in gave Jake an insurance policy.

The convoy headed for Sigma along a dirt track surrounded by rolling green fields and patches of woodland. He found it a welcome relief to be away from the tight confines of the forest, vegetation-hugged highway and claustrophobic bunker. From the sun's low position in the late spring sky, they had an hour of natural light left, making it roughly seven o' clock.

"You're quiet, Jake," Trader said.

"I've had a lot to absorb today. How long till we get there?"

"Ten minutes. It's over the next hill."

"Don't suppose you've got a spare watch?"

Trader unfastened his black plastic watch strap and handed it over. "Take mine. I've got a couple of spares at home. Anything else?"

Jake buckled it around his wrist and looked at the basic digital face. 18:45, Monday May 19th, 2205. Perhaps today's society didn't need that kind of grounding information, but Jake felt lost without it. The Fleet did that to a person.

With Trader wanting to engage in conversation, Jake decided to delve a little deeper into how the strongholds operated behind the curtain of solidarity. "A guard in Omega suggested the population clock wasn't as businesslike as what I've been led to believe."

"Oh? What did he say?"

"In Omega, you're only a number as long as Finch allows it, and there's something ugly under the surface."

"The theory behind controlling the population numbers in line with resources is sound. We never overstretch ourselves. It's worked for five generations, and all eight strongholds are signed up."

"What happens to the people turned away or the ones who get thrown out?"

"Some people are happy outside the system. We can't force them to take part in our society."

Jake shook his head. "That doesn't answer my question."

"It's not for me to make the laws in individual strongholds. I ensure their economies remain balanced by analyzing their resources and deciding on their trade prices. If Finch sees fit to kick people out, for whatever reason, that's his business."

"Seems to me like you're turning a blind eye to the Pol Pot impersonators like Finch. Have you seen his manor and back garden?"

"You underestimate him. I did too. After taking over Omega, he's doubled its size and beefed up defenses. He might be a weirdo, but he runs a tight ship. If that means a few people fall by the wayside, unfortunately that's how it is."

"People aren't just numbers that you can dismiss at your leisure. Where's the accountability?"

Trader rolled his eyes. "Drop the human rights bullshit, you're boring me. This is 2205, get used to it."

He lit a cigarette and lowered his window.

* * *

At the top of the rise, Jake caught his first glimpse of Sigma below. Built in a natural basin, its dark square walls had stone towers at each corner and surrounded an area similar to the size of Omega. Most of the properties packed to the left side had terracotta-tiled roofs. Warehouses and yards lined the right-hand side. A road ran up the middle of the stronghold to a three-story white stone building at its center.

"I take it that's the local lord's place?" Jake said.

"It's the administrative center. They're organized in terms of resource allocation and output. Makes my job harder when the likes of Kappa perform so poorly in comparison. They want to expand their clock to nine thousand, but we're blocking it at the moment."

"Who are *we*, and why is it being blocked?"

"I sit with the eight stronghold leaders every quarter. We review progress and decide on expansions or reductions, depending on how things are going. A unanimous vote is required to rubber-stamp any changes. The concern here is Kappa will become too powerful."

"Won't it cost you in the long run? You're potentially sentencing thousands of people to die in the wilderness and might create resentment in Sigma."

"Equilibrium, Jake. Remember the equilibrium."

Jake detected rising irritation in Trader's voice and decided not to press any further for the moment. He didn't have a problem understanding the logic behind the system. His issue was how it worked in practice. The idea that a life could be passed off as acceptable collateral damage on the whim of a fruitcake like Finch. Or that growth and ambition could be stifled in order to keep the status quo. At first glance, their monopolistic regimes were only a whisker away from communism.

Trader waved an arm out of his window as he approached the tall iron gates. They slowly opened, allowing the convoy access. He drove along the central tarmac road toward the administrative center. The yards on the right contained timber, bricks, dusty paper sacks and sheets of glass. Smoke pumped from the chimneys of two steel-constructed factories.

The smart stucco-sided homes on the left side of the stronghold started from just inside the stone wall, and were built in a grid system with small grassed front gardens surrounded by white picket fences. The terracotta roof tiles gave them a Mediterranean look.

"Nicer than Omega," Jake said. "Do they just trade the surplus?"

"One thing we can't stop is the strongholds keeping the best materials for themselves. What would you do in their shoes? I wouldn't expect Sigma to live in wooden bungalows while helping to build houses like this for Finch."

"They hold onto their top-end materials, and Finch gets to keep his prize carrots."

Trader laughed and coughed. He beat his chest three times with his fist. "Give it a couple of weeks and you'll come to appreciate the whole thing. We're meeting Sigma's governor now. Save the questions."

"No problem. He won't throw me in jail, will he?"

"She, and no, they don't have a jail here," Trader said coldly.

Jake didn't need to read too far between the lines to understand. Why build a jail when a person could be simply banished. The threat of it, especially with the increase in wastelanders outside, would be enough to keep people in check.

Trader parked outside the steps leading to the doors of the administrative center. The convoy rolled past, toward the other end of the stronghold.

A middle-aged woman with short mousy hair, dressed in black fatigues, walked out of the building into the fading light and acknowledged Trader with a nod. She looked at Jake and frowned. "Is that who I think it is?"

"Captain Jake Phillips of Endeavor Three," he said.

"My God, it's really you. How long have you been awake?"

"Less than a day."

"You must be a little confused."

"That's an understatement."

"I picked him up from Omega today," Trader said. "He got us into the western bunker, and I've got a few items for you. But there's a catch."

She groaned and shook her head. "There's always a catch with you. What is it this time?"

"Pete's got an injured leg and needs treatment."

"Okay, no big deal."

"Jake's joined my team, and we need a place for him. He led the assault inside the bunker."

"We've got thirty places on the clock. He sounds like a useful addition. Why do I get the feeling I'm not going to like the next part?"

Trader paused. Jake guessed the amiable governor was like an iron fist in a velvet glove to make a man like him hesitate over his next request.

"Come on, Trader. We're all busy here," she said.

"We found somebody in the bunker, and they also require treatment. I was hoping that you'd agree to take him in."

Her eyes narrowed. "What kind of injuries?"

"Ones of a mental nature. I have your goods from Theta and extra food and weapons from the bunker. Isn't it a small price to pay?"

The governor turned to Jake. "This is your idea, right? Trader isn't usually a kind-hearted soul. Did he tell you what happened last time I took in a crazy relic?"

"It's my idea," Jake said, attempting to hide his surprise at her question. "He's the only living link I have to the world I know. Trader didn't mention anything about other *relics*. What happened?"

"Eight years ago, we found him wandering around outside, shouting like a madman. I agreed to attempt his rehabilitation. He locked himself in a house and refused to come out. After a week of passing food through the window, my patience snapped, and we broke in."

"I heard stasis could have that effect if you're in for extended periods," Jake said. "I think I'm all right."

"You're lucky," she said. "He made a small bed for a teddy bear using pieces of wood and a cushion, a life support machine out of a tin box and some plastic tubes, and connected them to the teddy's mouth and wrist."

"I see what you mean," Jake said. "Where is he now?"

"He wouldn't leave the teddy, claiming it needed his treatment. When we removed it from the property, he hung himself with a leather belt. Do you see my reluctance at the request?"

"Just give him a few days. That's all I'm asking."

"I'll think about it," she said and turned to Trader. "I'd like to talk with you in private."

Trader nodded. "Jake, you'll find a bar around the back of the building. It's got a blue light outside. Tell them I sent you. I'll be ten minutes."

Jake stood for a moment, replaying the sobering story about one of his former colleagues through his mind.

The governor gave him a stern look. "If you want me to consider your request, you'll do as Trader says. He might be your boss, but while you're in Sigma, you're under my rules."

"Okay," Jake said. "Trader, I'll see you in ten minutes."

He didn't want to antagonize his chance of safety after his experience in the forest and on the highway. It grated on him that they'd immediately assumed the roles of his masters, but he had no choice. His favorite motto *Improvise, adapt and overcome* would just have to be trimmed to the first two words for now.

* * *

Light streamed out of the bar's four large opaque windows, dark figures sat inside. It had the same design as the houses in Omega, although twice the size. Jake stood under the blue light above the entrance in the chilly spring air and listened to the faint buzz of conversation occasionally punctuated by loud laughter.

The door swung out and a man dressed in a purple jumpsuit staggered past Jake. A rush of warm air mixed with the smell of stale beer simultaneously escaped into the quiet street. The man leaned against the wall and lit a cigarette.

Jake propped the door open with his hand.

A man at the bar looked over his shoulder. "Were you born in a barn?"

"Excuse me?"

"Shut the damned door."

Patrons, all dressed in the same clothes as the smoker, sat at eight round wooden tables on the right side. A few glanced up after the man's shout. A few had filthy faces. Jake guessed they were factory workers having a drink after a shift. To the left, six people perched on high metal stools at the copper-plated bar. The walls were painted in dark green emulsion and had four old-fashioned gold-plated light fittings attached just above head height in each corner.

He decided to act as naturally as possible to avoid attracting any unwanted attention. The barman rubbed a glass with a white towel and whispered something to a man sitting opposite him.

The conversation quieted to a hush. Jake creaked across the floorboards toward the bar. He looked at the unbranded spirits attached to the wall behind it. Each bottle had a white sticker with the type of liquor written in blue marker pen.

The barman, a stout bald man with a slug-like mustache, threw his towel over his shoulder. "Can I help you?"

"Trader sent me. Do you have a glass of water?"

A couple of the men either side of him snickered.

"We've got beer, whiskey, rum, gin and vodka," the barman said. "What would you like?"

It felt like the whole pub focused on his position. A middle-aged man with a greasy brown mullet and beard leaned over. "Why don't you give sleeping beauty a whiskey? That might put hairs on his chest."

The barman stifled a laugh, slammed a shot glass down, and filled it. Jake nodded and hunched over it, keen to avoid eye contact. The drink smelled like a postman's sock, and he twisted the rim in his fingers.

Mullet pulled his stool closer. "It ain't gonna drink itself, sleeping beauty."

His boozy breath barely masked his body odor. Jake turned to face him. "It wasn't funny the first time. I'm just here for a quiet drink."

"You hear that, boys? Sleeping beauty's here for a nice quiet time."

Most of the thirty people gazed over, but none reacted to Mullet's apparent joke. He spun back around and glared at Jake.

Jake said to the barman, "Has a local village reported an idiot missing?"

Mullet sprang from his stool. Its legs screeched across the tiled floor. He stood next to Jake and held his arms out. "You want a piece of me, asshole?"

Jake tensed, ready to defend himself, but hoped Trader would walk through the door. One of his faults was not being able to bite his lip in these types of situations. He hated bullies or people who tried to intimidate others.

A tall lean man with receding black hair rushed over from one of the tables and pressed his hands against Mullet's chest. "Easy now, Walt. You've had a lot to drink, and you're on a final warning. Go home before you do something you regret."

"He called me an idiot, Roy. We can't let him just walk into our bar and start insulting us."

Roy pushed him further away. "You don't know the deal he's got with the governor. Seriously, have an early night."

Mullet scowled over Roy's shoulder. "Me and you are not through yet, history man."

Jake shrugged and drank his whiskey. He swallowed and screwed his face up as it burnt the back of his throat. It tasted like hot alcoholic vinegar. The barman went to refill the glass. He held his hand over the top of it. "One's fine, thanks. Trader'll be here soon."

Mullet stopped at the door. "Show him the statue. Tell him what we do with it."

"Call it a night, Walt," a woman said from a table. She glanced sympathetically toward Jake. He acknowledged her with a single nod.

Roy pulled a stool beside him. "Sorry about Walt. He's like that with anyone after a few drinks."

"No problem. He's not the first person I've met like that. What's with the statue?"

Roy's face reddened, and he bowed his head. "Nothing. He's had too much to drink. I'd take his word with a grain of salt."

"Why don't you show him?" the barman said.

"Trader will be here soon. He doesn't need to see it."

When something piqued Jake's curiosity, he had to know. Besides Mullet, the people in the bar didn't display any signs of aggression, so he felt comfortable pushing. "He's not here yet. Surely it can't be that bad?"

"All right," Roy said. "It's in the yard. Follow me."

He led Jake to the back end of the bar and along a tight corridor.

"Are you from Sigma?" Jake asked.

"Born and raised. I work on the central heating systems. I guess this all seems crazy to you?"

"It's more like going back in time, rather than forward."

Roy paused at the rear entrance and looked over his shoulder. "How do you mean?"

"You have the construction, electricity, firearms, vehicles, farming and basic technology. But you don't have things like cell phones, the Internet and television."

"We might one day. They'd only provide a distraction at the moment. The strongholds create what we need to survive and defend ourselves. I'm sure if we put our heads together, we could get nonessential items working, but they're a waste of resources."

"Understood," Jake said. Roy's statement made a lot more sense than some of the other logic he'd heard since waking. With a limited population, they had to prioritize. "How do you wind down? Do you play any sports inside the walls?"

Roy clicked a switch on the wall and opened the door. "We use this for entertainment after a few drinks."

A light illuminated a small enclosed yard outside. Six steel barrels lined the left-hand side. The two closest to the bar had tubes running from the top of them, through a gap at the bottom of the wall. A bronze statue sat on a stone plinth at the far end. Jake moved closer to get a better look.

The inscription plate read *A gift from Epsilon to our brothers in Sigma*. A cast of an Orbital Bomber had a bust of a man welded on top of it. He had *Phillips* on his name tag. Jake felt for his own tag and shook his head. He couldn't believe they made a statue of him and his ship.

"They sent it here thirty-five years ago," Roy said. "The old governor kept it outside the admin building for a couple of years, but people kept vandalizing it. He used to put it back when Epsilon visited, but it was soon forgotten about."

The statue's head had red paint splashed across its lips and dints in the forehead and cheeks. Four loose wooden rings hung around its neck.

Jake looped one over its head. "What are these for?"

"It's a game." Roy pointed to a yellow line painted across the cobbles. "You stand behind that and try to land a ring over the head. The last person to do it has to get the drinks."

Jake smiled. At least he provided them with some form of entertainment. He found it a relief to see a human side shining through their functional society.

The door swung open behind him. Trader stood in the entrance.

"I see you've found your statue. You're in my spare room tonight. I'll show you to it."

Jake checked his watch. Just past eight in the evening and he didn't feel tired. Then again, he'd slept for decades. "What did the governor want?"

"If I had any information from my scout. I sent him south to try to find out why we're seeing an increase in wastelanders."

"And did you?" Roy said.

"He should be close to the radiation zone tonight," Trader said. "We'll see what he reports back."

"Is she taking in the man from the bunker?" Jake asked.

"For the moment, but if we find any more in the bunker tomorrow, we can't bring them back."

"What time are we heading off?"

"We're hitting it at first light."

Trader grabbed the ring from Jake's hand and tossed it at the statue. It bounced off its head and fell to the ground.

Chapter Twelve

Deafening blasts of gunfire filled the chamber. A high-pitched whistle rang in Skye's ears. The wastelander who entered, with an axe raised over his head, collapsed forward and slid down five rocky steps to the ground in front of the team. Children screamed in the chamber behind them. A pungent smell of nitroglycerin hung in the air.

Ryder sprang forward, grabbed the axe, and returned to the extended line. He moved along the back of it at a running crouch and stopped next to Skye.

"One of us has to make it out of here," he said.

Skye leaned her head toward him but kept focus on the entrance. "What do you mean?"

"There's a way out in the third chamber. Climb the wall on the left side and you'll find a small tunnel. It leads to the east face."

"Take the children. I'm staying here to fight."

"They can't make it up. At least you can warn people what's coming."

"I already have. They don't take it seriously."

"If they don't, you need to think—"

Skye fired at two wastelanders who jumped through the entrance. The shotgun blasted to her right. One went down straight away. A spray of blood spattered the cave wall behind him. The other clutched her stomach and attempted to raise her spear. Her head snapped back after a round drilled through her forehead, and she fell lifelessly to the stone.

"Keep your composure, guys," Ryder said. "They can't all get in at once. Take aimed shots and conserve your ammunition."

His team appeared calm under his confident leadership. The more Skye got to see of him, the more she realized he couldn't be the man described on the note in her pack. Whoever organized this mission had a different kind of axe to grind.

A spear sliced out of the dark, flew over the heads of the men in the middle of the rank, and smashed against the wall behind them. One of the men reached back and pulled it by his side.

"How much ammo have you got?" Skye said.

"About twenty rounds each. We haven't been to Epsilon for a while. We'll use their weapons as a last resort."

Skye looked along the line. All of the men and women held stronghold-produced weapons. "They gave you all this?"

"You're not all assholes. People should listen to Beth and Barry."

She didn't feel upset at the revelation. Nothing told her these were bad people, and who could deny them protection against wastelanders. Her thoughts were dangerous to express in a stronghold, but in the cave, under attack, only a heartless soul would deny the outlaws a supply of weapons. Skye felt conscious that the trip had started to change her, but she needed to finish it in one piece to make that change worthwhile.

Ryder swung his rifle up and fired. A wastelander clutched his neck and dropped to his knees. One of Ryder's team ran forward, raised her pistol, and fired in the wastelander's face. She quickly retreated back. So far they efficiently held firm. It was hard to imagine the attacking wastelanders outnumbering the amount of ammunition.

"If our ammo runs low, you're out of here," Ryder said.

"Let's hope it doesn't get to that."

"What happened this morning at Omega?"

Omega defense forces were not permitted to discuss any threats or weaknesses with anyone unless they had Finch's personal approval. Right now, she didn't care and felt part of a different team.

"Twenty attacked the northern steps. First time I've seen a group like that. Have you heard of Sky Man?"

"I heard the rumors ten years ago. Nothing since. We've seen them heading north in the last few weeks. Any idea what's going on?"

She shook her head. "Your guess is as good as mine, but it only means trouble for both of us."

The cave fell silent. Shotgun wiped sweat from his brow, opened up a box, and stuffed six shells into his jacket pocket. Two of the team carried out a tactical reload, switching their rifle magazines.

A collective scream pierced the silence.

Ryder pulled his rifle tight against his shoulder. "This is it, guys. Get ready."

Figures moved outside. One of the team pumped two rounds into the darkness. Seconds later, eight wastelanders rushed through the entrance. The first two jerked and fell as rounds ripped through their bodies. Two darted to the right, two to the left. More poured through the entrance behind the first wave. The cave reverberated with the cracks of gunfire.

Skye twisted left, following a wastelander through her sights, and fired. He slumped against the wall and clutched his hip. Ryder fired at the other. In the corner of her eye, she saw one dive straight over the steps and land with a dull thud in front of the team. Shotgun fired at him from point-blank range.

She fired at the injured wastelander and struck him in the temple. Ryder took care of the other one on their side.

The team in the center continued firing. More wastelanders ran in. The ferocity of their suicidal attack didn't slow. The initial charge must have encouraged others waiting outside. They continued to advance without fear.

An axe spun through the air. One of Ryder's men let out an anguished cry. Skye glanced across. He fell backward with the axe buried in his chest. A woman turned to give him attention.

"Leave him," Ryder shouted. "Grab his ammo and continue the fight."

One of the men ran, skidded next to the casualty, and slipped his magazine out of his rifle. He replaced it in his own, turned and fired.

A large wastelander, dressed in dark brown animal hide, stopped in the entrance and held a metal tube to his mouth. Skye shot him in the stomach. He dropped to one arm before slumping on his face. She only had five rounds left. If they kept coming, the others would soon run out too.

Shotgun loaded two shells and fired at a wastelander who jumped from the ledge. Her shoulder jerked to the side, and she fell flat on her back.

"Cease firing," Ryder shouted.

No more ran through the entrance. Skye could hear them grunting at each other outside. Twenty bodies lay inside. Ten around the mouth of the cave, five in front of the team, and the others spread on either side. Two of the wastelanders groaned and tried to pull themselves along the ground.

The man hit by the axe coughed up blood, and it ran down the side of his pale cheek. He probably wouldn't live to see the sun rise. None of them would if the wastelanders continued to attack. A woman edged back and placed a hand on the wounded man's shoulder. He placed his quivering hand on top of hers and closed his eyes.

"Ammo check. One at a time," Ryder shouted.

"Five rounds."

"Seven."

"I'm out. Any spares for a rifle?"

The team carried on shouting the numbers in turn. The numbers didn't get any higher. Ryder tossed a full magazine along the line. "Split this between you. It's all we've got."

A flaming hay bale slid in front of the entrance. A wastelander must've shoved it. It rolled forward, tumbled down the rocky steps, and bounced in front of the team. Hot embers shot across the floor, and smoke puffed into the air.

One of the team pulled off their ragged old Omega jacket and beat it against the bale. Skye focused through the thin smoke at the entrance. Another flaming bale spun into the cave and rested on the ledge.

Three wastelanders tried to sneak up behind it. The team fired. Only a wastelander or a fool would think an object like that would provide cover. The smoke rising to the ceiling and slowly lowering was a bigger problem.

Ryder grabbed her shoulder. "Time for you to leave."

"I'm staying. This is my fight too."

"Don't be stupid. If this is a sign of things to come, you need to warn your people."

The team members on the far right fired. A wastelander fell in front of them. Skye hadn't run from a fight in ten years. It didn't feel right.

"I can't leave you here like this."

Ryder pulled Skye to a standing position and stared into her eyes. "I haven't got time to argue. Get the hell out of here and make a difference."

Skye turned and ran. She entered the second chamber and glanced to her left. Parents comforted their scared children, but didn't look in a much better state. She thought about turning and ignoring Ryder's order, but deep down she understood his logic. As much as it pained her heart, somebody had to survive and tell their story.

She kept on running to the third chamber. Gunfire rattled behind her as the attack continued.

* * *

Skye found a good foothold in the rock and hoisted herself higher. She told herself not to look down. After climbing thirty feet up the wall, a cool draft from the tunnel brushed against her face. Sporadic fire echoed through the chambers, becoming less frequent, but crucially still continuing. They hadn't been overrun yet.

While she never suffered from a fear of heights, falling from here would cause serious damage. A bead of sweat ran down her temple. She reached up and gripped a small outcrop and pulled to check its sturdiness.

Her left foothold crumbled, and she tensed against the rock face. Small pieces dropped and peppered the ground below. Skye's heart thumped against her chest. She scraped her left foot against the rough surface, searching for another foothold. After finding solid rock to take her weight, she paused to catch her breath.

Twenty more seconds of ascent would do it. Wind groaned through the tunnel above her. The ceiling wasn't much higher. She flexed her tired muscles and braced herself. A child screamed in the second chamber.

She placed her right foot into a fissure, gripped the side of it with her hand, and sprang up to a small ledge. This allowed her to stand and observe below. The flames on the torches had reduced in size. Thin gray smoke drifted through the entrance. Nothing moved below. Three single shots rang out.

Skye grabbed a six-foot cream-colored stalactite with her left hand. It immediately came loose and dropped. Dust puffed from the ceiling, and she blinked to clear her eyes. The stalactite shattered into pieces on the rocks below.

She looked up for a more reliable grip. Two small darker rocks jutted from just below the tunnel entrance. One last push to make it; then the hard work really started. Once outside, she had to negotiate her way back through the dark alpine forest, through a half a mile of barren wasteland to the SUV that Rhodes loaned her.

At least she still had five rounds of ammunition left. Ryder's team probably had that between them. If shots were still going off, wastelanders were still coming, and they would soon run dry and resort to hand-to-hand fighting.

Skye reached up and grabbed the ledge. She placed her foot higher up the fissure, gritted her teeth, and raised herself into the tunnel, landing on her belly. A breeze chilled the sweat on her brow, and she let out a deep breath.

A shallow stream of water ran along the bottom, dampening her uniform. She crawled on her elbows and knees along the cramped space. A large man would struggle to get through, but Skye quickly made her way along the twelve-foot passage to the outer entrance and brushed a leafy branch to one side.

She knelt behind a bush next to the rock face and listened. Wastelanders grunted and shouted to her left. Far enough away that she could slip away in the opposite direction undetected.

Moonlight shining down from the star-studded sky provided good visibility. That was both good and bad. Good so she could retrace her steps once out of the forest. Bad that her silhouette would be more easily spotted.

Two dull cracks came from inside the cave. The outlaws were still fighting, but that also meant that the wastelanders were occupied.

Skye unslung her rifle and moved away from the bush. Picking her way down through the first part of the rocky forest wasn't going to be easy, but at least it provided more places to hide from any stray wastelanders. After that, crunching over scree would be noisy. Without her knife, only her wits and rifle protected her. A shot fired in a wastelander-occupied area attracted them immediately.

She clambered over a rock, stooped low to keep her shape as small as possible, and ducked between the trees.

An owl hooted. A dark figure stood from behind a rock and gazed up. Skye darted behind a tree and held her rifle to her chest.

She heard an extended grunt. A wastelander. She wondered how many were in the forest. This one was only ten yards away, in her direction of travel.

He sniffed and growled. She couldn't move from behind the tree without him seeing her. She didn't want to give him the chance to charge unseen. There was only one thing for it.

She swung around the tree, aimed and fired. He toppled backward as the shot echoed through the forest. Wastelanders roared in the distance. She looked to her left and saw shapes moving toward her. They were less than one hundred yards away.

Skye turned and ran.

Chapter Thirteen

Carlos bumped along a damaged highway with dimmed headlights. The last remnants of daylight departed, and he had to stop. Traveling one hundred miles south of the strongholds meant any artificial lights would only attract trouble. He steered between two smashed sections of the barrier, pulled his SUV behind a small group of trees, and crunched up the handbrake.

Trader gave him clear instructions. Keep going until you find something. He'd already patrolled for three days, covering a wide area. Wastelanders were around in small groups, most heading north without any signs of the reason.

Being a scout had its perks, like avoiding the crap jobs in the strongholds and their strict rules, and having plenty of free time to explore. This was its big downside. Searching hostile territory with the risk of being poisoned by radiation.

Carlos regretted reading books. His life would've been much easier if he just accepted the world, instead of obsessing over the trappings of the destroyed society. It gave him a craving for freedom and adventure. As a scout he could search old buildings and scratch his itch.

He grabbed a Geiger counter off the passenger seat, folded it under his left arm, and slipped his gun out of his holster.

The last nine readings were all standard background radiation levels. He'd taken one every ten miles after leaving Sigma, and was approaching the Californian border. He elbowed open the door handle and crouched behind a tree.

He listened for any suspicious sounds like wastelanders prowling or sneaking up to attack. After hearing nothing apart from the collective chirp of crickets, Carlos swept the probe near the ground. The needle on the display flickered higher. This region was still outside the known fallout area, but part of it may have been carried north by precipitation, causing a rainout zone.

He returned to the SUV and opened the rear passenger door. Trader had found an old CBRN suit and respirator in a compartment of a battered old ship and supplied him with it. Carlos wasn't one hundred percent sure it would work, but it was better than nothing.

The disruptive patterned jacket felt light around his body. He slipped on the trousers and tied the velcro fastenings, snapped on a pair of black rubber gloves, placed the respirator over his face, and tightened the hood around it.

Every breath gently sucked the mask tighter toward his face. Moonlight provided reasonable visibility from a clear night sky. He decided to patrol and grabbed his gun and antique night-vision goggles. Wastelanders were less active at night. They preferred to hunt during the hours of daylight. More chance of spotting movement and going straight on the attack.

He followed an exit road for half a mile, keeping his silhouette hidden below the rising ground to his right. It led to the remnants of a small town. Trees and plants grew out of the shells of the houses still standing. Dust piled up against their walls. Nature was in the process of reclaiming this place.

The solidly constructed buildings in the cities were always more interesting. The ones that weren't destroyed by the Axis' conventional onslaught usually had some interesting items lying around. The snow globe he'd found in a Portland apartment took pride of place on his SUV dashboard.

Something clanked along the road in the opposite direction. He slipped inside a collapsed ruin and crouched behind one of its broken windows.

Firing would be a stupid idea. It would only draw more trouble. Carlos would wait for the wastelander to pass. They often beat things with sticks to check if any animals were hiding in the wrecks or ruins.

Footsteps neared. He peered to his left. The shaggy hair, hunched gait and metal bar in the person's hand told him all he needed to know. Carlos fumbled on the floor and picked up half a brick. If the wastelander came close or spotted him, he'd have to take him out the old-fashioned way. In these situations, a gun was a weapon of last resort.

The wastelander, a male, stopped and sniffed the air like a dog. The further south he traveled, the more like animals they became. The ones near the strongholds used to be almost human and spoke pigeon English, although they had the same uncompromising aggression.

Carlos' breathing intensified. Condensation clouded the edges of his plastic eyepieces. He squeezed a finger under his respirator and smudged it away.

The wastelander turned to face his building and raised his metal bar. He ran for the house and threw himself against the wall, a few feet to Carlos' right. The whole structure shuddered. Dust fell from the exposed roof beams and showered him.

He gripped the half brick tightly and raised it. The wastelander sniffed again and moved toward the window. Carlos edged back and waited.

The wastelander put his head through the window. Before he had a chance to look around, Carlos slammed the brick down on top of his head. The wastelander grunted and slumped against the frame.

Carlos learned ten years ago, as a teenager, to never give these people a second chance. His friend did and it cost him his life. Luke showed an injured wastelander mercy; his reward was a slashed throat. He smashed the brick down twice in quick succession. His rubber glove glistened with blood. The wastelander grunted and twitched.

He pulled the unconscious body through the window and dragged him out of sight. Carlos couldn't afford the wastelander to follow him or report back to his group, if he had one. This was the most unpleasant part of his job. He swung the brick down five more times to make sure he wouldn't be compromised until they found the body.

His mutated friends would probably sniff him out eventually, so Carlos decided not to hang around. He wiped his glove on a faded dangling rag that used to be a curtain and exited through a rear entrance.

The frame of a swing set poked out of the top of the waist-high grass. He waded through it, brushed a section of rotting fence to one side, and came out on another former neighborhood road barely visible below the weeds.

Two cracks, sounding like distant gunfire, echoed in the distance.

Carlos ducked behind the rusting skeleton of a vehicle and looked south.

A pair of glowing red lights hung in the night sky and slowly descended. Somebody firing flares. He hadn't seen the wastelanders do that before, and he'd observed a lot of their behavior. Most of it involved a relentless hunt for food and soft targets from the clean zone.

Another flare arced into the sky. Carlos wondered if it was a distress signal. Only a fool would be living this far south. He raised his gun and crept forward to investigate.

Carlos moved into a sparsely wooded area and gently stepped between the trees in the direction the third flare came from. The moon cast eerie shadows across the dusty ground and branches creaked overhead. The town disappeared behind him, and the trees quickly thinned out. He looked around for some natural cover. The ground rose to his left.

A distant tinny-sounding voice broke the silence, carrying on the gentle breeze. The flares dropped out of sight. A vehicle engine revved. The voice became louder and faded away again. Carlos dropped to the dirt and crawled on his hands and knees to the top of the rise.

Half a mile to his right, two vehicles had their lights on full beam.

Standard design Omicron SUVs with open tops. Whoever it was had come from a stronghold. They headed across the wasteland at a speed of around five miles per hour.

A figure stood on the backseat of the rear SUV. They held a megaphone to their mouth and shouted through it. *What they hell are they doing?*

A sizzling light came from the front vehicle. Another flare shot into the sky. Carlos leopard-crawled closer along the ridge. These people had a death wish.

The voice became more audible as the vehicles drew level with his elevated position. A figure on the front SUV reached inside a crate and threw objects on the ground.

"Free food. Shelter. Weapons. All you can eat. The Sky Man urges you north. Defeat the people who want to oppress you. They have unlimited supplies."

Carlos scanned behind the vehicles. The recognizable shapes of wastelanders darted after the SUVs and picked up the boxes. Two ran alongside the rear vehicle. A muzzle flashed twice, followed by the report of both shots. Both dropped to the ground.

"Do not approach the vehicles. The next stop-off point is twenty miles north. We have food, water and weapons. Keep your distance. We are here to help you."

Thirty wastelanders appeared out of the gloom, fifty yards behind the vehicles. Some carried a box, others picked up the recently discarded ones. They kept their distance and followed, half jogging.

"We will reach our destination in four hours. The Sky Man will honor you with food. He is preparing you for battle against your mortal enemy. The Sky Man will give you what is rightfully yours in exchange for loyalty."

They were being lured toward the strongholds. Worse still, by Omicron vehicles. Somebody was trying to destroy their society from the inside.

The whole area moved behind the thirty wastelanders. Carlos tapped the side of his goggles and tried to refocus. Somebody cried in the distance, followed by two more shrill shouts. Seconds later, the whole air filled with a collective roar. The goggles weren't broken. Hundreds of wastelanders came into focus. Another flare fired in the air. More followed in a long disorganized procession. Thousands of them.

Carlos watched as they streamed past the ridge. He couldn't accurately estimate numbers because of the rolling ground.

A few stragglers on the flank reached the foot of his hill and trudged up. He had to get well ahead of this overwhelming force and warn everyone. They would need all hands at the walls to repel an invasion this size, and even that might not be enough.

Carlos had to get back to his vehicle immediately. He could race back up the highway and put decent distance between himself and the invading force. On foot, they would take two or three days to reach the strongholds. Wastelanders still had human bodies and would need rest.

Another flare shot into the sky in the distance. These weren't the only two vehicles collecting the savages. The odds could be insurmountable. If Carlos didn't make it back, he felt sure the strongholds would be crushed. They wouldn't be able to defend themselves without warning.

A man shouted through the megaphone, "Follow for a better life. Follow for victory. Follow the Sky Man."

A loud collective shout followed. They repeated the last few words. *Who the hell is the Sky Man, and how did he get his hands on the resources?*

Carlos ripped off his respirator, turned and sprinted for his SUV. The Geiger counter reading meant that he had a slim chance of being poisoned, but that paled into insignificance against the discovered threat. He had to move quickly, and running in a respirator was hard work.

He reached the SUV, didn't bother changing out of his suit, and started the engine. Through his open window he could hear the distant buzz from the mob moving north.

A surge of determination ran through him. If he didn't make it back to tell Trader, it could mean the end for humanity as they knew it. The continent would be left infested with wastelanders, and all hopes of forming a civilized society would be destroyed.

The SUV's wheels spun in the dirt, and the vehicle shot forward, through the gap in the broken barrier, back onto the decaying highway. He had enough gas to make it home without stopping, and that's exactly what he intended to do.

Chapter Fourteen

The first signs of daylight seeped through a gap in the curtains, casting light into Trader's cramped spare bedroom. Jake only managed a few minutes' sleep during the night. Sporadic gunfire rattled on the walls. The factory whistle blasted at four in the morning, and thoughts about the new world spun through his mind. The strongholds were too wrapped up in their original philosophies. He felt it was holding them back in terms of building a stronger, more cohesive society. Strength in numbers wasn't a bad thing, especially with a growing threat outside.

He heard a door open inside. Trader coughed three times, cleared his throat, and clambered downstairs. Jake threw his blanket to one side and sat up on the mattress. He checked his watch for the fiftieth time. Just past six in the morning.

He zipped up his flight suit, drank from a bottle of water on the windowsill, and gazed over Trader's compound buildings at workers trudging to and from a factory in their stained purple coveralls. The smell of cooking bacon wafted into the room, and his stomach growled.

Jake joined Trader by his frying pan in the kitchen. "Morning, chief. I thought we were hitting the bunker at first light?"

"Can't miss the most important meal of the day. Didn't the Fleet teach you that?"

"Depends on the situation, but I've never turned down a cooked breakfast."

Six bacon rashers sizzled in the pan. Trader forked out three and placed them in a fresh buttered roll. "There's coffee on the table. Help yourself."

"Thanks," Jake said and took a bite. It tasted exactly how he remembered, delicious. "Where do you get your meat and bread?"

"Each stronghold has their own livestock and bakery. Sigma doesn't own pigs. This is probably from Omega."

Trader opened wide and stuffed half of his roll into his mouth. Jake poured a coffee and gulped it down, warm and bittersweet, just the way he liked it.

"You ready to go?" Trader said. "I want you to lead the team today. Show them what you showed me in the first bunker. They'll respect you for it."

"Are you sure that's wise? I'm still a new kid on the block."

Trader stuffed the second half of the roll into his mouth. He tried to speak and paused after half-chewed food garbled his initial response.

"You've had years of training. My guys are good, but they're not at your level. I won't be here forever and need a safe pair of hands to pass my responsibilities on to."

"This is all a bit sudden, isn't it?"

"Things move quickly in 2205, Jake. Look at Pete; he was one of my better guys. He'll probably be crippled for the rest of his life and spend his time sitting on the rampart."

"You hardly know me."

"I saw enough yesterday. The way you took the initiative. You don't have any bias toward an individual stronghold. That's a key requirement to make things tick."

"Can't say I particularly like any of them at the moment."

Trader smiled and flashed his decaying yellow teeth. "That's my boy."

Jake reasoned that if he wanted to change the society for the better, it would be easier doing it from within. He couldn't go back so had to move forward. A few of Trader's team might be irritated, but it was nothing he hadn't faced before. After flying up to captain in the Fleet, he always had to deal with the scorn and bitterness of old sweats who didn't make it. His priority was always getting the job done.

"I'll do it. Who are you replacing Pete with?"

"We'll pick up a recruit from one of the strongholds. Sigma probably."

Jake thought about Skye from Omega during the night. He owed his life to her. Her slick exfiltration immediately impressed him, and she was exactly the kind of person he wanted watching his back.

"What about Skye? Can you bring her in?"

Trader swept his keys from the kitchen worktop. "Nope. Finch sees her as his little pet. I know she's good, but he won't let her go."

Jake finished his coffee and followed him out to the square in front of his house. The other team members were already by their vehicles. Thick gray clouds blanketed the dawn sky.

The growing daylight allowed him a clearer view around Trader's fenced-off compound situated below the northern Sigma tower. His team lived in a small five-story apartment block opposite his house; eight garages with rolling shutter doors, no doubt packed with goods that he exchanged between strongholds, filled the space between them on the left-hand side. The vehicles parked on the right, in front of the sturdy pair of wooden gates. One of the team pulled them open.

"Straight to the west bunker, guys," Trader said. "I'll be the forlorn hope. Keep your distance and sound your horn if you see any wastelanders."

A few of the team nodded. They climbed into the five SUVs and two trucks.

Trader and Jake jumped into the lead vehicle. He wound down the driver's window and lit a cigarette. Jake wound his window down too. He didn't mind people who smoked, but liked to avoid it first thing in the morning.

The convoy rumbled along the main road through the center of Sigma. Most people didn't even acknowledge it. They were probably used to seeing it leave and arrive at the stronghold every day. The main gates started to open when they reached within one hundred yards. Trader didn't need to brake and maintained his steady speed until they hit the road outside.

"How are you planning to distribute the weapons?" Jake said.

"Haven't decided yet. They're still in the truck. I'll give some to Epsilon for them to reverse engineer the design. Theta could do with—"

The radio crackled. "Trader, this is Carlos. Do you copy?"

Trader grabbed the mic from its central housing on the dash. "Carlos, do you have something for me?"

"We need to meet. Urgently."

"Where are you?"

"Heading north. I had to take a detour. Can you make it to Kappa for two o'clock?"

"What's the rush?"

"I can't say over the open airwaves. But you need to come."

"Give it to me on an urgency scale of one to ten. We've got a busy day ahead of us."

"Ten."

"I'll be there."

Trader placed the mic back. He held a clenched fist out of his window and thrust his foot against the accelerator.

Jake could taste the burning clutch plate in the back of his throat as the vehicle roared and sped up. They bounced over a rock, and his head brushed against the roof. He held his hands against the glove box to keep himself steady.

"Better buckle up," Trader said.

Jack pulled the plastic belt across his chest and clicked it in place. "Who's Carlos? Sounded important."

"He's my scout. I sent him south to see if he could find a reason why so many wastelanders were heading north."

"Why couldn't he say over the radio? I doubt they use them."

"When you make a move in this world, you better be damned sure you know the facts. I've got my suspicions, but I want to hear what he has to say first."

Jake frowned. "That's about as clear as mud. If you want to bring me along, you need to start being straight with me."

"I don't want to cloud your judgment. I will say that Carlos doesn't exaggerate. I've got a feeling we might need those extra weapons in the bunker."

Trader turned right at a fork in the road and headed west along a dirt track.

* * *

The team only encountered one wastelander on their way to the bunker. The convoy stopped, and somebody put an end to the danger with a sniper rifle. The track didn't take the most direct route; instead it snaked through the open countryside, avoiding any forested areas.

As Trader approached the bunker, Jake could see the shattered remains of a town in the distance. An Axis ballistic missile must have reduced it to a few jagged walls rising from piles of rubble. Most wooden structures were either flattened or burnt out. Foliage tangled and choked the mess.

"Is most of the country like that?" Jake said.

Trader sighed. "Pretty much. Total damned mess. The cities took the brunt of it, but they hit most areas."

"Just seems pointless. It guaranteed their own destruction."

"It was their last roll of the dice. They were losing. Desperate people do desperate things."

Jake still couldn't wrap his head around it. They must have known the consequences. The crew in the Orbital Bomber always dared each other to open the instructions safe, but they never did. It didn't take a genius to work out what they would be required to do. He wondered who was on watch in January 2077 and if they let rip with their missiles.

All of the fencing around this facility had fallen. The only signs of its former existence were a few of the steel supports spaced at irregular intervals around the perimeter.

Their SUV rattled over the previously flattened gate and stopped a few yards short of the topside building. The rest of the convoy arrived two minutes later, at quarter to nine in the morning.

The group surrounded Trader by the hood of his SUV. "Same as before. Jake is gonna get us in there and lead the clearance work. Stay on guard until we open up the loading doors. Tess and John, you two come with us."

The red-haired man organized the team again in a defensive formation around the building. Trader passed Jake a spotlight.

"Getting a sense of déjà vu?" Jake said.

"Let's hope we don't find another frazzled soul in here. We can't take them back."

Jake clicked on the light. Excitement built inside him again. These stasis pods might still be intact. System failures were bound to happen, but lightning striking twice in such close proximity seemed unlikely. If people were to be brought out of stasis, the time was now, when they were needed to rebuild and properly organize.

"Can't take our time either," Trader said. "Kappa's three hours' drive from here. We'll load the weapons and lock the place up for later."

Jake nodded, headed into the entrance, and made straight for the corridor. The gloomy interior had the same design as the previous building. Mold covered the formerly white plastered walls, and the fetid odor of damp rotting floorboards hung in the air. He reached the end room on the left and shone in his spotlight. The tiles were removed around the open hatch.

He turned back to Trader and his two team members. "Did you leave it open?"

Trader nudged past him and drew his gun. "No, we didn't."

Jake joined him at the edge of the hatch, shone his light down the shaft, and felt a cool draft against his face. "Either the structure's compromised or the loading doors are open."

"Let's go with option B first. I don't want to get caught climbing the stairs if someone's down there."

"Any idea who it might be?"

"Out here?" Trader said and looked down the shaft. "Doubt it's wastelanders or a stronghold team. We might have a third player."

"Seems unlikely," Jake said.

Trader ignored him and headed back out. Jake followed and climbed into the passenger side of the SUV. "Is there something you're not telling me?"

He gave Jake a lingering glare. "I've got no idea who or what opened that hatch. Let's hope for both of our sakes that it was a curious wastelander who has long gone. Because if it isn't, we might have a new group in town with plenty of weapons."

"Or the people inside decided to make a break for it?"

"Come on, Jake. Don't you think that's a bit of a coincidence?"

Jake shrugged. "I woke up, didn't I? If this place was still operational, they'd have somebody on shift. Maybe they saw you visit and decided to move?"

"I've visited here five times in the last year."

Jake thought for a moment. If somebody opened this place up from the outside, it had to be a captain or above that knew the code, meaning a person from his generation. He could find out who by accessing the mainframe inside the bunker, but decided to keep the idea to himself until they established more facts.

Trader twisted the key, slammed the SUV in gear, and punched the accelerator. The wheels screeched against the corroding asphalt, and they shot forward, away from the old parking lot. He plowed through the long dew-soaked grass, bumping over small pieces of debris, straight for the green mound that shielded the ramp leading to the loading doors. Jake always thought the design pretty pointless. Before the war, people from the road would still see vehicles heading behind it.

He swept around the edge of the mound and drove ten yards down the ramp. Both chunky black doors at the bottom of the hundred-yard-long, thirty-degree slope were wide open with the locking mechanism disabled. Lights were on inside. Somebody with knowledge of the management system must have done it.

Jake jumped out and aimed down the ramp with his clunky gun. Trader seemed to take most things in his stride, including the nervy cryptic message from his scout a few hours ago, but the latest development had him on edge. He moved with urgency to the back of the SUV and waved his team around him.

"Follow Jake and me in staggered groups of two. If you hear gunfire, get your asses down the ramp. Make sure two of you stay here to guard our rear."

"Mind if I get a weapon from the truck?" Jake said.

Trader gestured his Epsilon-manufactured rifle toward the closest. "Nothing wrong with what you've got, but if it makes you feel better, they're in that one."

Jake holstered his gun, weaved his way through the cluster of SUVs around the entrance, and climbed into the back of the truck. He grabbed a rifle from a portable rack, checked the working parts, loaded a magazine, and clicked it into the housing. He felt a lot more comfortable handling a familiar weapon. A rifle also gave him extended range, to take out any threat from a distance.

He jumped back out and rejoined Trader. The team of eighteen split to either side of the ramp and spread against the walls at five-yard intervals. Jake shouldered his rifle and walked down the ramp toward the bunker's entrance.

A patch of grain spread across the surface halfway down. Food supplies had been removed recently; otherwise the rain would've washed them into the metal drain at the bottom. Trader moved to the left-hand loading door and waved him forward. He continued inside and surveyed the warehouse. The shelves were mostly empty, apart from cleaning materials and utensils like plates and cutlery.

A hollow pop came from Jake's right. He crouched and aimed at the elevated control room. Sparks spat against its window. If somebody trashed the console, it was only a matter of time before the system went into emergency lockdown.

"Trader, we need to move fast; otherwise we'll end up sealed in here."

"How long have we got?"

"No idea. It could close at any moment. What are our priorities?"

"Weapons first. Your call after that."

Jake crossed the warehouse floor. More electrical snaps came from the control room. The lights flickered overhead. He headed straight for the door on the other side that led to the armory, food chambers and living quarters.

The window of the fresh food preservation chamber still felt cool to touch. Inside, condensation dripped from the open doors of the twenty silver storage units. A thin coating of water covered the red vinyl floor. Somebody emptied this recently, perhaps in the last twelve hours.

Jake pressed his thumb on the armory access panel. Oxygen hissed from the vents inside. The solid black door punched open. Trader squeezed past Jake, entered the room, and placed his hand on his forehead. All racks were empty. A couple of green synthetic slings lay on the floor.

"Who the hell …" Trader said.

"A captain or above," Jake said. "There's no other explanation. This door wasn't forced, and it explains why the loading doors are open too. If I can access the system in the control room, I can find out from the access logs."

"How's that going to help?"

"They might be registered to this facility. If not, I can get you a photo. You might recognize them from one of the strongholds."

"It's impossible. I'd know about it."

"Would you? I think we at least need an idea who it is." Jake thought it could be a team from another bunker, maybe now all awake and gathering arms to protect themselves. "Let's check the stasis pods, find out if we've still got people here or not. That's an easy one to rule out first."

Jake jogged back along the corridor, turned left up the stairs, and passed through the living quarters. All beds were neatly made and showed no signs of recent activity. He grabbed the rails and jumped down the metal spiral staircase to the stasis chamber.

A red light winked above all sixty open pods. Jake wanted to turn away, but he couldn't. Some of the bodies were still in position with stab wounds in their coveralls. Others slumped on the ground in front of their pods; most had visible injuries. A man lay in the middle by the console with a snapped spear in his chest.

None were in an advanced state of decomposition. Trader moved alongside Jake as he surveyed the scene. "Wastelanders. How did they get in here?"

Jake shook his head. There was more to it than that. He rolled the pointer on the console, and the screen lit up. *Officer C3431* activated a waking procedure on pod one at 21:37 yesterday evening, and the rest every thirty seconds after. He shuddered when thinking of how events must have played out. A systematic murder. Every half a minute, a drowsy inhabitant waking and receiving a knife or spear to the chest.

A growing anger bubbled inside. One of his own instigated the slaughter. He pointed to the screen. "I need to get to the mainframe and get an ID on this murdering scumbag."

Trader crouched and inspected the spear. "Are you sure there's no other way this could've been done? The spear's definitely wastelander."

"Maybe stasis sent C3431 crazy? I don't know, but if we have a trained officer working with the wastelanders and he has armed them, we've got a serious fight on our hands."

Jake vowed to get justice for the men and women lying in front of him. He didn't check the names to see if he recognized any; that wouldn't help. Whoever did this had already made it personal.

Trader stood and placed his hand on Jake's shoulder. "Do what you need to find out—"

The lights flickered overhead. Half didn't come back on. An electronic beep pulsed through the facility-wide address system.

"We need to get the hell out of here," Jake said.

They had sixty seconds to reach the loading doors before the bunker automatically closed. Without any technical skills to repair the system and a lack of supplies, it meant a quick death.

Jake ran back through the living quarters, along the corridor, and threw open the door to the warehouse. Trader lagged behind, wheezing after him.

He waited and grabbed Trader's arm. He provided Jake's safety and a chance to change things in his new environment. If Trader didn't make it out, all that was gone.

"Get your ass moving," Jake said.

"I'm seventy years old, goddammit."

Jake dragged him across the warehouse toward the ramp. The doors began to close, creaking and screaming on their steel winding mechanism. Team members peered through the gap and encouraged them forward. They made it through with twenty seconds to spare.

Trader rested his hands on his knees and slumped against the exterior wall. Jake watched as the doors rumbled inward and locked together with a hollow thud.

"Do we need to go all the way back to the other bunker to access their system?" Trader said.

"Is Kappa close?"

"It's south, closest places are Omega and Epsilon."

"I think we need to find out as soon as possible," Jake said. "If I can log in to my ship's comms console, I have captain's access and can look up the officer ID. Can you get me in and out of Epsilon without them turning me into a tourist attraction?"

"Yes, but we need to go to Kappa first. I've got a horrible feeling what Carlos has to say might be linked to this."

Trader trudged up the ramp. Jake followed and found it hard to disagree. The cold-blooded killings and wastelander weapons were enough evidence that something coordinated was being planned against them. They were facing a well-armed, unknown enemy who recruited the very people who wanted to destroy their society.

Chapter Fifteen

Skye kept low and clambered over rocks. She paused behind each one and looked back up the hill. At least five wastelanders were searching for her. They spread through the trees and headed down in an extended line, springing around trunks and leaping over obstacles. She had to time her movements when the closest turned in another direction.

A gunshot cracked from the plateau. Skye hugged a pine and peered around it. The wastelanders stopped and looked back up the hill. Two approached each other. One pointed up, the other down. A third joined the debate.

She edged back and felt her boot sink into loose scree. The trees thinned from here, providing less cover, but the gunshot gave her a chance to put some more distance between herself and the hunters. Any closer on this ground and they would hear her every move.

Skye kept her rifle trained on the figures and weaved backward. A stream gushed through the forest to her right. She remembered it being on her left when she first tracked her way toward the camp.

The wastelanders continued to argue amongst themselves. She adjusted her course to the most direct route to her SUV. It was parked behind a semi-collapsed wooden barn, covered in a moldy piece of blue tarpaulin she found inside, next to a rusty egg-sorting machine.

A bird burst from a tree between her and the wastelanders. Its harsh caw carried through the forest. This ended the wastelanders' debate; they fanned out again and continued down. Skye didn't want them an inch closer. In a couple of minutes she would be on open ground with half a mile to travel to the barn.

She moved back with more urgency, keeping focused on the descending shapes. They would see her soon, but every second she moved faster, the distance became greater. She needed every yard possible for a sprint to the SUV. Her boots skidded against the scree, and she reached the edge of the forest.

The options for cover turned to rocks and shrubs for the next thirty yards. After that, she only had a knee-high field of gently swaying grass.

A wastelander made the decision for her. He let out a guttural roar and bounded in her direction. This alerted the others, and they immediately followed.

Five of them and five rounds. One or two missed shots in the dark and it would be hand-to-hand fighting. Without her knife, her only weapon against their axes and spears would be using the rifle as a club, like Phillips did outside the walls of Omega.

Skye decided to sprint for her vehicle. If any got close, they would be the ones to receive the contents of her magazine.

She focused on the ground as she pounded over the last of the thinning scree. Bright moonlight flooded the area, and she forcefully raised her feet to avoid them being snagged in the long grass.

Wastelanders snarled and shouted behind her. The distant barn didn't seem to be getting any closer. She glanced over her shoulder. Three of them dashed out of the forest, two hundred yards behind her.

Her thighs burned and she pumped her arms. Her lungs felt at the bursting point, but adrenaline kept her going. The ground became uneven and she tried to look for obstacles in the grass.

Skye's ankle twisted after she stepped on a rock. She staggered to her left, reached forward, and just managed to maintain her balance. A sharp pain shot down the side of her foot every time it connected with the ground. Her only option was to clench her teeth and try to ignore the pain.

She wondered how so many wastelanders managed to converge on the outlaws' camp. Either hundreds or even thousands were swamping the area, or this was another assault organized by Sky Man. If it was, it can't have been a coincidence that she'd been in all three locations. If she escaped her pursuers, Rhodes had questions to answer.

The wastelanders sounded closer as she approached the SUV. Skye didn't look back and felt for the keys in her pocket. Thankfully Ryder's men didn't take them. As soon as she reached the side of the barn, she dropped to one knee, twisted and aimed. Two were fifty yards away. She could hear their feet swishing through the grass.

Skye fired at the first. The round stopped him in his tracks, and he crumpled to the ground. The second wastelander dived in the grass. Three others following did the same. She reached over and dragged the tarpaulin off the SUV.

Four areas of grass twitched in front of her. The wastelanders were crawling forward. These were probably northern ones. Less suicidal but still deadly.

Skye fumbled with the keys in the SUV door. The internal lock popped up. She didn't bother to check on her attackers' progress, just jumped into the vehicle, slammed the door, and punched down the lock.

Her hands trembled through fear and exertion as she tried to put the key in the ignition. She took a deep breath and told herself to switch on. The engine roared into life, and she flicked on the headlights.

The four wastelanders stood, probably sensing she was about to get away. They collectively darted straight for the front of the vehicle. Skye slammed the SUV in gear and thrust her foot against the accelerator.

She jerked in her seat and gripped the steering wheel as the SUV shot forward.

Two wastelanders dived out of the way. One stood like a rabbit caught in her headlights. The bull-bar crashed against him, and his screaming body disappeared underneath her vehicle.

The only wastelander left standing smashed her axe against Skye's window as she sped past. The window splintered, and she felt tiny pieces of glass shower her face, but it held. The SUV plowed through the field, and she turned right toward the road.

The luminous arms on the analogue clock told her it was half past four in the morning. Omega and Zeta had to act. Rhodes needed to give her some answers.

* * *

After driving an hour along a bumpy dirty track, Skye hit an old highway. Zeta was only five minutes from here. She blinked and rubbed her dry, tired eyes. The drop in danger level had given her a chance to think. She considered if she'd trusted Ryder too easily. He seemed genuine, but his claims were hard to believe. After a few minutes of arguing with herself, she put it down to his cynical view of her world and the way it operated.

She believed the outlaws sourced weapons and ammunition from Epsilon, but decided to keep that to herself. Twenty-four hours ago, Skye thought she was beyond corruption. Now she knew about three serious treaty breaches. An illegal Omega-Zeta trade and distribution of weapons to people outside of a stronghold, these two didn't bother her. The expendable resource pool did, if Rhodes told the truth. *How many other strongholds were circumventing the rules?*

Skye felt her chin drop as her eyelids drooped. She snapped her head up and lowered her window to allow chilly spring air to rush inside the vehicle. Anything to keep awake for the last few minutes, until she could grab two hours of sleep behind Zeta's walls.

She finally reached the raised ground leading up to the dark stone wall and solid oak gates. The first signs of dawn appeared on the horizon. After she got some sleep, Skye planned to have a busy day. First, she would question Rhodes again. He put forward a convincing argument to kill Ryder, and spoke as if he'd witnessed some of the events. Second, she planned on speaking to Finch about Ryder's claims.

Two SUVs and a truck parked outside the gate. Five people in royal blue jackets stood around them. Members of the Omega Force. None were scheduled to visit Zeta today.

As she pulled level with the rear vehicle, she saw local officers, in their crisp navy uniforms, aiming their weapons at her team. This was a highly unusual state of affairs. Skye had only seen a standoff like this once before. Three young soldiers from Theta went AWOL, and her team found them in a derelict factory.

She slammed on the brakes, grabbed her rifle and jumped out of her SUV. One of the Omega guards looked back at her and shrugged. He was in the convoy she left with last night. Skye told them not to wait.

Two orderlies, dressed in green medical center scrubs, carried a casualty through the gates and headed for the truck. None of the three she delivered yesterday would be fit to travel back to Omega. They'd needed serious treatment. She headed over to check who was on the stretcher.

A Zeta guard, with a handlebar mustache, stepped in front of her and blocked her path to the truck. Another followed close behind and lowered his rifle toward her.

"Who are you?" Handlebar asked.

"I'm Lieutenant Skye Reed from Omega. I have important news for your governor. What exactly is going on here?"

He stepped back and drew his pistol. "Put your rifle on the ground and raise your hands."

Skye froze. His actions were so alien she didn't know how to react.

"I said, put your rifle on the ground and raise your hands. Now."

She shook her head, placed down the rifle, and locked her fingers around the back of her neck. "I'd like to know what's going on here?"

"I have orders to arrest you on sight. Please step away from the truck."

"Arrested on what charge?"

He jerked his pistol to the right, encouraging her away from the Omega team and their vehicles. "Conspiracy and illegal trading."

"You've got this all wrong. Let me speak to Governor Harrison."

"Get the other two loaded," an officer shouted at the orderlies. "I want them out of here as soon as possible."

They both scurried back through the gates.

"Got any other weapons?" Handlebar said.

"Just the rifle. Outlaws took my dagger."

"I don't believe you." He moved around behind her. "Keep still while I search you. My friend over there can get nervous."

He ran his hands along her arms and legs, patted down her back, and moved his hands around to the front of her body.

She looked over her shoulder. "Just watch where those hands go, buddy."

"She's clear," he said to the guard in front of her.

"What evidence do you have against me?"

"You can explain to my commanding officer. He's the one who wants you arrested."

"I need to speak with Governor Harrison."

Handlebar laughed. "He doesn't deal with bottom feeders like you. Move toward the gates."

He shoved her in the back, and Skye stumbled forward. She glanced across to her driver. He sat cross-legged in front of his SUV and raised his bound wrists. "What are we supposed to have done, Lieutenant?"

One of the guards kicked him in the chest. "Stop talking, traitor."

SIXTH CYCLE

Handlebar continued to shove Skye in the back, even though she didn't need encouraging through the gates. If they met again on more equal terms, she intended to give him a taste of his own medicine. This had to be connected to Rhodes. Finch wouldn't put her in a situation like this.

They passed the guardhouse, didn't sign in, and headed for a smaller side building attached to the headquarters. He bundled Skye through the door and directed her into a small windowless room with red walls.

Handlebar pointed at a plastic chair behind a scratch-covered metal table. "Sit down. He'll be with you shortly."

He slammed the door behind her. Skye slumped on the chair and let out a deep breath. A minute later, muffled chatter came from outside.

The door swung open. A stocky man with a buzz cut and general's flashes on his epaulets walked in and sat down in front of her. He didn't say anything at first and just glared. Skye kept eye contact. She wouldn't be bullied by Zeta thugs.

"How long has Omega been planning an attack on Zeta?"

Skye frowned. "Excuse me? I have no idea what you're talking about."

"How many men are working with Rhodes?"

"How should I know? He works in your factory."

"How long have Omega been supplying insurgents?"

"You're gonna have to help me out here. Has Rhodes done something? I only met the guy yesterday."

"Don't lie to me, Lieutenant. Governor Harrison was more than a little suspicious about your private meeting with Rhodes. When we raided the factories, we found out he's disappeared, along with your shipment. Was the plan to support them in a coup, or is this a precursor to an attack by Omega?"

"I was asked to deliver that shipment by Governor Finch. I have no idea what was inside. I'm not aware of any attack or plan against this stronghold."

He rested his elbows on the table and leaned forward. "Where were you last night?"

"I was in the hills to the east. I had a private mission to take care of some outlaws. It seems that your foreman set me up. They weren't who he led me to believe."

"Are these outlaws part of the plot to attack Zeta?"

"No. I was told they were enemies of Zeta. Rhodes asked me to kill their leader. He said they had been attacking your outlying fields and you were doing nothing to protect the workers."

He smiled and shook his head. "What outlying fields?"

"You don't have any outside the walls?"

"We'd be mad to do that. I suppose Rhodes told you this?"

"Yes. I met him yesterday with your governor. If I had anything to hide, why would I do that?"

As much as she hated to admit it to herself, she believed the officer about the fields. Rhodes had gone missing, which suggested he was the one who came up with the lie and set her up to be killed in the eastern hills.

Skye knew Finch too well to think he had anything to do with Rhodes' true intentions. If Rhodes meant to help out the workers in Zeta, he had a funny way of going about it.

The general relaxed back in his seat and unfastened his top button. "Did you kill the outlaw?"

"No. Turns out he's not the bad guy we should be worrying about."

"Are you saying outlaws are the good guys?"

"Rhodes gave me directions to their camp. We were ambushed shortly after I arrived. I managed to escape. They have women and children."

"Ambushed by who?"

"Wastelanders. Maybe a hundred."

The general let out a heavy sigh. "Let me get this right. You're claiming that you escaped from the largest wastelander attack in history. But nobody can verify it?"

"I assure you the threat is real. Twenty attacked Omega yesterday morning. I have no idea about any internal plot to attack this stronghold. If I were you, I'd be looking outside the walls."

"The governor is straightening this out with Finch at the moment. I'm sure you see my problem. You turn up with an illegal trade, and the next thing, Rhodes is gone. You realize he's a known rabble-rouser?"

Skye shrugged. "How would I know? I'm sure he set me up, so I'd like to ask him some questions too."

"By wastelanders? Pretty unlikely."

A thought struck Skye and she took a sharp intake of breath. If Rhodes did know about the wastelander attack, he probably knew Sky Man. She wanted to find both of them first.

"Are you okay?" the general said.

"Fine. Any idea where Rhodes might be?"

"We think he might be hiding out in one of the apartment blocks. We'll find him. Don't worry about that. When we do and make him talk, we might be paying you a visit."

"If you do, make sure you bring him along."

He shook his head. "That's not gonna happen. If I were you, I'd pray that Finch has a good story lined up, or you might be spending the rest of your life working our hemp fields."

The door swung open and a guard walked in. The general winced after he offered him a weak salute.

"Sir, the governor has sent an order to release Lieutenant Reed and her people. They are to leave Zeta immediately."

"I haven't finished with her yet. We still don't know what was in that crate."

The guard passed him a piece of paper. Skye watched as he ran his finger along the lines of text. "It seems Governor Finch has secured your release. If it was up to me, I'd take you to our cells for a real interrogation."

"I'm glad it's not. Just be on the lookout for wastelanders. If I get to Rhodes first, I'll let you know."

"Final question. What was in the crate? Don't tell me it was tools."

"I honestly don't know. I intend to ask Finch when I get back."

Skye also wanted to know his relationship with Rhodes. She guessed, like her, Finch also swallowed Rhodes' crap about wanting to help people. But she needed to be sure. Especially now she suspected Rhodes' link to Sky Man.

The general waved his hand toward the door. "Get her out of my sight. Make sure their convoy leaves immediately."

He stood and eyeballed Skye as she walked past him. She hoped he took her warning about wastelanders seriously, for the good of the workers if nothing else. She walked out of the half-open gates and hoped it would be another four years until she returned to Zeta.

* * *

Skye lay on a spare stretcher in the back of the open truck. She gave orders to wake her when they were in radio range of Omega. All three casualties were still in bad shape, and she wanted a treatment room prepared in the barracks.

After drifting in and out of sleep for twenty minutes, the truck braked hard. She sprang from the stretcher and grabbed her rifle.

A vehicle door slammed. Footsteps approached. Somebody talked to the driver. She waited for a minute and the conversation continued. Looking at the casualties and becoming increasingly impatient, Skye jumped off the back and walked around the side.

Trader turned to her. "I hear you've been up to mischief?"

"I'd call it something else."

Phillips leaned against the open passenger door of Trader's SUV.

"You need to come with me," Trader said. "I need to hear about it."

"I need to speak to Finch first."

He raised his sunglasses and lacked his customary smile. "You're coming with me."

Chapter Sixteen

Trader had the idea of stopping and searching the truck. After what they found at the western bunker, Jake thought it a smart thing to do. Even more so, now they had Skye, a capable member of the Omega Force, in the backseat of the SUV. He glanced at her in the rearview mirror. She rubbed her eyes and yawned.

"Foreman Rhodes you say? I've dealt with him a few times," Trader said.

"They think he was part of a coup. I delivered a crate, and he gave me the mission. I swear either he or somebody else set me up in those hills."

"I'd keep your powder dry for the moment, Skye. Wastelanders are building in the area. Whose idea was it for you to go up there?"

"Finch sent me to Zeta because Rhodes wanted me to kill an outlaw rapist. Turns out he's no rapist, and he hasn't attacked them."

"Doesn't surprise me. Some of them are good people. What did you deliver for Finch?"

She sighed. "I should've checked the crate. I know the punishment for illegal trade. Do you think Finch had anything to do with Rhodes? I don't see it like that."

The SUV screeched to a halt. Trader's left eye twitched. The convoy rolled up behind and stopped.

He slammed his hand against the steering wheel. "The last thing we need at the moment is that idiot Finch playing his silly games. There's trouble on the horizon, Skye. Bigger than any tin-pot coup. We all need to be pulling together."

"I heard two wastelanders in the forest talking about Sky Man. Do you mean that kind of trouble? Because if you do, I've got your back on that one."

"Yes, that kind of trouble. Finch certainly knows how to pick his moments to screw me around. Leave him to me."

"Could either of those two be C3431?" Jake said.

"No," Trader said. "Both have been around as long as I can remember."

"Who's Sky Man?"

"He's a myth."

Skye poked her head between the front seats. "Come on, Trader. That's bullshit and you know it." She turned to Jake. "Ten years ago he destroyed my settlement with a small army of wastelanders. I heard two northern ones mention his name yesterday morning. It explains the growing numbers in the area. I know it."

"We've just come from a mass slaughter," Jake said. "An officer in the Fleet, C3431, is working with wastelanders. Could he be Sky Man?"

"Where was this?"

"At an Allied bunker. They were all taken out of stasis and killed."

"He did the same to my settlement. Only two of us survived."

"Did you get a look at him?"

"I only heard his name—"

Trader shook his head. "You're putting two and two together and getting five. Ten years is a long time in this world. We'll wait to see what Carlos has to say."

Jake remembered Trader telling him how they liked to not repeat historical mistakes. It seemed they were well on their way to doing so. Many regions and countries had fallen in the past because of infighting and division while a larger threat loomed and struck. Finch and Rhodes sounded like they were opening up a dangerous fault line in the thin veneer of solidarity that existed between the strongholds.

Trader pressed the accelerator, and the SUV continued along the dirt track through rocky terrain. Hills rose either side, but hiding places to mount a close-quarter ambush were limited. Jake scanned both ridge lines for signs of movement. Somebody out there had the western bunker's rocket launchers, and the Omicron-constructed SUVs provided little protection from a direct strike.

Seeing the bunker victims cut deep, but it did raise the prospect of other places still being operational. Jake knew of two more in Wyoming he could explore, once the opportunity arose. Trader providing safety and an enemy slaughtering his former colleagues committed Jake to this fight. He wanted revenge and the prospect of a future.

They snaked up to the southern ridge, across a barren plateau, and Kappa appeared in the distance below them, only half a mile away. This stronghold looked unlike the rest. Its high oval walls were constructed out of concrete blocks. A natural lake hugged the eastern boundary, plowed fields surrounded the rest.

"It used to be made out of timber," Trader said. "Those blocks are eight deep."

"What kind of trouble were you all expecting?" Jake said.

"Don't misread our motivations. The walls you've seen allow people to sleep safely at night. Wastelanders have been a constant threat."

Jake turned in his seat. "I want to thank you for yesterday."

"Just doing my job," Skye said. "I guess you've had an interesting twenty-four hours?"

"Interesting is one way of putting it. It still hasn't all sunk in yet, but I'm only sitting here because of you."

"I saw you fighting them off. You were doing fine."

Jake liked her modesty. She could've just turned a blind eye to his plight, like the others he initially spotted on the rampart and in the pillboxes. But she didn't.

Trader checked his watch. "Twenty minutes to our arranged meeting time; he might be here already." He grabbed the mic and depressed the button. "Carlos, this is Trader, do you copy?"

The radio crackled. "This is Kappa gate. He arrived fifteen minutes ago. I recognized your convoy coming down the hill."

"Thanks. Where's he waiting?"

"The cafeteria. I'll open up the gates."

"Roger."

A sound like a fire bell rang in the distance. The gates opened. Trader sped up after reaching flat ground and headed straight for them.

* * *

The cafeteria reminded Jake of a prison block from the outside, with small rectangular windows positioned near the top of cream-painted concrete walls. The smell of cooking meat drifted through a gap in the large blue metal door at the front. Most other square buildings in Kappa looked the same, neatly constructed in a grid system around tarmac roads.

"Skye, wait with my team until I've finished talking to the governor," Trader said.

She nodded and walked back to the team standing around their vehicles. A thin-faced old man in a smart brown uniform, flanked by two armed guards in dark gray fatigues, strode up the street.

Trader leaned toward Jake. "Herbie runs Kappa. He's got a short fuse, so let me do the talking."

"Bit of a running theme with the leaders."

"Do you expect wet politicians? Get with the times, Jake. Don't say anything to anyone about the western bunker until we visit your ship at Epsilon."

Herbie stopped three yards short of them and peered above his black-rimmed glasses at Jake. "When did you take Lenin out of his tomb?"

"Yesterday morning. I picked him up from Omega."

"What have you got for me, Trader?"

"I've come here to check on clock and stock."

"It hasn't changed from your last visit. We're still at capacity. If you don't support me at the next general meeting, you can forget your men being serviced in our cafeteria."

"It's not just my decision, Herbie, you know that."

Herbie scowled. "Don't take me for a fool. Get me my five hundred increase or dine in Finch's soup kitchen."

"Things are going to change. You can trust me on that."

"Change the record. We're seeing more wastelanders by the day. I need to protect my people."

"I've got eight new rifles and five hundred rounds of ammunition for you in the back of my truck. We recovered them from the eastern bunker."

Herbie's stern expression softened, and he focused back on Jake. "Is that one of the rifles on your shoulder?"

"It's Allied standard 5.56 with an effective range of four hundred meters," Jake said. "They're pretty straightforward to use."

"What else did you find in there?" Herbie said. Jake paused and waited for Trader to do the talking. "Has the cat got your tongue? Answer me."

"Some basic supplies, but we didn't have room in Trader's trucks."

Herbie glanced between them at Trader's team waiting outside the cafeteria. "Have your men fed and watered, then come to my house. I'll brief you on our wireless tech project. Gaining access to that bunker might give us the breakthrough we need."

"Thanks. I'll be over in twenty minutes."

Herbie spun and headed back up the road. Trader turned to his team and indicated toward the blue metal cafeteria door.

"He's a prickly character," Jake said.

"We caught Herbie in a good mood, but he means well. He's always looking at ways of advancing what they have."

"Which is stunted by the population restrictions and trade. I can see his frustration."

"Short term loss for long term gain, Jake. We have to build solid foundations before branching out. It'll sink into your stasis-fried brain eventually."

"I love a good cliché as much as the next man, but I don't think arbitrary caps are your answer. What happens if a stronghold breaks the rules?"

"It hasn't happened yet."

"Haven't we just picked up a passenger who has been involved in Finch's idiot games?"

"Our treaty commits the other seven to war against the offender. That tends to keep the status quo. You'll get it in the end."

"Sounds like you've got one coming. Maybe you'll get that in the end?"

Trader jabbed his finger at Jake's chest. "You need to keep those dangerous thoughts to yourself."

* * *

Trader's team, dressed in their brown cargo pants and sweaters, sat on orange plastic chairs around a long rectangular table at the far end of the cafeteria. The tennis-court-sized room filled with the noise of Trader's team, clanking spoons against bowls as most hungrily devoured the stew served from a steaming hot plate at the opposite side.

Trader led Jake to a small table in a dark corner and waved Skye over. A young man with greasy brown hair, dressed in filthy khaki trousers and a black shirt, hunched on one of the four chairs around it. He blew on and sipped from a steaming mug of coffee. When Trader approached, he looked up and pulled out a chair.

"Meet Carlos," Trader said and sat next to him.

Carlos extended a scarred dirty hand. "You're Phillips, right?"

"Call me Jake."

"Who are you?" Carlos said to Skye.

"Skye Reed, from Omega."

Carlos glanced at Trader.

"You can trust her," Trader said.

"I don't feel like trusting anyone at the moment."

"You've had my mind racing since this morning. What did you find that can't be said over the airwaves?"

"It's bad, boss. I mean, really bad."

"Go on."

"Have you heard of Sky Man?"

Skye leaned forward to speak. Trader held out a hand to stop her. "Just tell me exactly what you saw."

"Omicron SUVs firing flares to attract wastelanders. They threw out food, luring them north, and shot any who got close. A guy shouted through a megaphone that Sky Man would help defeat the oppressors and give them unlimited supplies."

Trader rested an elbow on the table and rubbed his chin. "Interesting…"

"I knew it," Skye said. "This matches up with what I heard in the forest and the attack on the outlaws. Any idea who it might be, Trader?"

"It could be anyone. If they've waited ten years to strike again, I'm guessing some planning has gone into this."

Sky grabbed Trader's arm. "He killed my family. I want to be the first to know."

"We're all going to find out soon enough. Don't let emotions rule your thinking. Making the wrong move at this moment in time could prove fatal."

Jake understood Skye's desire. He had similar feelings burning inside, but Trader was right. Beating an enemy like this required smart planning. At the moment, they were one step behind. They had to find a way to get a step ahead, and visiting the ship in Epsilon might achieve it.

"Do you know any stronghold down a couple of SUVs?" Carlos said.

"I only hear if they need a new one. Did you recognize the voice or see any marks on the vehicles?"

"It was dark and too dangerous to get close."

"How far away are we talking?"

"A hundred miles when I saw them last night. They could be here tomorrow night. You have to put out an all stations call to organize our defenses."

"It's not as simple as that," Trader said. "Do you mind grabbing some coffees?"

Carlos sighed and pushed away his chair. "Whatever."

He placed his hands in his pockets and headed for the hot plate.

"I thought wastelanders lacked intelligence and couldn't be organized?" Jake said.

"Imagine being in a lion enclosure with a sack of meat," Trader said. "You can feed the lion for a while. It might even pretend to be your friend. When you run out of food, or it doesn't want what you're offering, it's over."

"The southern ones are more ruthless," Skye added. "Most don't even know we exist. I've seen what happens when a large group are shown a settlement. It's not pretty."

"Can they be trained to use firearms?" Jake said.

"Some probably can," Skye said. "Did they take some from the western bunker?"

Jake nodded. "Sixty rifles, twenty pistols and ten launchers. Plenty of ammo too. If C3431 is Sky Man, and he's from one of the strongholds, I think we need to make it an immediate priority to get to Epsilon and find out who he is."

"I'm not putting out an all stations call until we've established his identity," Trader said. "If we have a traitor in our ranks, who knows what he might have up his sleeve?"

"You're sure he's from a stronghold?" Jake said.

"Look at the evidence. Wastelanders are being led north by someone in our SUVs, a bunker close to the stronghold is raided for weapons, and what Skye heard in the forest. I don't believe in coincidences."

Carlos returned and placed three mugs on the table. "You need to warn people tonight, Trader. Give them time to prepare for what's coming."

"How many wastelanders did you see?" Trader said. "A few hundred?"

"Thousands. They could pick us off one at a time."

Skye puffed her cheeks and sat back. "Do you mind if I go out for some air?"

"Be my guest," Trader said. "We're heading to Epsilon in thirty minutes. I don't want to be traveling in the dark."

She stood and walked out of the building. Jake thought about the prospect of thousands of wastelanders attacking a stronghold at the same time. From the defenses he'd already seen at Epsilon, Omega, Sigma and Kappa, they were spread too thin and would be quickly overwhelmed.

"We need to pool our resources," Jake said.

"What do you mean?" Trader said.

"Bring the populations of other strongholds behind the walls of Omega. Line the ramparts with a large armed force; otherwise they'll quickly lose a war of attrition."

"They won't abandon their own places," Carlos said. "Especially at such short notice."

"He's right," Trader said. "There's personal pride at stake."

"Pride won't save their lives," Jake said. "Sometimes you have to lose something in order to win. Blow the gates of the other strongholds, take out the supplies and carry out a scorched earth policy so they have to attack Omega. We'll cut them down before they get inside."

Trader and Carlos exchanged glances. One of the team rushed through the door and made her way over to the table. "Trader, did you give permission for Skye to take one of our SUVs?"

"No. Tell the gate not to let her out."

"It's too late for that. She's already gone."

He clenched his fist and thumped the table. "Round up the team. We're heading out immediately."

"Where do you think she's gone?" Jake said.

"She's a lone wolf. I'm guessing to do her own investigations. Let's just hope it doesn't lead her to Sky Man. The last thing we need is for him to get an early heads-up that we're onto him."

Jake had another motive for going to Epsilon. He wanted to find out how he came out of stasis. He had a growing feeling that his waking was more than simple fate.

Chapter Seventeen

Skye pulled off the main route, half a mile from Omega, and bumped along a disused road through the forest. She wanted to confront Finch on her own terms. If he was looking for her, guards at the front gate would send an immediate message to his mansion. She didn't believe him to be complicit with Sky Man and his plans, but the stronghold's safety had to come first.

She reached a derelict church and parked the stolen SUV around its side. Skye remembered being brought here as a child. People from her settlement and Omega would meet every Sunday morning to exchange food and socialize. It hadn't been used for ten years and had fallen into a state of disrepair. Paint peeled off the dull white planking, moss covered the roof tiles, and the stained-glass windows were coated in dust. A filthy tattered flag hung limply from the top of a rusty flagpole outside the faded red front doors.

Skye locked the vehicle door and headed through the forest toward the steps. Trader would be furious about her theft. She hoped he would understand that if Finch was dirty, she wanted to hear it for herself. He took her in and treated her like a daughter. It seemed impossible he could be involved with the very man who killed her parents, but she had to be sure.

Shafts of late afternoon sunshine radiated through the canopy, highlighting small clusters of midges busily swarming just above the forest floor. Skye maintained a high level of vigilance while she weaved her way between the trunks and headed for the steps. She knew most of the guard on that part of the rampart and could tell them not to report her return, if Ross wasn't around.

The dark imposing walls were only two hundred yards away. She decided to approach directly in line of sight of the pillboxes. They might have faced more attacks in the last twenty-four hours, and she didn't want a nervous guard taking a potshot at her.

One of the guards on the rampart acknowledged her with a wave. Skye breathed a sigh of relief and jogged to the steps. Sam Bennett appeared from the left pillbox. He nodded at her but didn't smile as she climbed to meet him.

"You look like death warmed up," he said. "Where the hell have you been?"

"Long story. I need you to do something for me immediately."

"Sure. Whatever you want."

"Destroy the outer steps. Use whatever you can."

Sam glanced down and gave Skye a confused look. "Have you fallen on your head? What's going on?"

"Thousands of wastelanders are heading north. Trader's scout confirmed it this afternoon. We need to destroy our weak point."

"Thousands? Are you sure?"

"Positive. Yesterday's gonna seem like a picnic compared to what might arrive tomorrow."

"You know I can't do it without permission. Ross will tear me a new ass."

Skye considered that Ross, being a coward, would do anything to save his own ass before he went after anyone else's. Ross had witnessed Sky Man's ruthlessness first hand, and when he found out the same might happen to Omega, with no place to run, he wouldn't argue about destroying the easiest way into the stronghold for an attacking force.

"Just find a way, Sam. Let me take care of him."

He looked in either direction and stepped closer. "We could both lose our tags for this."

"We could both lose our lives if you don't. Do you trust me?"

"Yes … I do … but—"

"But nothing, Sam. I'm going to see Finch. Whatever happens, this needs to be done."

"I can't get my head around it. How did thousands get together and know to come here?"

"I don't have time to explain everything. Where's Ross?"

"The governor's manor. Finch ordered him up this morning."

"Good. Things need to change around here, regardless of what I find out in the next twenty minutes."

He paused for a moment and nodded to himself. "Good luck. I'll do what I can here."

"Thanks, Sam," Skye said. "Hopefully I won't need luck, but Finch has some questions to answer."

She turned and ran down the inner steps. Sam called her back, no doubt wanting to find out more, but her friend would have to wait.

* * *

Skye pushed open the wrought-iron gates at the front of the governor's mansion. She couldn't think of a diplomatic way to confront the man who acted like a father for ten years.

The front doors opened. Ross walked out and put on his cap. He looked at Skye, grimaced and strode toward her. "Where the hell have you been?"

"Finding out that we're in serious trouble."

"We're not in serious trouble. You're in serious trouble. Finch is furious. He told me about having to bail you out in Zeta."

Skye wondered if this man ever had a single thought that didn't involve his own self-interest. "We've never seen eye to eye. I have always doubted you, Ross, but I'm going to have to trust you for this to work."

"What are you babbling about?"

"I've just ordered Sam Bennett to destroy the steps in front of the barracks."

He moved closer and his belly brushed against Skye's jacket. "You did what?"

His breath stank of a mixture of cigar smoke and alcohol. The rewards for being Finch's unquestioning stooge.

"Thousands of wastelanders are heading right here. We don't want to give them an easy way in."

"You can't expect me to believe that. If they've gone ahead and done it, Finch'll take your tags for sure. Even you won't get a pass for an action like that."

"They'll overrun us if we don't do it. You don't have anywhere to run this time. You can deny what happened ten years ago to Finch, but you can't to me. I know the truth, and you need to face up to it. Sky Man is coming."

Ross shook his head and sneered. "You've lost it this time. Do you know how insane you sound?"

"Would you accuse Trader of lying? Because that's what you're gonna have to do if you don't listen to me."

"Why didn't you radio ahead and speak to Finch? We've been trying to contact you for hours."

"I turned it off, and he can't know about it."

"Why not?"

"He might be involved. I know somewhere inside of you is a man who wants to protect his people. It's time you be the hero that Omega thinks you are."

Ross gently gripped Skye's arm and led her to the side of the mansion. "Do you have any proof to your allegations?"

"Nothing solid, but he's linked to a man who sent me to the outlaws' camp. Wastelanders attacked in force after I arrived. Would you call that a coincidence?"

He looked down and palmed his forehead. "It can't be true. Can it?"

"Something tells me that you're having doubts about Finch. Seriously, Ross, this isn't time for playing games. Our survival's at stake, along with everybody else in Omega. He might have nothing to do with it, but we need peace of mind and to prepare our defenses."

"He was acting weird just now. Distracted. More than just the usual butterfly stuff."

"Come with me. You need to hear this too, because if he's involved, we're taking command."

Ross shook his head and paced around the gravel path. A smile stretched across his face. "I'll come with you."

"Do you find this amusing?" Skye said.

"No, I'm not the one taking the risk."

"It's worth the risk. Not confronting him would be far more dangerous."

Seeing the hemp fields in Zeta as a mature adult, fighting alongside the outlaws, and learning about Epsilon's role in arming the outlaws drove a wedge in Skye's total acceptance of the stronghold system. The more she thought about it, the deeper her doubts became, but they were nothing compared to the ones she had about Finch.

She led the way through the mansion's front doors and headed straight for Finch's study. Ross followed, mumbling to himself about the craziness of what he just heard.

Skye knocked twice on the office door.

"What? Can't I get any peace today," Finch shouted.

"It's Skye. We need to talk."

"Come in. I've been waiting for you."

She took a deep breath and entered. Finch slumped behind his desk in a brown paisley robe. His hair stuck up on one side, as if he'd just gotten out of bed. A quarter-full whiskey bottle and empty glass sat on the desk in front of him.

He glared at her and drummed his fingers on the table as she approached.

"The flutterby has returned," he slurred. "Maybe Ross was right about you. Perhaps I need to pull off your wings?"

"We need a serious talk, Alexander."

"You don't get to call me that today. The convoy told me you've been with the Trader. Why?"

"I went to Kappa with him and Jake Phillips."

"I specifically asked for you to return straight after your mission and debrief me. Are you turning into a Cloudless Sulphur Caterpillar?"

"A what?"

"They kill and eat their own. What did the toad want?"

"If you mean Trader, he intercepted the convoy and asked me to join his, as he has some concerns over recent events. I went because I do too."

Ross, standing behind Skye, cleared his throat. "May I offer an opinion?"

"No, you may not," Finch said while keeping his focus on Skye. "What are your concerns?"

"About the mission you sent me on. Rhodes specifically."

Finch's lips curled into a snarl. "What exactly is it I'm supposed to have done? The ridiculous ramblings of Governor Harrison got to you? He tried to accuse me of assisting a rebellion inside his walls. I simply made a trade with good citizens asking for weapons to defend themselves against roaming outlaws. Weapons their own people wouldn't provide. How was I supposed to know they were planning on using them to oppose his rule?"

This was the first mention of weapons. Skye wondered how he would react if another governor armed people of Omega behind his back. He also didn't seem his normal self today, if any of his behavior could be classed as normal.

"I was told someone from Omega contacted Rhodes to warn him about his arrest. Was it you?"

"No I didn't. Who are you to question me, even if I did?"

Normally his comment would be correct. The politics and coups of strongholds were none of her business, but the looming threat and wastelander attacks on Omega, the outlaw camp and bunker, coupled with his connection to Rhodes made it Skye's business. She decided to reveal more of what she knew and observe his reaction.

"Thousands of wastelanders are heading for Omega."

Finch clenched his fists and rested them on the table. "Who told you that pack of lies?"

"Trader. One of his scouts has seen them. They could be here by tomorrow evening."

"I've scouted the area myself and found no evidence. Has it crossed your mind that he might be lying to you? It's in his interest to build up a threat so he can line his pockets based on false fear. Don't tell me he's caught you on his sticky tongue and sucked you in?"

He shook his head, twisted off the bottle's cap, and poured himself a whiskey.

"I don't believe you," Skye said.

She never thought those words would come out of her mouth, but believed every one of them. Finch threw his glass across the room. Skye dodged to her right and it shattered against the wall behind her. He looked at the damp patch on his right arm, picked up the bottle, and unsteadily moved toward her.

Skye braced herself. She wasn't going to stand there and let him hit her with it.

"How dare you call me a liar?" Finch said. "I've done everything for you, and this is how you repay me? Listening to that greedy toad over your own *father*!"

"My father was Thomas Reed. An honest and good person. Murdered by Sky Man. Did you know about the wastelander attack on the outlaw camp? Because if you did—"

Finch's face reddened and he crossed his palm over his chest. Skye took a step back. His breath hissed through gaps in his gritted teeth.

"Captain Ross, has this bitch spread any of these lies since arriving back in Omega?"

Skye turned to Ross and hoped he'd seen enough to realize that Finch was increasingly unhinged and up to something. They hadn't established what, but his evasive and aggressive answers showed more than they told.

"I don't know, Governor," Ross said. "She accosted me when I walked out of the front doors."

"Don't lie to me, Ross. I've had quite my fill of that today."

Ross edged away from Skye. "She told the guard to blow the outer steps in preparation for a wastelander attack, sir."

"Was it that little turd, Bennett?"

Skye didn't answer. She should have guessed that Ross would be a coward.

Finch nodded. "Inform Bennett to cease any such activities. Have him come to the mansion to speak with me. Her lies can't be allowed to spread. She's obviously in league with the Trader, in a scam to take over Omega."

"Yes, sir. I'll do it right away."

"Ross, listen to me, he's lying to you. He's lying to all of us. I saw the attack on the outlaw camp with my own eyes in the hills. Someone is bringing them north. Arrest Finch, and we'll find out the truth together."

Ross looked at her and back at Finch.

"Cuff her," Finch said.

Skye ran for the door. Ross reached out and grabbed the back of her jacket. She turned to strike him, but Finch dived at her and forced her against the wall. Both of them pulled her hands behind her back and she felt the cuffs tightly crunch around her wrists.

Ross spun Skye around. Finch grabbed the chain around her neck, ripped her tags off, and dangled them in front of her eyes. "She won't be needing these. Captain Ross, please take her to the cells. That's an order."

Ross grabbed the back of Skye's arm and opened the door.

"Wait a moment," Finch said. He moved to an inch of Skye's face. "You'll never be clever enough to get the better of me."

He pressed his tongue against the bottom of her cheek and slowly licked up, then turned to Ross and nodded. He led Skye from the office to her future as an outlaw.

Chapter Eighteen

A light dust storm brushed across the convoy as it crunched along a gravel road toward the distant forest. Shafts of late afternoon sunlight poked through the clouds, creating a strange amber atmosphere. Jake wound up his window. Trader's smoking was more bearable than grit in his eyes.

If Epsilon were worried about Jake's escape denting their population clock, they were about to receive a larger and more immediate threat to their numbers.

"If the comms console doesn't work, what's the plan?" Jake said.

"We warn everyone tonight. If the strongholds are prepared to move, they can't afford to be caught in the open tomorrow evening."

"A hundred miles is a long way on foot. That's fifty miles a day if they get here by then."

"Wastelanders are human, but they're being purposefully driven. I'd be surprised if they took their time getting here. Thank God for Carlos."

Jake glanced over his shoulder at Carlos sleeping on the backseat. "How do you think Epsilon will react?"

"I'm guessing they'll initially resist. You're going to help me convince them. It's your plan. We don't have any experience with battles, only skirmishes."

"Not being funny, Trader, but I was their exhibit for forty years. Why would they listen to me?"

"We're going to need a single voice to lead. They know me as a Trader, a middleman. Strongholds won't take orders from each other. You're an Allied officer with military experience. Can you think of a better candidate? We start selling you now."

They approached a rickety wooden signpost at a fork in the road. Left pointed to Epsilon, right to Omega. Trader steered left and cut through the forest. Driving through countryside wasn't an option as the stronghold lay in the middle of it. Jake remembered that much from his escape.

Feeling slightly more comfortable in Trader's company, and not knowing a thing about the man's history, Jake took the opportunity to probe. If he was to take the role forward, he wanted to know whose shoes he filled.

"I don't know anything about you," Jake said. "Tell me a bit about yourself?"

"There's nothing much to say."

"Let me be the judge of that. How did you get the job in the first place?"

Trader groaned and flicked his cigarette out of the window. "The old Trader took me under his wing, a little like what I'm doing with you."

"But you didn't come out of a stasis pod in the middle of a stronghold."

"That's true, but I wasn't really part of any society. I used to scout for Sigma, and he took over those duties, so I ended up in his team by default. I rode with him and learned how he operated. You can't say there isn't any value to how things are set up."

"I'm not saying there isn't value, but the day you stop reviewing potential ways to improve things is the day that a decline starts. Do you have a wife? Kids?"

"I'm married to this job. The team are my kids."

"I know that feeling."

Jake joined the Fleet Academy as soon as he could. When the threat of war escalated, he grew deeper into his training as part of an Orbital Bomber crew. The last thing he wanted to do was to leave a family looking at the sky and missing him.

Dust thinned due to the protection of the trees, and the surface allowed them to increase their speed. Jake checked his watch. Half past four in the afternoon probably gave them twenty-four hours to organize a robust defense, although they didn't have a minute to waste.

"I was thinking about how I woke—"

Trader hit the brakes. The SUV's wheels locked and scraped against the road surface. Carlos bolted up.

A spear arced through the air toward the windshield.

Jake pressed himself against the door, out of the trajectory line. The spear's point hit the center of the glass a second later, causing a chip with small shatter lines around it. It fell, clanked against the hood, and rolled off the side.

He kicked the passenger door open, shouldered his rifle, and scanned the area. Trader blasted the horn, and vehicle engines roared in the distance.

A figure darted from behind a rock to a nearby tree. Jake focused his sights on it. Another moved forward in the gloomy undergrowth, creeping through a group of ferns. He switched his aim and fired three rounds. A gurgled scream echoed through the forest.

The vehicles rumbled up behind. The trucks' breaks hissed. Trader's team piled out and surrounded their own vehicles. Jake gave a crisp hand signal toward the area he saw the first figure move.

A muzzle flashed in the forest. Rounds peppered the SUV behind them. Each impact created a hollow tinkle. One of Trader's team fell clutching their thigh.

Something whistled through the air. Jake heard a small clink. A metal dart with red flights stuck in the SUV door next to him.

The area cracked with gunfire as the team returned fire. Rounds whizzed through the forest. Bark chipped off trees. The figure behind the trunk fell to all fours and tried to crawl away. A rifle hung around their shoulder. Jake placed the wastelander's head in his front sight, let out a deep breath, and fired. The figure collapsed.

If more were armed in hidden positions, the team were sitting ducks. Two men scrambled behind the SUV with Trader.

Jake jumped to his feet. "Give me covering fire."

He sprinted across the road for the tree line and crouched behind the first pine he reached. Rounds from the team zipped through the forest. The enemy casualty was dressed in a clean Allied overall. This wasn't a colleague. The man had grimy hands and cheeks, tangled greasy hair and red welts on his face. It gave Jake a sense of satisfaction that he gained a little bit of justice, but he wanted a lot more.

Footsteps thudded on the damp forest ground. Another wastelander, in a badly fitting Allied uniform, hobbled away carrying a thin metal tube.

Jake quickly surveyed the immediate area. Without detecting further signs of movement, he held out a hand to stop the team's fire. He wanted to stamp out the risk of blue on blue while giving chase.

The team stopped firing. He gestured them to the casualty and headed deeper into the forest. The female wastelander, with long mousy hair, wasn't attempting to hide and held her blood-soaked left arm as she staggered through the trees.

Jake crouched and aimed. Something inside stopped him pulling the trigger. She was still a human, albeit a dangerous one. Trader wheezed up behind him, leaned against a trunk and fired. The woman flopped to the ground.

"Don't even think about having sympathy, Jake. She'd skin you alive given half a chance."

"Did you notice the uniforms?"

"Couldn't miss them. They must've been part of the bunker raid. Sky Man's wastelanders in the local area."

"Which means we could be facing more rifles and rocket launchers. I suggest we get out of here before the cavalry arrives."

Trader peered through the trees. "We could wait and ambush them. I'll get the launchers from the truck."

"No. Save them for tomorrow. That's when we're going to need them."

"Epsilon it is."

Jake found it slightly odd how they were prepared to go with his decisions so quickly. He accepted strongholds hadn't been involved in battles yet, but they had experienced skirmishes. Regardless of how his increasing authority came about, he enjoyed leading by example and knew they had a fight on their hands. If they accepted him to lead the battle against a wastelander invasion, so be it. It would give him influence after victory, to organize a better society without clocks.

It also gave him a chance to face down a former fellow officer who was now a cowardly traitor.

* * *

Trader took a less cautious approach for the last twenty-five minutes of the journey. He pushed the SUV's suspension to its limit, bumping through potholes and crashing through pools of water. Jake maintained a vigilant watch on the forest to either side until they reached the gates of Epsilon. It felt like a week had passed since he last saw the walls, not a day and a half.

The gates opened with a loud mechanical click. Four guards stood inside the entrance and glared into the SUV as Trader drove past. Jake leaned down and covered his face with his hand.

"Seriously, Jake, you've got nothing to worry about. They like you."

"It didn't seem like that when I escaped."

"The last thing they would've wanted is for you to get butchered by wastelanders in the forest. I'll take you straight to Barry and Beth. We'll need their permission to access the ship."

"The governors?"

"They don't use titles here. Just names."

Trader drove along a smooth paved road between the brick-built foundry and the hundreds of tightly packed houses. All were twentieth-century style with hipped roofs and narrow alleys running between them. It looked more like an old-fashioned industrial town than any of the other strongholds.

A noise like a foghorn blasted from the factory.

"Home time, better get out of the way," Trader said.

He sped up toward the woodland cloaking the ship, and stopped next to the end house. It had a neatly trimmed lawn at the front, surrounded by a colorful flower bed.

"One thing I've been meaning to ask," Jake said. "I hardly see any people around in the strongholds. Where do they all go?"

"Most places have curfews after work. Before you say anything, it's for the good of the people. If a wastelander manages to get in, the guard need a clean shot, and we don't want to put the workers at risk."

"What about the bar in Omega?"

"You can go directly between buildings. We can't have people wandering close to the walls. We have to preserve what we have in the best possible way."

Jake thought about questioning the supposed best way, but decided better of it. At the moment, they had a bigger and more immediate concern. Being an effective leader wasn't all about fighting, it was choosing battles wisely and avoiding them if they had no chance of a positive outcome. The restrictive ways of the strongholds were irrelevant if they couldn't overcome Sky Man and his plans.

He followed Trader down a garden path and stood outside a red-painted front door with the gold letters *B&B* screwed onto it.

"Don't let their friendly appearance fool you," Trader said. "Anyone who runs a stronghold has to be tough."

Jake smiled. "I'm starting to like your early warnings. Are you going to introduce me to anyone who doesn't require a caveat?"

Trader shook his head and straightened his gray bushy beard. He gave the door three sharp knocks and stepped back.

"Give me a minute," a woman called from inside.

Jake turned and watched men and women stream out of the factory in their blue coveralls and head for their houses. Some went to a large building next to the factory and returned outside with children. A few glanced across at Jake and Trader before disappearing through their doors or along alleyways.

The door opened and a man and woman stood in the hallway. Both were slim with gray hair and dressed in the same coveralls as the workers.

The man squinted at Jake and smiled. "You've returned, Captain Phillips. I'm Barry, and this is my wife, Beth."

Jake shook his bony, liver-spot-peppered hand. "Nice to meet you both. We've come here on on important business."

Beth stepped forward and rested her hand on his shoulder. Jake's instinct told him to flinch away, but he maintained his position in front of the threshold.

"We were your guardians for forty years, Captain," she said. "You have nothing to fear in Epsilon."

"We'll always have a place for you on our clock," Barry said. He looked at Trader and frowned. "If the others keep insisting that we use the damned system."

"You're not fans?" Jake said. "I've only been—"

"This can wait," Trader said. "Can we come inside for a chat after looking around the ship?"

"Sounds urgent," Beth said. "What are you hoping to find? All loose objects were taken years ago."

"It is urgent. Very urgent. Jake needs to access the comms console. What I'm going to tell you has a direct consequence. We don't have much time."

"Very well, Trader," Barry said. He unclipped a handheld radio from the side of his coverall, depressed a button on the side, and held it to his mouth. "Epsilon guard, this is Barry. Trader and Captain Phillips will be accessing the ship. No need to raise an alarm."

"I hope you find what you're looking for, Captain," Beth said. "We're looking forward to talking when you return."

Jake found it slightly strange that they acted like they knew him and spoke as if he was a returning son. He did feel grateful that they'd brought his ship inside a stronghold and kept him alive. "I have a few questions for you, like the fate of the rest of my crew."

"Can't help you with that," Barry said. "You were the only one left. I'm sorry."

"Until later." Beth smiled and closed the door.

Trader glared at Jake. "Don't lose focus and start your own private investigations. Our priority is to identify the rogue officer and act accordingly."

"I won't. Do you know how I can get into the cockpit? I found the port door jammed when I first came out of stasis."

"There's a staircase on the opposite side that leads to the front of the ship."

"Keep your fingers crossed that it works, because the one in the stasis chamber didn't."

"The screens are readable. Loads have tried to access the system. Epsilon had to rope the area off to stop people from playing with the controls."

Jake didn't want to waste any time and headed straight for the woodland. A well-beaten path led through the middle, straight to the rickety wooden staircase.

Trader moved ahead after reaching the clearing and turned left on a gravel path that circled the ship.

He stopped, lit a cigarette, and blew smoke in the air. "I remember when this used to be popular."

"I remember when it used to fly."

Jake wondered how many humans had visited Endeavor Three, inspecting it like a zoo or ancient pyramid, with him as the main exhibit. The Orbital Bombers used to be the pride of the Fleet. The crafts that would ensure their long-term safety, and it was considered an honor to be part of the crew. They were never designed with voyeuristic pleasure in mind.

Walking past the smooth nose cone at the front of the ship, Jake could see both staircases. The original one he descended and another that climbed to the starboard side emergency exit. Viewing the symmetry of both from the front made it look like a ramshackle roller coaster had been built through the vessel.

Trader screwed his cigarette end into the ground with his heel. He ascended the fifty creaking wooden stairs, and Jake followed closely behind.

Climbing this side of the ship gave Jake a view of the southern end of the wall. He remembered that Epsilon had just under three thousand inhabitants and knew they wouldn't have a chance of holding such a large circumference against an attack from a larger group. An assault could try to establish a breach in several locations, or take a spot on the wall using ladders, allowing the enemy to stream over. Nothing changed his mind about pooling resources. The second part of his Epsilon mission would be to convince the stronghold to move, survive and win.

Trader leaned against the entrance and took a few deep breaths. "Through there … Door's open."

It only seemed like two days ago that Jake sat in one of the two black leather seats in the cockpit, viewing Earth from orbit. Everything looked the same, although the leather, gray laminated controls and blue interior were all slightly faded and an odor like polish hung in the air. He scanned the flight controls first. All were in the manual landing position, so they were purposely brought down by a pilot.

A small dark green square winked on the comms console. The only unit to have power in the cockpit. This wasn't unexpected on skeleton settings, although the beacon signal on landing would've been futile in terms of expecting a response. Once bunkers went on lockdown, they didn't respond to distress signals.

Jake sat at the stool and hit the keyboard. The password prompt flashed across the screen in light green letters.

He input his password, and the main screen fired up. It confirmed the date as May 20th, 2205. From here, he accessed the file manager, opened up the ship's monitoring folder, opened up the stasis log, and read through the last ten events.

A crew member activated all pods for waking procedure in 2165, apart from Jake's. Nothing then until yesterday morning, when the same crew member activated his waking procedure. C1437. He now had two officers to look up. More importantly, his suspicions about the coincidental nature of waking were justified.

"What you looking at?" Trader said.

"Looks like we've got another officer on the loose. He woke me up yesterday morning."

"You're kidding me."

Jake ran his finger across a line on the screen. "See for yourself."

Trader leaned forward, and Jake received a waft of stale smoke while he whispered the text to himself. "Did you see anyone in Epsilon you recognized?"

"I didn't hang around to check out faces."

Jake didn't know what to make of the latest revelation. If a member of the crew woke him up, he couldn't understand why they disappeared straight after. He drilled down to the Fleet resource file, input his captain's passcode, the date of the moon landing, and a box popped on the screen asking for a surname or number.

He input C1437 first. The chance of an old friend or ally in the new world proved too much to resist. The pointer spun for a second and the information flashed across the screen. Jake took a deep breath.

C1437 – Flight Lieutenant Gary Mills – Pilot
D.O.B: 11.11.2045
Location: Endeavor Three

He stared at the picture of his fresh-faced partner for the Sixth Cycle.

"I don't believe it," Jake said. "Where the hell is he, and why did he wake me up?"

Trader shook his head. "Forget about that for now. Find out who Sky Man is. That's what we came for."

"You can't blame me for being a little surprised."

"How does it improve our situation?"

Jake shrugged. "No idea, but I'd like to know where he is and what he knows."

He closed down Mill's info and input C3431 into the prompt box.

The information flashed across the screen.

Jake leaned forward and shook his head.

Trader gasped.

C3431 – Captain Alexander Finch – Facility Manager
D.O.B: 04.10.2043
Location: Oregon

Chapter Nineteen

Late evening sunshine poured between the rusty bars of Skye's cell. She stretched her neck and enjoyed the last moments of warmth before spending an uncomfortable night on the cold stone floor. She craved sleep, but snorting and clucking from the pens and shed outside would probably keep her awake, when her mind didn't race over the events of the last twenty-four hours.

She peered at a distant section of the wall and hoped to catch a guard's attention. Somebody needed to listen to reason; otherwise they would be attacked without warning. Nobody came close to her cell, no doubt wanting to avoid being held guilty by association. All around the stronghold, people went about their usual early evening business, closing up the stores, returning from the fields, and changing the guard around the rampart.

Her neck felt naked without the tag chain. For ten years, Skye wore her tags as a confirmation of Omega citizenship. She never dreamed of them being taken away, especially by Finch.

Confronting him without support backfired, but she had little choice considering the impending attack. Her hopes rested with Trader and Jake. They knew what was coming. They would do something.

She hated feeling useless locked up in a cell.

Her stomach growled, but people in cells weren't served food. She thought about dining with Finch yesterday and shook her head. It made her feel stupid to know that all the time she sat there eating his pea and ham soup, he played her like a fiddle, making her do his corrupt bidding.

Skye stared at the ceiling. A small black spider busily spun a web in the corner around a captured fly. She felt just as trapped. Bashing her way through the decaying corrugated cover would bring a guard before she had a chance to escape.

Footsteps squashed through the mud toward her. She pressed her face against the bars and looked to the right.

Sam Bennett, looking unwashed with dark rings around his tired eyes, glanced around while approaching the cell.

"What are you doing here?" Skye said. "If Finch finds you, he'll take your tags."

Sam pointed his rifle at her. "This is just for show in case I'm being watched. Ross ordered us to leave the steps in place. Said you were lying about the wastelanders. I was sent up to the mansion for a meeting with Finch."

"Did he punish you for listening to me?"

"After he finished ranting about the lack of loyalty, he sent me back to the captain's tower. Ross told me that he took your tags."

Skye felt her neck again and remembered Finch ripping them away. She shuddered at the thought of him licking her face after doing it.

Sam gave her a sympathetic look. "I'm sorry, Skye. What I don't understand is why he's keeping you locked up. Why weren't you thrown out?"

There was only one thing that made sense.

"He wants to keep me quiet. Doesn't want me getting in contact with Trader or the other strongholds. I'm not crazy. The wastelander army is real. Can you get a message to Trader for me?"

Sam turned away. Two guards gazed over from outside a pillbox on the rampart. "He's promoted Ross to General of the Guard. He's in charge of all our defenses."

On the face of it, the promotion seemed ridiculous, but it wasn't if Finch wanted an ineffective commander. Ross didn't know his ass from his elbow and couldn't organize a fart at a curry-eating contest.

"That rat sold me out. You can't trust him an inch. He only acts out of self-interest and will betray you if it means another fat cigar in Finch's study."

"Tell me something I don't know," Sam said. He paused and sheepishly looked at the ground. "There's more ... I've been made captain."

Skye stared at his guilt-ridden face and tried to gauge if she'd misjudged him too. His reward for playing along would only be short term if he didn't listen to reason.

"Doesn't mean a thing if we get overrun and slaughtered this evening."

"Finch told me it was payment for my loyalty and silence. He said things were going to change and that he has big plans for our immediate future."

"He's right about the last part, but not in the way you think."

"I'm not buying his crap, Skye. If you and Trader both say this thing is happening, that's good enough for me."

Skye smiled and hoped he wouldn't turn when she requested a second time, "I could kiss you, Sam Bennett. Tell the Trader I've been locked up and Finch is hiding something. He'll know what to do."

"Okay. I'll take a vehicle out and contact him on his channel. Is there anything else you need me to do?"

Skye thought for a moment. "No. We've still got until tomorrow for him to get here and sort things out. Don't put yourself at risk. We need every good fighter available. If the Trader doesn't show by mid-afternoon, we'll have to launch our own coup and destroy the steps."

Sam nodded and slung his rifle. "I'll get right to it."

Skye breathed a sigh of relief and leaned against the wall of her cell. At least she had part of a plan in place. She disliked having things out of her own control, but her options were limited. Sam gave her a timely reminder that they had something good worth saving. Finch and Ross were the ones who needed to be banished.

Raised voices came from behind the chicken shed, followed by two dull thuds. A man cried out in pain. People were heading toward her. She smelled cigar smoke on the gentle breeze.

Ross and Finch, the latter dressed in old-fashioned combat clothing, dragged Sam by his arms to the front of her cell. He groggily tried to raise his head.

Finch kicked him in the jaw. "If there's one thing I hate, it's a traitor."

Sam slumped in the dirt and moaned through blood-soaked lips. Ross leaned down and handcuffed him.

Skye glared at Finch. "What the hell are you doing?"

"I'm repeating history. This animal has fallen into my trap."

"What's that supposed to mean?"

"In colonial Africa, Major Godfrey Finch used an excellent hunting method to capture his prey. He would tie a young boy to a tree and wait for a tiger to appear before shooting it. I am my forefather, you are the boy, and Bennett is my tiger."

Skye shook her head. "You need help. Sam came here to interrogate me for information as your new captain."

Ross sneered and ran his golden general's baton along the bars. "Once bitten, twice shy. Drop the act. We're not swallowing your lies."

"You're not a citizen of this or any stronghold," Finch said. "You have no rights under the terms of our treaty, and anyone found assisting you will also be made an outlaw."

"Why are you doing this?" Skye said. "Have you made a deal with Sky Man and his wastelanders?"

"My motivations are none of your concern. General Ross, please restrain Bennett."

Ross dragged Sam to his feet, gripping him by the shoulders.

Finch groaned. "Don't let him stand."

He kicked the back of Sam's legs, and he dropped to his knees. He looked up at Skye with fear in his eyes and opened his mouth, but no words came out of his trembling lips. Finch scowled at him, took a handkerchief out of his jacket pocket, and wiped blood from his right knuckle.

"General Ross, may I have your radio, please? I believe our good friend, the Trader, is probably well in range of Omega by now."

"He won't let you get away with whatever you've planned." Skye said. "It was one thing to take over like you did, I heard all about it from James Ryder, but you've gone too far. All of our lives are at risk."

Finch ignored her and snatched the radio from Ross. He switched it to Trader's channel and passed it through the bars.

Skye frowned. "What do you expect me to do with this?"

"Call the toad, tell him all is well in Omega and the wastelander army is heading straight past us."

She held it back toward him. "What kind of a fool do you think I am?"

"I thought you said their army didn't—" Ross said.

"Shut up, General. I can demote you as fast as I promoted you." Finch ripped his pistol from his holster and placed it against Sam's temple. "You'll do it, Skye, and be convincing, or I'll kill him."

Ross' eyes widened and he backed away.

"You're many things," Skye said to Ross. "But you can't let this happen. He's admitted about the army. That's one of your men he's pointing a gun at."

"I'm sure we can sort this out," Ross stuttered. "I mean, you aren't really going to shoot him, are you, Governor?"

Finch glared at Ross. "How dare you question me? This man is an outlaw. I have the right to kill him if I want. You need to read the treaty if you want to keep your position."

Ross looked down at his baton and avoided eye contact. "I'm sorry, sir. It won't happen again."

Finch nodded and focused back on Skye. "Call him now." He put a round in the chamber. "Five. Four. Three. Two."

Skye couldn't decide if he was bluffing, but she couldn't risk Sam's life on gambling the wrong way. She lifted the radio to her mouth and pushed the button. "Trader, this is Skye. Do you copy?"

The radio crackled. "Trader here, but you're coming through pretty weak. What the hell were you thinking running off like that?"

She looked up at Finch. He jabbed his muzzle against Sam's head.

"I'm in Omega with Finch. I was wrong about him. He's scouted the wastelanders, and they're bypassing our strongholds and heading north."

"Did he tell you this?"

Finch gave her a single nod.

"Yes. There's no need for you to worry."

"You're sure?"

"I'm sure, but we'll keep on the lookout."

"Thanks for letting me know. Tell him we won't be visiting tomorrow."

Her heart sank. The best she could hope for now was for Finch to release both of them to spend the rest of their lives as outlaws. Avoiding an army of wastelanders without weapons provided a bleak outlook for anyone outside the walls. The situation wasn't much better for the citizens behind them. They would be attacked without warning.

"Are you still there, Skye?" Trader said.

"I'm here. Where are you?"

"Epsilon with Jake and my crew. I'll contact you on Friday. Don't go running off like that again, okay?"

"I'll speak to you then. Skye out."

Finch held out his hand. "You've got quite a talent for lying. Give me the radio."

"Can we leave now?"

He flashed his uneven yellow teeth. "I'm gonna show you how we deal with traitors in my new system."

"Wait!" Skye said.

She sprang forward, thrust her hand through the bars, and tried to reach for his pistol. Finch leaned away and shook his head. He holstered his weapon. "I wouldn't waste a round of ammunition on a snake."

Relief washed over Sam's face. Finch grabbed the tag chain from around his neck and yanked it away. He passed the tags to Ross and slid a hunting knife from his belt. "This is how to deal with disloyalty."

He grabbed a chunk of Sam's hair and pulled his head back, exposing his throat. Sam tried to struggle to his feet and twist away. Finch grunted, shoved him back down, and plunged the blade into his windpipe. Ross gasped and put his hand over his mouth.

Sam let out a gargled cry. Finch sawed at his neck with the serrated edge for five seconds before letting him slump to the ground.

Blood pulsed from the wound. He coughed and looked at Skye through his flickering eyes and reached out his quivering right hand.

Finch crouched and wiped his blade on Sam's jacket. "This is the dawn of a new world. I will not tolerate treachery. He backstabbed me; I gave him the courtesy of doing it from the front."

Skye knelt and grabbed Sam's hand. His eyes closed and his grip loosened almost immediately. A mix of grief and anger rose up inside her. Finch wasn't even pretending to be official anymore, and Ross watched on like a frightened child.

"You're a monster," she said.

Finch slid his knife back into his belt and stepped over Sam. "You can stay here and watch his body rot while I decide what to do with you."

"Are you mad? Those are wastelanders coming, and they will slaughter all of us. They only work for Sky Man. Do you think he'll have mercy on you?"

Out of the corner of her eye, Skye noticed Ross slip away. Rather than facing reality, he still remained a yellowbelly. Finch glanced over his shoulder, but didn't seem concerned. He was probably confident in Ross' ability, or lack of it.

He edged closer. "You have no idea what I have planned. This is only the beginning. I had such great hopes for you. But now you'll have to watch Omega get slaughtered from your cell, just as you watched your settlement destroyed ten years ago."

"Are you that obsessed with power that you're willing to sell your soul? You'll be killed like the rest of us."

"I can assure you that I won't be dying tomorrow. I've been delivered into this world to cleanse it of predators. The strongholds are full of rats, lizards, toads, wasps and parasitic flies."

"You need help, Alexander. Release me and we can work through this together. Whatever you have going with Sky Man, he's tricking you. Think about what happened to my settlement."

Finch laughed and spread his arms. "You still don't see it, do you? I am Sky Man."

Chapter Twenty

Trader and Jake thumped down the ship's stairs and headed straight for Barry and Beth's house. At least Finch was still in Omega and didn't seem aware they had his number. Stasis must've corrupted his mind, like the poor man they came across in the eastern bunker yesterday, but Finch channeled his insanity in a dangerous way.

"I knew he was up to something," Trader said. "I never thought he'd lead the wastelanders here to destroy us, though."

"Certainly takes a special kind of crazy. He's either flipped or spent years planning this from the inside. I hope it's not the latter."

"What difference does it make? We should go for him tonight and put an end to his plans."

Jake checked his watch. Six in the evening meant they still had enough natural light to reach Omega. "If he's planned this for years, and Skye's mention of his previous attack suggests he might have, we need to tread carefully."

"What are you suggesting?"

"That we don't shoot immediately to Omega. Let's convince Epsilon to join forces, travel first thing tomorrow morning, and capture Finch. He might have something up his sleeve, but won't be expecting us to show up with three thousand people."

Trader pulled at his beard. "Makes sense, I suppose. The guard will quickly turn against him once they find out."

"Instead of putting out an all stations call, you can send Carlos out to the other strongholds to warn them tonight. Which other stronghold has the best defensive wall?"

"Sigma. I now see the logic behind Finch building the steps at Omega. He probably knew exactly what he was doing. Using us to build his infrastructure before replacing us with wastelanders."

"Will Carlos have time to get around the other six places and direct them to Omega and Sigma?"

"Probably not. I'll send Tess out to three—Omicron, Lambda and Theta—and tell them to go to Sigma. Zeta and Kappa can join us at Omega."

"Do you think they'll listen?"

"I'll brief them both to spell it out. Individually we die; together we pull through. There's nothing like a threat of destruction to focus the mind."

They rejoined the paved road. Barry or Beth must've seen them approach. She opened the door and waved.

"Did you have any luck?" she said.

"We better go inside," Trader said.

"That bad, huh?"

"Yes. That bad."

She led Trader and Jake along squeaky floorboards, through a thin, magnolia-painted hallway to a gloomy living area. The crudely constructed wooden table and chairs were nothing more than functional. A painting of Jake's ship hung on the wall. Beth lit three candles on a mantelpiece above an iron fireplace. Jake hadn't seen a working one in a house for years. Underfloor heating managed to get rid of the last retro ones in the 2060s.

"Take a seat," she said. "Barry's making coffee."

Jake pulled out a chair and sat at the table. Trader continued to pace the room, mumbling to himself about Finch.

Beth sat opposite Jake and fished a pair of glasses from her breast pocket. She breathed on the lenses and rubbed them. "Have you visited other strongholds?"

"I've been to Omega, Sigma and Kappa."

"What do you think?"

Jake didn't feel the need to hold back after picking up on Barry's previous comment about the clock. "I think the theory overrides the practicality."

Beth put on her glasses, making her eyes almost double in size behind the thick lenses, and leaned toward him. "Would you care to explain?"

"I understand the theory behind the clocks, trade and curfews, but don't think it's the right way to build a new society."

"These rules have kept us together for a few decades. Why do you think you know any better?"

"I'm only calling it as I see it. Artificially keeping the population down will mean possibly condemning people to death outside of your walls. Nobody has been clear with me about the policy on that. Trade agreements and balance are fine, but if you keep producing the same things and don't advance, it's crushing aspiration. It sounds like people are prisoners in their own homes too. What do you people do to unwind?"

Beth smiled and slapped her hand on the table. "We've been telling Trader and the other strongholds the same thing for years. They seem to think it makes us soft."

"I would say it makes you the opposite. Going against conventional wisdom to point out the potential problems."

She turned to Trader. "Did you hear that? You can't keep telling us we're wrong."

He stared out of the window and grunted a reply. Jake could understand his distraction. All of them faced a big problem.

Barry carried in four steaming mugs and a bowl of sugar on a metal tray. He placed them on the table and sat next to Jake. "One lump or two?"

"I'm okay, thanks."

"Are you going to tell us what's happening, Trader?" Beth said.

Trader sat at the table and sighed. "There's no easy way to put this, so I'll come right out with it. Alexander Finch is leading thousands of wastelanders to our strongholds. We can only defend ourselves if we fight together at the larger, better protected strongholds. Tomorrow morning, we all need to move to Omega."

Barry dropped his teaspoon on the table.

"Where did you get this information?" Beth said.

"Carlos found two of our SUVs encouraging them north. They mentioned Sky Man, who we found out is Finch."

"He led a group of local wastelanders to a bunker and murdered sixty of my colleagues," Jake said. "It contained rocket launchers, rifles and pistols."

Beth took a deep breath and held her chest.

"He was the guy who killed Tom Reed, wasn't he?" Barry said.

Trader nodded. "We need to start preparing tonight and move first thing tomorrow morning. Do you have plenty of weapons and ammo in your stores?"

"We've got a good stockpile. I just can't believe it."

"We've got children here," Beth said. "We can't risk moving them on the open road."

"I think you can," Jake said. "The alternative's not worth thinking about. It won't take a large force of motivated wastelanders long to scale your walls and overpower you."

Barry and Beth looked at each other. He reached over and squeezed her hand.

"Finch's offering them our strongholds as a reward, and is feeding them," Trader said. "I wouldn't be surprised if he came here first. Picked off the smaller places to build up weapons before hitting the larger strongholds."

"Which is why we need to take as much as possible with us," Jake said. "We can defeat them together. After that, I'd be happy to support your ideas about how we can move forward to create a better society."

Jake didn't throw out the last suggestion as an olive branch, he genuinely meant it. Epsilon were being held back and didn't like the restrictions of the stronghold treaty. If they were to come out victorious, he didn't want to lose the progressive part of society.

"You realize what you're asking us to do?" Barry said. "This has been home to a lot of good people for all of their lives. Don't tell me there's no risk of us never returning."

"I'm not going to lie to you," Trader said. "We don't know how many thousands of wastelanders we're facing, but if you can't return here, that means we're all screwed."

"We'll force their hand," Jake said. "If they want to defeat us, they'll have to take heavily armed ramparts packed with thousands of armed men and women. You can't cover enough of the Epsilon wall with the population you have."

"Do you mind if we discuss it in the kitchen?" Beth said.

"Not at all," Trader said. "I understand it's a big decision, but please consider the implications."

Beth and Barry left the room. Trader paced the floor again.

They returned two minutes later.

"Tell us what we need to do," Beth said. "Our priority is to protect our citizens, and if that means moving to ensure our survival, that's exactly what we'll do."

* * *

While Beth and Barry went to call the citizens together outside the factory, and Trader briefed Carlos and Tess about their immediate mission to the other strongholds, Jake took a spotlight out of the SUV and returned to the ship. He wanted to look around for extra weapons and see if the computer held any more clues.

Dusk had set in when he approached the woodland. A single cowbell tinkled outside the factory, calling the population out of their homes.

His plan was to get back to the meeting before it finished. Maybe he would spot Mills in the crowd. Perhaps he was staying low profile until establishing contact. Whatever his reason, he knew Jake would be around, he'd seen to that himself.

He clicked on the spotlight and returned up the stairs to the cockpit. The comms console cast a thin green light around the walls. Jake crouched on the stool and input his password. The screen glowed into life, and he accessed the ship's logs.

It continued on a normal pattern until January 2077, a month before his cycle. All ground communications ceased. The ship deployed its missiles at Russia. Mills never woke him for duty; instead, the young lieutenant programmed all stasis pods to permanent mode, apart from his own in 2165. He landed the ship before waking all but one of the crew.

Jake could understand his actions as far as not immediately landing, but Mills should have consulted him. He also couldn't understand why the rest of the crew left him. Some of them might still be alive. Hopefully not in the same deranged state as Finch, who must have also spent time in stasis.

Without any further leads on the console, Jake searched along the starboard side of the ship. Just like Beth said, all of the storage spaces were stripped of goods. The living quarters resembled a shell compared to his memory of the rooms. The six metal bunks were missing their mattresses, all lockers were empty, and the bathroom hadn't seen water for years.

None of the doors to the rest of the ship worked, and the edges of the engineering hatch to the hull had welded with rust. He would need more time and tools to carry out a proper inspection, if wastelanders didn't colonize the stronghold after they left. That was a concern he didn't want to air in front of the others.

Jake clambered down the stairs and headed back to the factory. He hugged the houses on the left and slowly approached. The citizens crowded around Beth and Barry, who stood on the hood of an SUV, giving them a speech. Something about securing their future.

All turned and faced Jake.

Barry waved him over. "Come here. We're just explaining about the wastelanders."

Jake pointed to himself, hoping he heard him wrong, but knowing deep down he didn't. One thing he was never good at was public speaking. Flying bombers, fine. Tactical planning and organizing an assault, good too, although he only ever went through simulation training and never fought a real ground war. They didn't need to know that.

"Come on, don't be shy," Beth said.

The crowd parted in the middle. Jake walked through them to the SUV. A few whispered to each other as he passed.

Barry reached down. Jake grabbed his wrist, stepped onto the bull-bar, and hauled himself up.

Beth put her arm around him and faced the crowd. "This is Epsilon's own Captain Phillips. He is going to lead us to victory tomorrow. We are moving to Omega to help defeat the invading force, and after that, we will redefine our relationship with the other strongholds to create a better community."

A ripple of polite applause followed. Jake hoped every word was true. He would certainly do his best, and hoped it would be enough.

Chapter Twenty-One

Skye stretched her back after spending a sleepless night in her chilly cell. At six in the morning, Omega citizens woke and carried out their usual activities, unaware that an attack might be coming later today. Finch was Sky Man. The words didn't sound right in her head. The man who took her in after the worst moment of her life that he made happen.

She glanced over at Sam's lifeless body. Finch had positioned him facing the bars and opened his eyelids. An undignified end for a good man and a friend. She vowed to avenge him if she had a chance. Her hopes lay with Trader, but they were slim considering Finch throwing him off his scent by forcing her to send a radio message.

Finch used to lecture her on justice. He told her a system required designing to protect humanity, building toward a new future, and learning from their past mistakes. At the time it sounded like he meant the strongholds; thinking back, she could see the chilling double meaning to his words.

Skye wrapped her fingers tightly around the cold steel bars and shook them in anger. "If anyone can hear me, you have to let me out. Finch is Sky Man. A wastelander army is heading to Omega. We have to act or we'll die."

She knew most would dismiss her as insane and pass off her words as the wild ramblings of a broken mind. People who'd lost their tags had snapped before. She sounded exactly like the desperate cries she had heard from the cells over the last ten years, and always assumed they were taking a bitter parting shot at Finch. Citizens had no reason to believe she wasn't just another criminal that abused the system.

A man walked around the side of the pigpen and poured a bucket of vegetables into the wooden trough.

"You have to listen to me," Skye said. "Your life is at risk."

He shook his head and walked away.

"Come back," Skye shouted.

The siren at the front gates intermittently warbled. Vehicles entering the stronghold. Skye hoped it was Trader and his team. He had the best group of fighters, and they wouldn't put up with Finch's nonsense. Not with so much at stake.

She peered through the gap in the sheds and hoped to see eight vehicles rumble past, straight to the mansion.

A low cloud of dust crawled toward Omega on the distant horizon. Another type of storm heading their way. Fewer people patrolled the ramparts during low visibility, as the wastelanders generally didn't attack and sought out shelter instead. This would leave them even more exposed in conditions of poor visibility.

Skye heard the distant buzz of vehicles. More than eight. Maybe Trader arriving with plenty of backup. That would be a smart move. Finch had two SUVs leading the wastelanders north, meaning others were involved in the plot.

A guard ran from the closest house, pulling on his jacket as he headed for the front of the stronghold.

"What's going on out there?"

He glanced at her and disappeared toward the road. Men and women shouted in the distance. She caught glimpses of them moving between buildings but had no clear sight beyond the sheds and a few of the houses.

A woman left the same house in her farming coveralls. Skye recognized her as Helen. They'd played together as children but drifted apart after she joined the force.

"Helen, come here."

She approached but stopped twenty yards short and glanced in either direction. "You know we're not supposed to talk to you."

"What's going on?"

"We've been ordered to converge on the front fields."

"Who has?"

"Everyone. Something big is going down. The whole of Zeta and Kappa has just shown up in a huge convoy."

Skye's heart raced with excitement. "Who ordered you?"

"I'm not sure. Bob received a call five minutes ago."

"Can you find out if Trader's among them and tell him I'm here?"

"I'm sorry, Skye. I can't do that. You know the punishment for assisting an outlaw."

"If Finch has anything to do with this order, you need to assume it's bad. He's organized a wastelander attack and might be herding you all together."

Helen sighed. "I'm sorry it's ended like this for you, but I can't risk losing my tags. You'll have to find somebody else."

She turned and walked away.

"Wait. The tags won't mean anything if …"

It was no use. She didn't want to listen. Skye couldn't blame her because she still believed in the system and Finch. Nobody wanted to lose their citizenship by helping an enemy of Omega. The whole rotten system needed changing. It had people living in fear, and the governors could do as they pleased, without question. They bent the original treaty wording to suit themselves, and Finch took full advantage of the situation while he hatched his plan.

The intermittent siren stopped. If Trader wasn't here, she had to put her faith in the officers of Kappa and Zeta. Skye wondered if Finch lured them here on purpose, to take them all out with one killer blow. She kicked the cell wall out of frustration, and a chunk of plaster dropped to the ground.

Ross hurried over and wiped his sleeve across his sweaty brow. "Lieutenant Reed, I'm going to need you to come with me, please."

She glared at him. "Have you come to kick me out? What dirty work has Finch got you doing this—"

"I was wrong about Finch. Trader confirmed thousands of wastelanders are heading here. Zeta and Kappa have come to join forces. It was Jake Phillips' idea. They're heading here later this morning with Epsilon."

Skye walked to the bars. "You've come to release me?"

"It's all hands on deck."

"Where's Finch?"

"I think he's in his mansion."

"I want to hear you say it."

"Say what?"

"Ten years ago at the settlement. Say it."

The color drained from his face, and he bowed his head. "I ran after seeing the carnage. I saw what the first wave of those monsters did and abandoned my post. We didn't have a chance. I know Sky Man's real, but I never thought he was Finch. I'm sorry, Skye."

"You're sorry? You're in command of our entire defense force now. It's time you acted like it. Let's arrest Finch and destroy those damned steps."

Ross fumbled in his trousers pocket and produced a key. He twisted it in the lock and the door creaked open. Skye couldn't resist her urge, sprang forward, and punched him in the stomach.

Ross groaned and doubled over. "I'll give you that one. Don't try it again."

"I need a rifle," she said. "We'll try to force him to call off this attack before it's too late."

He straightened his jacket and took a deep breath. Ross deserved a whole lot more, but that would have to wait. They headed toward the road leading up to the mansion. He called over a young male guard who stood next to the base of a wind turbine. "Give Lieutenant Reed your rifle, please. You can grab another from the barracks and tell the men to immediately destroy the outer steps. Jump to it."

"Yes, sir," he said, unslung his rifle, passed it to Skye, and jogged away.

She put a round in the chamber. "If Finch doesn't comply, I'm shooting him. When did you change your mind about him?"

"I didn't know what to do after he killed Bennett. I locked myself in the tower and thought about running today."

"But you didn't?"

"I don't want to live my life in fear anymore. When the other strongholds turned up and told me what was happening, I realized this would be our last stand."

Even a coward like Ross couldn't avoid this fight. He had nowhere to go. When Trader turned up, she would speak to him and arrange for Ross to be placed back in the ranks. If he survived.

Skye slipped through the mansion's wrought-iron gates and crunched up the gravel drive toward the open front doors. She couldn't understand Finch's lunacy. Two strongholds had turned up to fight his arranged invasion, and he sat inside with the entrance wide open, probably sipping whiskey and puffing on a cigar.

"Don't let me down this time, Ross."

"You can count on me. It all changes today. If we pull through, I'll stick to the stronghold treaty."

Skye shook her head. He still didn't get it. She swung around the Venetian doors and aimed inside. Nothing moved in the entry hall.

She moved across the squeaky polished tiles and entered the corridor that led to Finch's office. Skye used to think the varnished wooden floorboards here gave a comfortable, old reassuring creak. Now they were advertising her approach.

Two of the paintings lay on the floor. The glass covering her favorite, the ship at sea, was shattered in pieces next to it, and the painting had a twelve-inch tear in the middle, like somebody had put their foot through it.

Finch's study door was closed. Ross would have to use his bulk to force his way in if she found it locked. Skye waited outside the door for him to catch up. He wheezed along the corridor, pointing his pistol at the five hung sash windows as he passed each one.

She nodded at him, twisted the handle, and burst through the door. Finch wasn't here. One of the brown leather chairs sat on top of the smashed glass coffee table. Books scattered in front of the empty shelves of his mahogany bookcase, and the butterflies were missing from the display cabinet, leaving darkened silhouettes on the faded purple velvet.

Skye lowered her rifle and moved behind his desk. She opened the drawer and found a green journal.

Ross picked up an empty glass bottle and sniffed the rim.

"Watch the corridor," she said.

He paused for a moment. Skye glared at him until he moved to the entrance. Ross' reluctant support didn't wash with her. All of his second chances were used up, and she had a bullet with his name on it if he didn't comply.

She unfastened the journal and flicked it open. The first few pages were filled with pencil drawings of butterflies; each had strange philosophical rants below in shaky writing. Finch accused Skippers of taunting him with their erratic flight behavior, and Pygmy Blues of purposefully hiding from him.

He wrote *Sky Man* repeatedly from the middle pages onward. Most were stained with rings from his whiskey glass. The final picture was a crude sketch of himself emerging from a cocoon. Skye felt like she was looking into the mind of a maniac. The naked figure, with two antennas on his head, held a globe in one hand and a spear in the other.

A floorboard groaned overhead. Skye snapped the journal shut and stuffed it in her thigh pocket. The heads of Zeta and Kappa, Trader and Phillips needed to read about the kind of mind that worked against them.

She shouldered her rifle and immediately rushed past Ross. If Finch was upstairs, she wanted to get to him first. Make him call off the attack and then get revenge for her parents. His deceit left the strongholds' laws in tatters. No treaty would stop his execution.

SIXTH CYCLE

Skye crept up the staircase and headed straight for the location of the noise. The back of the mansion. Finch's bedroom.

Ross followed, keeping a safe distance. She expected nothing more as she approached the open bedroom door. A woman's faint sobs came from inside.

Skye crouched by the door and nudged it open with her left hand.

Mary, the housekeeper, sat in the corner with her head in her hands. Dried blood crusted around her nostrils and stained the front of her white dress.

She looked up at Skye with tears in her eyes. "Have you found him?"

Skye knelt next to Mary and put an arm around her shoulder. "Everything is gonna be okay. What happened?"

"I woke at three this morning to banging coming from his study. When I went to investigate, he threw a paperweight at my head and chased me to the bedroom. He hit me …"

Skye clenched her teeth. "Where is he?"

"He went back downstairs, and I heard the front door open two hours ago. I didn't dare investigate."

Skye turned to Ross, who peered around the door. "Have you checked with the front gate to see if he left?"

"Not yet. I thought he was here."

"You thought wrong. He might be crazy, but he's not stupid."

Ross clipped his radio off his belt and held it to his mouth. "Omega gate, this is General Ross. Do you copy?"

"Yes, sir."

He gave Skye a smug smile, not realizing how meaningless his rank had become. "Has Governor Finch left this morning?"

"Two hours ago on a mission to gather resources. Said he'd be back later this afternoon."

Ross lowered the radio. "Guess we have our answer."

"We need to get to the front and start organizing our defense. Call a meeting with the other stronghold leaders, get them to send their guard to man the ramparts, and confirm we've destroyed the steps."

He gave her a false smile. "Are you telling *me* what to do?"

"Yes. Now get to it. We haven't got any time to waste."

Chapter Twenty-Two

At seven in the morning, half an hour after first light, a convoy of fifty vehicles lined up along the road inside Epsilon, ready to leave. Children squeezed into the back of Trader's trucks, along with every available weapon in Epsilon. Jake estimated that they had around five hundred rifles and pistols along with thousands of rounds.

Two hundred armed men and women of the Epsilon guard, hundreds of factory workers carrying rifles, and Trader's team lined either side of the packed vehicles, providing protection for their two-hour trip to Omega.

Jake sat in the lead vehicle with Trader and Carlos. He'd returned at five in the morning with good news. The strongholds were converging on Sigma and Omega. All agreed to maintain radio silence until Trader reached Omega and transmitted a status about Finch.

Trader raised his arm out of the vehicle window and casually swung it forward. He hit the accelerator and sped through the open gates. Jake looked over his shoulder at the convoy rumbling forward.

"Did you come across any wastelanders?" Trader said.

"None, which is weird," Carlos said. "The local ones must be gathering somewhere."

"Hopefully they're not planning an ambush on our route," Jake said. "How many do you think are in the area?"

Carlos shrugged. "Impossible to say. A few months ago I'd say a handful. Today, maybe hundreds. It's what's coming that worries me."

The low early morning sun glared through the windscreen. In the distance, a large creamy cloud hugged the horizon.

"Got a dust storm on the way," Trader said. "Should hit by the time we reach Omega."

"That's all we need," Carlos said.

"It's not necessarily bad," Jake said. "We work out how to turn it to our advantage rather than worrying about it."

After rolling along for an hour, the thin front end of the storm reached them. Trader assured Jake it would get a lot worse.

Gunfire crackled ahead of them.

Trader slammed on the brakes, and they came to a halt. Jake wound his window down and listened.

The sporadic distant cracks continued.

"Could it be another stronghold on the move?" Jake said.

"On this road? I doubt it."

One of Trader's team appeared at his window. "What do you want us to do, boss?"

Trader turned to Jake. "We need to clear any blocks in the road."

Jake clicked off his belt, opened his door, and put a round in the chamber. "Trader, Carlos, we'll scout the way ahead. The rest can take defensive positions around the convoy until we find out what the situation is."

The team member nodded and ran back to the convoy. Trader and Carlos joined Jake at the front of the SUV. He peered ahead but couldn't see further than two hundred yards. Beyond that, dust shrouded the road and forest.

"We move through the trees until we spot any signs of movement. From there, we observe until we can figure out the position and strength of what we're facing, and then we come up with a plan. Okay?"

"You got it," Trader said.

Carlos nodded and shouldered his rifle.

Jake moved into the cover of the trees, to try to remain undetected. The soft forest floor would also quieten their advance.

He checked the ground in front of him, careful not to step on any branches or twigs as he weaved between trunks, focusing on the ground ahead.

Shots split the air, becoming louder but less frequent.

Jake slowed his pace and crouched behind a trunk after seeing a faint flash through the dust. Trader and Carlos knelt on either side of him behind two other trees.

A burst of automatic gunfire rang out. Two figures appeared out of the gloom. Moving slowly and deliberately, switching their aim to different parts of the forest.

Jake crept over to Trader. "They look too efficient to be wastelanders. Any ideas who they might be?"

Trader stared over his sights as the figures closed in. "Doesn't look like any stronghold guard. But I agree, they're moving with too much precision."

The figures stopped after two shots cracked behind them. They both crouched by the side of a rock and swept the area with their rifles.

Jake looked left after hearing the noise of velcro tearing. Carlos opened a pouch on his belt and pulled out a pair of goggles. He planted them against his eyes and adjusted the focus.

A man called out, "Over here. We're clear."

Two more figures joined them.

Carlos put the goggles back in his pouch. "They're outlaws. I don't know what the hell they're doing here."

Jake leaned toward Trader. "What kind of reception are we going to get from them? Do they run with wastelanders?"

"No. They're just like us but live outside the strongholds. I wouldn't exactly call them a friendly force, though."

"If the shit's hitting the fan today, they're going to be in the same situation as us. I'm going to talk to them."

"It's too risky. They don't attack convoys. We should wait until the firing stops and proceed."

"They must have run into wastelanders, right?"

"Yeah, but they won't talk to us."

"They will when they hear what I've got to say. It's about time we all started working toward the same objective."

"Omega won't allow them entry."

"We'll see about that."

Jake got to his feet and prepared to move.

Trader grabbed his shoulder. "Don't do it."

Jake brushed his hand off and sprang forward, hunching between trees, and skidded to the ground behind a rotting trunk.

He looked over the top of it. The outlaws seemed unaware of his presence and chatted amongst themselves. "This is Jake Phillips. I'm fifty yards north of your position. Do you need any help?"

All four scrambled behind the rock. Two aimed over the top of it.

"Thousands of wastelanders are heading this way," Jake said. "We're all in this together. I'm here to assist you."

"We've dealt with an ambush," a man replied in a gravelly voice. "Go back to where you came from."

"I'm serious. All eight strongholds are converging on Sigma and Omega. You're welcome to join us. You won't survive out here if the wastelanders catch you."

"What did you say your name was?"

"Jake Phillips. I'm not associated with any stronghold, and I'm telling you the truth."

"We saw them approaching the southern hills this morning and were on our way to Epsilon. Are you the guy from—"

"Yes. I was their tourist attraction, but I'm from their lead vehicle. We're heading for Omega."

"Are Barry and Beth with you?"

"Yes. I'm coming out. Don't shoot."

Jake took a deep breath and stood. He held his rifle to one side and approached the rock. Two outlaws maintained their aim. A man with a graying beard stood behind them and slung his rifle.

"You're risking your ass coming over here. We could've mistaken you for wastelanders."

Jake stopped ten yards short and looked across the faces. Three bearded men and one woman. All eyed him with suspicion. He addressed the man at the back. "I could say the same thing to you. Our convoy is half a mile back. Join us and I'll take you straight to Beth and Barry."

The man shook his head. "This ain't gonna work. Finch won't let us into Omega."

"Finch is behind the attack. He's drawing wastelanders north, promising them the strongholds and resources after they defeat us."

He stepped from behind the rock and looked Jake up and down. "If you're lying to me, you're the first one who gets it."

"Don't you think it's time we all came together? How long till the wastelanders get here?"

The man checked his watch. "Four hours. Is Finch still in Omega?"

"As far as we know. He doesn't know we're onto him, yet. We'll turn the guard and take him. The only way we can save ourselves is to defend their walls. Fighting on open ground isn't an option, but I think you know that."

"That's why we were going to Epsilon. They're the only decent place out of all of the damned *strongholds*."

"This is our chance to change things. Fight with me, and we'll create a better society. Today, we all have to put our ideologies to one side."

The man looked at his team, turned and whistled. Thirty more outlaws appeared through the dust. The ones at the back covered their rear as they gathered around the leader. He jumped to the top of the rock and addressed them.

"We're joining a group on their way to Omega. Before any of you complain, Finch is behind the attack, and Epsilon have cleared out to join forces with Omega. The way I see it, we don't have any other options."

"We could head north," a woman said.

The man shook his head and held his hand toward Jake. "We can't avoid a force that size forever. Phillips claims it's a chance for us to change things. I believe him. Barry and Beth are in the convoy, and we know they want the same thing. It could be the opportunity we've waited a long time for."

The group talked quietly among themselves.

"Are there any objections?" the man said.

Nobody replied. Jake couldn't blame them for wanting to take advantage of the situation. Some of these people were probably stronghold outcasts; others perhaps preferred their freedom away from the imposing systems in place. Putting all of that on the line in return for survival and a better life was a fair price.

"Follow me," Jake said and headed back to the convoy.

Trader and Carlos broke cover when he returned to their position.

"Trader, fancy seeing you here," the man said. "Bit out of your comfort zone, isn't it?"

"Ryder, finally decided to join the good fight?"

Both men squared up to each other. Jake pushed them apart. "Save it for the wastelanders. I take it you two know each other?"

"He's part of the corrupt system," Ryder said. "Most of my people killed in the last few days were kicked out of strongholds for daring to have a different opinion."

"You're nothing but a second rate Robin Hood," Trader said and turned to Jake. "His notional idea of *freedom* doesn't exist. He robs from the hardworking to feed the deluded."

Ryder's eyes narrowed, and his hand jerked against his rifle. "Watch your tongue. There's nothing stopping us killing you right here. Accidents happen in the forest."

"Get a grip of yourselves," Jake said, not wanting the situation to escalate any further. "I'll take you to Beth and Barry. You can protect their part of the convoy."

Ryder took a step back and gave a single nod.

Jake set off back to the convoy, concerned about their new fragile alliance, but pleased the situation didn't descend into violence. It was clear that feelings ran high between the outlaws and the establishment.

Trader walked alongside him. "What do Beth and Barry have to do with it?"

"The outlaws were going to Epsilon. I'm guessing for protection behind their walls."

"Impossible. It's against the rules."

"Don't be so naïve, Trader. If they are decent people, I wouldn't be surprised if they reached out to Epsilon, and they provided help in return. I'd do the same thing."

"We can't disintegrate what we've built because of a single attack. You need to understand that our structure worked for years."

Jake stopped next to the SUV and looked him in the eye. "You need to understand that things change, sometimes for the better."

* * *

Most of the Epsilon citizens didn't seem surprised at the emergence of the outlaws from the forest. Trader's team surrounded him while he briefed them. Beth and Barry gave Ryder a warm welcome, and the outlaws fanned out around their vehicle.

Jake climbed back into the SUV, and they continued toward Omega. Trader clenched his jaw and kept his focus on the road ahead. Jake could understand the old man's mixed feelings. Everything he worked for during the last few decades was falling apart. Trader kept shaking his head and grunting until the wall of Omega came into view.

The gates remained closed when they neared. Trader stopped and ripped up the handbrake. "Do you want to take it from here?"

"Get your men ready with the rocket launchers and wait. If Finch is still here, we might need them. Going back to Epsilon isn't an option."

Four men stood either side of the gates on the rampart. Jake exited the SUV and walked forward.

"Identify yourself," a man shouted.

"Captain Jake Phillips. I'm here with a convoy from Epsilon. We also have a group of outlaws."

"The outlaws stay outside. The rest of you can enter."

"That's not going to happen," Jake said. "Is Governor Finch inside?"

The men on the rampart looked at each other. One disappeared from view. Jake glanced along the left-hand side of the solid stone wall. The outer steps leading to the barracks were demolished. A positive sign that the stronghold had already started preparations.

Ryder, Beth and Barry crunched along the road and stood by his side.

"Is there a problem?" Barry said.

"We'll find out shortly," Jake said.

Skye looked over the rampart. "Ryder, what are you doing here?"

"We're here to fight," he replied.

"Do you have Finch?" Jake said.

"He's gone. Kappa and Zeta arrived here an hour ago and told us about your plan."

"Are you gonna open the gates or leave us out here?"

Skye looked to her right. Jake cringed when the intermittent siren blasted to signal the opening of the entrance. The gates clanked open, revealing a hive of activity inside.

Jake left the others to return to their vehicles and walked inside. At least one hundred SUVs were parked inside. Some blocking the road, others around the barracks and bases of the towers, most parked by the inner wall in four rows of ten. Men and women stood around them, dressed in their stronghold-colored coveralls, cleaning weapons and talking in groups. A couple of hundred people queued up next to an extended wooden table. Steam belched out of three large metal pots. A man in a white apron poured green liquid into bowls and handed them out.

Over a thousand citizens and guards ducked behind the front section of the rampart with their weapons ready. More spread around the sides as far as Jake could see. Skye raced down the steps and approached him.

"Have you brought guns from Epsilon?"

"Yes. We've got some rocket launchers too. Nice to see that you've already started arranging things. How many guns are we short?"

"Four thousand."

"We've got five hundred. The rest will have to use whatever they can get their hands on."

She gave him a resigned look. "I hope you don't mind helping give a crash course in weapons handling. We'll split them into groups of ten."

"No problem. We need to start right away."

The convoy snaked through the gates and parked alongside the other vehicles by the inner wall. The siren above the gates stopped after they slammed shut with a dull thud.

Wind gusted through the stronghold, bringing a thick sheet of gritty dust. Jake turned away and wiped his eyes. He surveyed the interior of the stronghold and thought about the best way to defend against an assault. A distant scream echoed through the forest.

Chapter Twenty-Three

Guards and civilians on the rampart focused outside after hearing the single scream. If anyone dared question Ryder's entry, they would answer to her. The fact that he turned up with Jake didn't surprise her. She liked him from the moment she met him.

Skye twisted her ponytail up into a bun and fastened it in place. The growing amount of dust being carried on the wind surrounded the stronghold in a thick cream cloud. She watched Jake shield his eyes and scan the internal area. Ryder joined him and pointed toward the inner wall.

She raised her newly acquired radio. "Advanced sentries. Do you see the enemy force?"

"Only two. We'll let you know and fall back when we see them coming."

"Thanks, Skye out."

She'd stationed ten of the guard outside the stronghold walls to give them a decent warning of an oncoming force. They'd given her advance warning of the Epsilon convoy's approach.

"Smart thinking," Ryder said. "I never got a chance to thank you for helping me out in the cave."

"I'm sure you would've done the same thing."

"What's the arrangement around the walls and the secondary plan?" Jake said.

"I've called a meeting with the governors of Zeta and Kappa. They're expecting to hear from you."

He turned to Trader. "Are you coming for the ride?"

Trader leaned out from the trunk of his SUV. "You know what you're doing. Skye, are you okay with me distributing weapons and organizing a few things?"

"Sure thing." She turned to Jake. "What's he organizing?"

"You'll find out shortly, but it's for the best. We discussed our options last night."

She held the radio to her mouth again. "Governors' meeting at the tower in two minutes. Skye out."

"How the hell do you all manage to keep any form of decent communication if you all use the same channel?" Jake said.

"Each stronghold and Trader has one. As we're all here, I don't see what choice we have. Maybe you can show us a better way after we get through this."

"We split them into sections and use one as a command channel," Jake said. "Are we out of Sigma's range?"

"Yes. We'll have no problems."

Ross moved alongside her and extended a hand. "Hello again, Captain Phillips."

Jake put his hands in his pockets. "We meet again, Captain Ross."

"General Ross. I'm the senior officer around here."

"Finch promoted him before he left," Skye said, not able to resist verbally kicking him again. "When this is all over, I can't see him keeping his sparkling new gold baton."

Ross scowled but didn't answer back. He must've known deep down that he only held his position because he was Finch's patsy, and that his rank held zero weight with Skye.

"I remember him from Monday," Jake said. "I hope he isn't in a position of responsibility today?"

"You just wait a minute," Ross said and stepped toward Jake. "You can't speak about me like that. I'm a general now. I outrank you."

"I don't know who you outrank, but I know it isn't me."

Skye caught Jake's eye and gestured her head toward the tower. He gave her a slight nod and walked around Ross.

"Skye," Ross said, following them. "We're both Omega officers. You can't let him come here and speak to us like this."

Skye sighed and spun to face him. "You're not coming to the meeting as acting governor. Do you think Harrison and Herbie will stand for it after you spent years slurping Finch's toe caps until your tongue turned black?"

"I'm the senior officer here."

"You were Finch's senior officer."

"I'll find a job for you," Jake said. "Don't worry about that."

Ross clenched his fists, and his lips curled into a snarl. Skye turned and headed for the tower with Jake. This time, Ross didn't follow. His redemption would have to come on the battlefield.

Skye led the way up the spiral stone staircase and entered Ross' former office. The two governors were already there, dressed in their sharp navy and brown suits. Harrison sat behind the desk and gave her a suspicious look. Herbie gazed at a painting on the wall. She noticed Jake looking down at the animal skins on the floor.

"Yep. They're his."

He smiled. "Thought so."

Herbie looked over his shoulder. "I hear this was your idea, Captain Phillips?"

"That's right. Trader's scout confirmed the wastelanders being led here. We found out Finch was responsible by checking my ship's records in Epsilon. His army has rifles, pistols and rocket launchers stolen from the western bunker. We can't fight a force like that on open ground without sustaining heavy casualties, and you can't defend your individual walls against thousands with the numbers you have. The idea is to defend and take them out here. Even up the odds."

"Finch admitted it to me last night," Skye said. "There's no doubt he's coming."

Harrison leaned forward. "Who put you two in charge?"

"You can have Finch's puppet or me and an experienced military man," Skye said. "We haven't got time to debate the state that Finch left Omega in."

She pulled Finch's journal out of her pocket and threw it on the table. Harrison picked it up, licked his finger, and flicked through it. He reached the final page and frowned.

"Beyond defending the wall, what else can we do?" Herbie said.

"What's the situation on the ground at the moment?" Jake said.

Skye grabbed the stronghold plan from the side of the office and rolled it out on the desk. "We've split the Omega Force and some armed civilians on the north wall by the gates and on the south wall. Kappa are covering the east, Zeta the west."

"Looks solid enough to me," Harrison said.

"But not very dynamic, and I don't see a fallback," Jake said.

Harrison sat back in his chair and grunted.

"What are you suggesting?" Herbie said.

"Split your areas into two sections each, so they can each use a dedicated radio channel. They need to communicate along their own parts of the wall without confusion. Each local commander can use the Trader channel to report any serious threats of a breach."

"Make sense," Herbie said. "I'll take one and two."

"Three to six," Skye said.

She looked at Harrison. He rolled his eyes. "I can count, goddammit."

"Skye, you take twenty of your team and use them as a mobile force to plug any gaps. I'll use Trader's team to do the same thing. We also need to position a firing squad in front of the gates. If the wastelanders manage to blow them, we need an immediate response to stop them flooding in."

"And if your plan fails?" Harrison said.

Jake pointed to the middle of the map. "We fall back to the inner circle, reduce the perimeter size to account for casualties, and fight them to the death. Tell all of your local team what the retreat command means. We can put Ross and Trader to work with the remaining citizens on preparing fallback defenses."

Herbie, who watched and nodded as Jake spoke, headed for the door. "You've got it all worked out. I'm a man of business, and I know when I see the best plan. I'll go and brief my team. Harrison, I suggest you do the same."

His footsteps echoed down the staircase. Skye felt relieved, but could understand his acceptance. As Jake spoke, she felt like part of a slick military operation for the first time since she'd been in uniform. She expected Harrison's arguments and Herbie's ego to block any serious decisions, but having an experienced neutral, who knew what he was talking about, knocked the wind out of Herbie's sails.

Harrison remained in his chair, though. "I just want you to know that if this plan works, everything goes back to the way it was. Your governor turning traitor isn't going to ruin our system."

"We've got a chance to make things better, Harrison," Skye said. "You must be able to see that things aren't working."

"That's Governor Harrison to you. I'll go along with the suggestions for the good of the strongholds, because it has merit, but after we defeat this force, we're returning to business as usual."

"Your population clocks are outdated," Jake said. "I'm sure they worked when you were filling your strongholds up. What purpose do they serve now?"

Harrison narrowed his eyes. "What do you know about it? We have to balance resources. While you were sleeping, we were the ones protecting the population."

"And now you cast them out or refuse them entry? I think you need to face reality."

He probably didn't want to lose his little empire. Covering the western side of Omega was his way of achieving it. Skye didn't want to waste any time having a philosophical debate about the wrongs of the system. They all had work to do, and time was running out.

"Did you find Rhodes?" she said.

Harrison smiled. "Last night. Cowering in a warehouse. I had him branded until he confirmed what Trader's scout told us."

"Where is he?"

"Hanging by his neck from our front gate. Don't think I take security lightly. We found a group of Finch's traitors on our way here, in two SUVs. After I questioned them, they were executed on the side of the road."

"Carlos told me about them," Jake said. "They won't be missed."

Skye's radio crackled. "Falling back. Falling back. Falling back. Wastelanders heading from the north."

Harrison sprang from his chair and pushed between Skye and Jake. They looked at each other and followed.

* * *

Skye sprinted for the section of rampart by the gates. She pulled her jacket collar up to avoid swallowing mouthfuls of dust. The level of visibility had decreased, but she could see figures climbing to the rampart to take their positions with their new weapons. Jake split away to brief Ross and Trader. She guessed Ross might jump at the chance to help organize a defense that they might not need. If they did, whether Ross was in charge or not, everyone was in serious trouble.

She raced up the steps and pulled out her radio. "Omega section commanders. Join me by the gate tower immediately."

Men and women lined the walls as far as she could see, and she could hear their collective quiet chatter. The main gates cranked open two notches. Outside, figures appeared from the gloom and headed for the opening. A minute later it cranked shut with a dull thud. Skye couldn't see or hear any wastelanders. Because of conditions, she could only see twenty yards into the forest beyond the clearing surrounding the perimeter.

Footsteps slapped along stone. Two men appeared through the dust and crouched next to her. Both young corporals. A vehicle revved in the distance, heading from the southern wall. Its headlights stabbed through the murky atmosphere as it approached and skidded to a halt. A man and woman joined them by the tower.

She pointed at each in turn. "Channel three, four, five and six. That's your team's allocation for local communications. Use Trader's channel to report if you need assistance or see other sections getting overwhelmed. If you hear the 'retreat' command, fall back to the inner circle. Any questions?"

Nobody said a word.

"Okay. Send five of your team here to take part in a mobile group. I'll use it to plug any gaps. Pass the channel info along the line and call me if you have any problems."

The two from the south headed straight for the SUV. One ran back along the rampart. The fourth section commander remained and looked at Skye with a wide-eyed expression while fumbling with his rifle. "Did you say channel four?"

"Yes, and don't worry. If you come under serious pressure, call me and I'll be there."

He nodded and headed back to his position.

Wind howled between the rustling trees, carrying distant cries. Jake, Trader and Ross climbed the stairs.

"Shouldn't you two be working on the inner defense?" Skye said.

"The citizens know what they're doing," Trader said.

"He's a bit annoyed that I've taken his team," Jake said.

Trader shrugged. "He's given the old man an easy job. It's no skin off my nose."

Ross didn't say a word. He looked to be quietly seething until a single shrill scream came from the forest. Ross staggered back and nearly fell off the rampart. Jake grabbed his arm and pulled him from the edge. "If you're gonna die, at least do it the right way."

Ross shrugged off his grip and stared over the wall. Trader edged next to Skye and held out his pistol.

"You need to be getting back, Trader."

"They've already started. Did you really think I'd miss out on the fun?"

Shouts grew louder in the forest. Weapons clicked along the rampart. Skye caught a brief glimpse of vague movement through the trees.

The shouting grew into a single booming chant.

Two words repeated.

Sky Man.

The name that haunted her since childhood no longer held the same fear. The nightmarish creature that haunted her dreams was now flesh and blood. A dream was bulletproof; Alexander Finch wasn't.

SIXTH CYCLE

Somewhere in the forest a whistle blasted, and the shouting stopped. Skye and her fellow strongholders silently waited on the wall. The invaders did the same outside. Skye's team began to gather below the steps. Ten of them so far. That would have to be good enough.

"I'm going to brief the team at the gates," Jake said. "Back in a minute."

"What's that?" somebody a few yards along the wall said.

Jake stopped and pushed next to Skye. She peered into the forest. Something flapped through the air and slowly came toward the wall.

A single figure appeared from the gloom, waving a white flag.

Alexander Finch dropped the pole and spread his arms.

Chapter Twenty-Four

Finch stood in front of the walls of Omega, his walls, and lowered the red handkerchief from in front of his face. Like a Monarch butterfly, his bright display of talents proved enough to warn off the predators from the other strongholds until he could hatch his plan. If they dared to try to eat him, they would quickly find out about his toxicity.

The rampart bristled with weapons. Maggots jealously glaring down at a superior being that would bring them justice. Behind him, five thousand wastelanders waited in the forest. Caterpillars that would chew their way through the strongholds before changing into his perfect creatures.

Patience brought this moment. Years of hiding his revulsion at the sick society. Stasis transformed him. He evolved and transcended during his period of metamorphosis. Now it was time to stamp out the predatory Neanderthals and lead the world into a new era. No more trivial trades. No more dealing with pathetic issues. No more pretending to like the backward species that plagued Earth.

Ross, Skye, Trader and Phillips stood on the rampart by the gate. Even if they formed into a hive mind, and he wouldn't put it past them, they still wouldn't be clever enough to beat his army. He smiled and pointed at them. "You four. Get down here now and hear my terms."

"We don't negotiate with the enemy," Phillips said.

Finch laughed. "You're nothing but a dried-up relic. I used to be like you until my deliverance. I'll give you two minutes to get your worthless asses down here."

They had no choice but to surrender. He would send them north, away from their precious resources, and have them hunted to extinction. They didn't care about the Xerces Blue dying out. He didn't see why he should feel differently about them.

"We're ready to fight you," Skye said. "Give it your best shot."

Finch shook his head. "What happened to that young sweet innocent girl that I took in ten years ago?"

"After killing my family? You've got some balls."

He didn't need balls to convince Skye to play along. Once inside the Omega system, he acted like a pitcher plant. People couldn't resist his sickly sweet external juices and always fell into his trap. Her annoying parents resisted and paid the price. He already claimed the piece of skin on her cheek for his new display cabinet, and planned to cut it from her corpse. That particular trophy would remind him of the suffering he went through in Omega.

She aimed her rifle at him. Ross grabbed the muzzle and pushed it to one side. Once an obedient fool, always an obedient fool. Even now he had him wrapped around his antenna. The only thing he could never work out about Ross was that as a spider, he should've acted differently. Nature worked in mysterious ways.

"This is your last chance. Come down and hear my terms, or I launch five thousand wastelanders against you, and they will kill every man, woman and child inside."

"We've got the populations of Kappa and Zeta here," Trader shouted. "We outnumber your forces and have the whole wall covered."

He knew the fools wouldn't understand that he'd already anticipated their clumsy strategy. He had enough guns spread behind him to keep the ramparts occupied while the rocket launchers smashed open the gate. Hundreds of wastelanders would be cut down during the assault, but enough would break in to slaughter those inside. Weak citizens didn't have the experience of hand-to-hand combat. Wastelanders were raised to fight with axes and spears. A diversionary attack on the south side would keep the stronghold forces split.

Finch checked his watch. He decided to give them the time it took his second hand to complete a full revolution.

Somebody fired from the rampart. He felt a searing pain in his left arm. Blood dampened the arm of his purple turtleneck sweater. He gritted his teeth and looked up.

Phillips lowered his rifle. He failed to transcend in his stupid ship, and now he dared take a jealous shot.

Finch pointed at him and walked backward toward the edge of the forest. "You're first, caveman. I'll skin you alive."

Skye raised her rifle. Ross didn't stop her this time. Finch turned and ran for the cover of the trees. A round hissed over his shoulder, nicked his neck, and snapped off a small branch in front of him.

He dived behind the nearest tree. Time for the bastards to pay the ultimate price. Finch waited a few moments to catch his breath before moving deeper into the forest.

The first wave of wastelanders waited, panting in angry anticipation of taking what was rightfully theirs. Half the front rank carried the rifles he liberated from the bunker, the rest gripped their spears and axes. The jagged and rusting blades were a pleasant sight. Nothing would give him more pleasure than to see them plunging into the bodies of Skye and Phillips.

They would never be capable of seeing the genius of his plan.

The local wastelanders spoke with the ones just south of the strongholds. In turn, they passed the information further south, and so on, communicating in increasingly broken English until even the savages who were incapable of decipherable speech got the message. Finch's offer fanned down hundreds of miles, and he received the required response. All he had to do after that was direct them to their salvation.

This was their moment. An opportunity to take the rich, unsoiled land denied to them by the snobby cretins who still tried to hang on to the old world. He would no longer be the only sane person in the stronghold asylum.

Two of the accomplished wastelander speakers gathered around him. His newly appointed generals. One looked at the wound on his arm. Finch kept a straight face. He refused to show signs of pain.

"Take a thousand south and hit the stronghold in ten minutes," Finch said to the ugliest caterpillar. "Don't commit everyone. It's just a show of strength to keep their forces from concentrating on the main assault. Do you understand?"

"Yes, Sky Man. I go now."

Finch patted him on the shoulder. "Good man."

He left to organize his troops. Finch wiped his hand on his trousers. If the wastelanders proved themselves today, the glorious battle would continue. More bunkers lay to the north, and possibly more settlements. Testing his theory about an all-out assault proved successful ten years ago when he crushed Tom Reed. Nobody would stand in his way once he spread his wings.

"We are ready to charge, Sky Man."

"Take half of our rifles to the left flank. Fire at the pillboxes and lead the moths to the light. I'll command the rocket launchers and main body. When I attack, sweep round and join me through the gates."

The general frowned. "Who are the moths?"

Finch squeezed his eyes shut and rubbed his temples. "Just take half of the rifles to the left and attack. Do not let your men charge until we have established a hole in their defenses."

"I follow your command."

"Excellent."

The general trudged away and directed a group to join him. Some of them looked confused but eventually followed. Wastelanders weren't used to being coordinated, but they were learning. After seeing the value of his leadership, they would only follow with a greater resolve and smash everything in their path.

* * *

Finch stood in front of the main body of wastelanders. He waved the ten forward who were armed with rocket launchers. Teaching them how to use them had proved a painful experience, but destroying the infrastructure inside the western bunker during the early hours of this morning would give him a sense of satisfaction. It wouldn't match the feeling of watching the people inside meet their end, though.

He spent ten years in that godforsaken place after waking. Ten long years, without any help from his supposed colleagues. Their sleeping bodies in the stasis pods mocked him. They looked so stupidly unaware that a man translated to a higher level watched them every night, thinking about how to end their lives.

He followed a scouting group back to Omega after seeing them on the loading camera doors. Destiny presented itself in the form of a stallion standing outside the original stronghold gates. He would be a Trojan horse and bring about the destruction of the inferior race. The rest was easy, and he expected nothing less. If any of the maggots had half a brain, they would recognize the symmetry of his planning. Like two beautifully colored wings of a Sunrise Monarch flapping the devolved humanity to their judgment, the ten years in the bunker matched the ten years between his assaults on society.

Finch crept between the trees until he had a clear view of the gates. The dust storm gave him the perfect cover to get the launchers close enough to score direct hits. Whoever had transformed him probably sent the storm as a gift.

Wastelanders lined up behind the trees either side of him. He held up his hand, and they primed their weapons.

He looked over his shoulder at the advancing army between the trees. An unstoppable force once he created the breach. Every stronghold would regret the day they met Alexander Finch. Sky Man. The Butterfly King.

Chapter Twenty-Five

Jake scrambled down the steps to brief the forty guards behind the gates, and collect his mobile team. If the wastelander army managed to blast through, the guards would provide a crucial first response and would have to hold firm for the initial onslaught. An open breach would lead to chaos. The force on the rampart would have to fall back if that looked likely. Being drawn to a single area of the wall would create gaps elsewhere for the enemy to stream over. He would join the gate defense with his men and hoped the rest of the wall followed the command instructions.

Trader had done as asked and positioned two of his team at either end of the extended lines with rocket launchers. The rear guard formed up fifty yards behind the entrance, behind a roadblock of SUVs.

The gates were an obvious target, although it was impossible to second-guess a deranged lunatic like Finch. He had some nerve walking up to the walls like that. It wasn't the actions of a cautious man who thought he would lose or face a difficult fight.

Jake stood in front of the men and scanned the expectant faces. "You already know what's behind those walls and what they want to do to you. If they smash the gates, the outcome will rest on your shoulders. I will join you with my team, and together we will show them what we're all about. Finch will only win today over my dead body. Hold your nerve, and we'll pull through."

A few gave him a determined nod. He returned the gesture and jogged over to his group, who waited for him by the base of the wall. Skye's team waited there too.

She approached him. "Where do you want us positioned?"

Jake looked around the defenses, walls lined with guards disappearing into the haze in both directions. Other than the gate, he couldn't think of another obvious weak point. Geographically splitting the teams so they could quickly support any hot areas made the most sense. "Cover the southern section. I'll stay here. Keep in touch and call me if needed."

"Okay. Good luck," Skye said.

"Same to you."

He waved his team up the rampart. "Let's go, guys."

Jake positioned them to the left of the gates to increase the firepower. Citizens and guards stood around them, shoulder to shoulder in quiet anticipation. Two thousand were armed with conventional weapons. Two thousand more had improvised weapons like tire braces, hammers and bricks to throw at the invaders. They were instructed to take the rifles or pistols of any fallen comrade.

"Any sign of the enemy?" he said to a man in an Omega royal blue jacket.

"Nothing since the governor."

Finch was no doubt briefing his cohorts after his terms were refused. Jake couldn't detect a single movement in the forest. A strong breeze continued to whip dust across from east to west, and the storm showed no signs of easing.

Trader and Ross had left to finalize the organization of the inner ring. The last line of defense if they lost the wall. They were busy smashing up five houses and sharpening improvised spears out of the shattered planks of wood.

A collective roar came from the forest. Thousands of feet pounded against the ground, along with the noise of hundreds of branches being snapped out of the way.

Jake shouldered his rifle and scanned between the trunks through his sights.

Gunfire erupted to his right. They were attacking the former site of the stairs in front of the barracks. People on the rampart returned fire. A few threw bricks at the forest, but they all fell short. His team of sixteen, crouching behind the first line of defenders, looked at him for direction.

"Hold your position," Jake said. "Finch is an idiot if he thinks we'll pull people away from the gates. The pillboxes will do their job."

A spear arced out of the canopy and thudded into the ground in front of the wall. An eager Omega guard fired into the gloom.

Jake grabbed his shoulder. "Conserve your ammunition for a clean shot. You'll have plenty of opportunity."

If wastelanders were going to use the launchers, they had to move further out of cover to accurately hit the gate. To get a straight shot, they would need to either stand on the road leading up to Omega or fire from the edge of the tree line. Without experience, firing through a cluster of trunks would be high risk.

The sound of gunfire echoed from the southern section of the wall. Clever, Jake thought, but not that good. Finch bragged about the number of wastelanders involved in the attack. He didn't have the numbers to successfully attack from two fronts. He felt confident that Skye could organize a defense against a probing maneuver.

Jake switched his radio to the command channel. "What have you got at the south?"

"Enemy firing from cover," a crackly male voice said. "No immediate danger."

Two wastelanders sprinted onto the road leading to the gates, with Allied rocket launchers on their shoulders. Nobody required prompting. Shots rattled from either side of Jake. Both of the enemy collapsed to the dirt. Two more wastelanders broke out of the shrouded forest and attempted to retrieve the weapons. They met the same fate.

A flash of light and loud explosion boomed between the trees. A plume of white smoke belched out of the canopy fifty yards away. Jake hoped it was a wasted enemy rocket and checked the increasingly darkening sky for projectiles.

Gunfire continued in the area around the demolished steps. Finch, being a commissioned facility manager, only had basic combat training because of his support role. His madness probably magnified his own ability in his stasis-fried head. Jake felt confident that Finch could only dictate terms by weight of numbers rather than tactical genius.

A shot split the air closer to his location. One of the guards cried out and collapsed backward, clutching his chest. A citizen knelt by his side.

Twenty wastelanders darted behind trees close to the edge of the forest. They aimed rifles around the trunks. Rounds peppered the wall and whizzed above it.

The rampart returned fire, taking single shots as instructed. If Finch only had the weapons and ammunition from the bunker, he would run out before the stronghold. But nobody could confirm if he shipped out more to co-conspirators beyond the recovered cache in Zeta.

Jake aimed at a wastelander. Before he had a chance to fire, a rifle cracked to his side and the bearded man's head flipped back. He dropped to the ground with a twist.

The war cry from the forest grew louder. Hundreds of savages charged toward the edge. The front lines, extending a hundred yards in length, burst into the open and carried fifty wooden ladders toward the wall. The rampart cracked with deafening gunfire.

Wastelanders dropped to the grass and writhed on the ground. More followed out of the forest in a constant flow. They threw axes and spears, and picked up the ladders of their fallen comrades.

A woman, dressed in an Omega Guard jacket, fell to her side and attempted to grip the stem of a spear that punctured her chest. An axe twisted through the air between Jake and one of his team and smashed into an SUV's windshield behind the wall.

Jake tracked an enemy in his sights and pulled the trigger. He didn't have time to check an enemy's fate. The weight of the advance meant the guard were concentrating their fire on stopping the ladders hitting the wall, leaving the wastelanders in the forest free to take shots at them.

Citizens threw their bricks and rocks. A man in a blue coverall dragged a prone guard away from the edge of the wall by his collar and grabbed his rifle. One of Trader's team took a round to the throat, toppled back, and fell from the rampart.

A ladder brushed against the wall to Jake's right. His team fired at two wastelanders who attempted to climb. He grabbed the ladder's rough arms and thrust it away from the wall.

More wastelanders continued to charge out of the forest. Jake glanced along the wall and noticed a few ladders propped against it. Another two guards were hit and dropped to the ground. They were holding, but couldn't sustain this effort for a long period. It seemed

Finch decided to throw everything against them in a battle of attrition.

Jake felt conscious that he had to keep an eye out for wastelanders armed with rocket launchers. He ducked down and moved closer to the gate in a running crouch. Wastelander weapons continued to fill the air, most hitting the wall or flying overhead.

He pressed his radio to his mouth. "Skye, what's the situation on the south?"

"Same as before. They're firing but not coming out. What about you?"

A round ricocheted on the wall next to Jake and sprayed small chips of stone against his cheek. The screams below sounded close. In the building crowd on the grass outside, any of them could have a launcher.

"You need to get your team over here. This is the main point of attack."

"Roger that."

He glanced at the attackers and guessed over two thousand had rushed forward. A quarter were down, but more numbers were reaching the ladders. He pumped rounds into three who attempted to hoist a fallen ladder next to the gatehouse.

Ten yards to his right, a man changed his magazine and leaned over the rampart. A wastelander's arms appeared and dragged him over the wall. Two of Trader's team rushed forward and took care of the threat.

"Herbie, Harrison, what's your situation?" Jake shouted into the radio.

"No sign of the enemy," Harrison said.

"Send half of your force to the north."

"Negative," Harrison said. "We will hold our section of the wall."

"Herbie here. I'll send half of my team. Out."

Jake shook his head. Harrison wouldn't have anything to defend if they didn't reinforce the thinning defenses on the north wall. He obviously didn't understand the meaning of a dynamic defense.

Jake swept the area for any wastelander carrying a bulky green tube. His biggest concern was with all of the force occupied on the closest threats, it would give them more space and time to position their launchers and destroy the gates. Dust continued to impair his vision as he continued to search and fire.

A hundred members of the Kappa guard streamed around the rampart from the east. Jake crouched to change his magazine and said to the front two, "Over there, guys, fill in the gaps."

They nodded and continued forward, firing at targets as they went.

A loud explosion boomed from the edge of the forest. A split second later the gates shuddered as a cloud of fire and smoke rose above them.

"Damaged but holding," a voice called out.

Jake put a round in the chamber and leaned over the wall. A wastelander dropped his launcher, picked up a battle-axe from a casualty, and ran for the gates. Others below the wall and on the edge of the forest were distracted by the loud explosion. They turned and followed.

He emptied his magazine into the group. Others joined him and fired. Jake glanced along to the pillboxes in front of the barracks. Wastelanders were over. Ten of them wrestled with Omega guards and citizens. Skye and her team raced up the track from the captain's tower to the fight, pausing to shoot and running for the inner steps. He knew he could rely on her.

Jake searched the forest again. They couldn't afford to take another hit, especially with wastelanders converging on the gate.

Another loud boom echoed from the forest. He only got a chance to see the backfire in the gloom before a rocket exploded at the gates. Wastelanders fell in front of it. They didn't care if they made casualties of their own people, as long as they broke through. The gates gave a loud metallic groan.

Jake continued firing through the smoke left by the rocket. His team did the same. People cried out in pain along the rampart. He felt they were hanging on by the skin of their teeth.

He lifted his radio again. "Harrison, send half your men. Now."

No response.

Skye's team had successfully retaken the ground by the inner steps, but wastelanders had scaled the wall between the two positions and swung their weapons at the decreasing number of defenders. Bodies littered the bottom of the inner wall and spread along the rampart.

He looked to his left. One of the gates leaned in. One more strike would do the trick. Most of the wastelanders headed for it.

A throng had already gathered after the explosion. Every available man and woman close enough to have them in their sights fired into the crowd. As the front wastelanders dropped, others climbed over the top of them and threw themselves at the damaged gate.

Skye's team had retaken the middle section of the wall, but the only way to bring more strength to the fight and ensure superior fire against the continually increasing numbers was to retreat to the inner wall and start again. Harrison would be committed to following the order unless he wanted to be left in the open with wastelanders attacking from his rear.

Another earsplitting blast ripped through the air, followed by an immediate explosion by the gates. A gust of wind cleared the smoke, revealing a pile of dead wastelanders. The survivors outside, and the others approaching, paused momentarily, probably wondering if they were next in line to be killed by their own side. The gate swayed and screamed on its huge hinges.

Jake raised the radio. "Retreat. Retreat. Retreat."

* * *

The surviving citizens and guard clambered down the internal ladders and stairs and sprinted across the fields toward the inner ring. A few turned and fired at wastelanders who climbed over the rampart. Most outside were focused on the gate.

Jake led his depleted eight-man team to the SUV roadblock on the road leading from the gates. All forty stationed by the vehicles had held their position.

He waited for the repeated calls of retreat to die down on his radio. "Trader, how's that firing step looking?"

"We're good to go. How many more are coming back?"

Jake glanced through the dusty air. Most were close or already in the inner ring. "Not many more than you can see."

"We've got good numbers from the south and west."

"Higher concentration to the north. I expect a frontal assault."

"You got it."

Two wastelanders descended the stone steps near the gate tower and charged the roadblock. They were quickly brought down by a hail of bullets. Jake carried out a tactical reload and checked his watch. At half past six, they would soon be losing natural light, adding to the already poor visibility.

Another explosion boomed to their front. Shrapnel slammed into the SUVs. A man leaning over the hood next to Jake twisted to the paving and his legs twitched. One of the iron gates dropped through the smoke and crashed to the ground. He felt the paving shudder below his feet.

"Prepare to fire your launchers," Jake shouted.

He squinted into the thinning smoke. Everything seemed silent for a moment.

The first wastelander appeared through the shroud. One of the team dropped him with a single shot. A roar followed and a hundred rushed forward. Fifty yards and closing.

"Fire!"

Both launchers boomed. One rocket zipped down and exploded in front of the advance, cutting down the front of the mob. The second slammed against the remaining gate, and the explosion smashed it off its hinges.

All forty men stationed behind the roadblock and Jake's remaining team fired into the enemy assault. The front twenty fell, but it didn't deter their comrades. They stumbled over the casualties and continued forward to meet the same fate.

Jake detected movement in his peripheral vision. Wastelanders were climbing the wall by the vacated pillboxes and appeared on other sections of the north wall. They risked being outflanked if they stayed for too long. Although their fire kept the frontal attack at bay, they would also run out of ammunition soon. This wasn't a suicide mission.

He pushed the button on the side of his radio. "Trader, do you have everyone back?"

"Not sure. I think so. How many are coming through?"

"Hundreds. Be prepared."

Jake dropped the radio and continued to fire. The weight of wastelanders entering the stronghold was too much for their roadblock to hold. Some would start getting through. They spread to either side of the clustered vehicles after seeing their straight advance along the road come to a bullet-ridden halt. A spear skidded along the paving, slid under the vehicle, and shot out by Jake's left boot.

"Fall back. Fall back," he shouted.

The team turned and ran. None stopped to look back. They could hear the shouts and the rapid footsteps behind them. A few seconds' pause would be fatal. Wastelanders crossed the fields from the pillboxes and darted through the gloom.

Jake neared the inner ring. Trader encouraged them forward, waving through a thin gap in the wall. Gunfire rattled as wastelanders came into the vision of the firing step.

If they couldn't stop them here, it was all over. Jake hoped they'd caused enough damage to weaken the enemy forces. If they still had numbers similar to the initial assault, they were all in big trouble.

He let the team file through the gap first, flicked his rifle to automatic, turned and sprayed the closest pursuers. Others dropped around him as rifles cracked overhead.

"Jake. In. Now!" Trader said.

He scrambled through the dry stone wall. Trader pulled him clear, and an SUV parked in the gap.

A group of civilians with makeshift spears gave him a nervous look. Herbie ran along a line of the Kappa guard and shouted encouragement. Ross waved citizens back between the bungalows. Skye stood on the fire step to the right with her team and glanced over at him. He gave her a single nod.

Jake reloaded with his last full magazine. He had to carry on the fight.

Chapter Twenty-Six

Skye aimed at a charging wastelander and fired. Adrenalin pumped through her veins as she searched for her next target. She wondered how many more could attack. Hundreds lay outside the wall, but hundreds more headed for the inner ring. Shadows moved through the dust. Her team didn't have enough rounds left to take speculative shots. She ordered them to only shoot at confirmed targets.

After retreating to the newly formed defense five minutes ago, she led her five surviving team members to the fire step, where they replaced citizens on a section of the inner wall facing north. She watched Jake's group hold off the initial internal assault against an invisible enemy while she caught her breath. Wastelanders appeared through the gloom, giving chase as the team fell back from the roadblock. Now they were all inside; the final battle lines were drawn.

Ross ran around like a headless chicken behind her. "They'll kill us all. We need to keep shooting."

Nobody listened. It was obvious what they needed to do.

Skye turned back to him. "Collect a few citizens and start refilling magazines. We're gonna need them any minute now."

He paused for a moment, nodded and rushed away. Better to have him do something useful than be a distraction. Jake had already ordered others to do the reloading, but she wanted Ross out of the way. They couldn't afford any confusion.

An increased rate of fire came from her left. The wastelanders were attacking the west side. At the moment, none got close enough to the northern side to effectively use their spears and axes.

Wind gusted across the stronghold. The air became clearer. They needed this kind of break if they were to survive.

The stronghold outer wall slowly came into view across the casualty-infested fields. Wastelanders lined up in front of it, perhaps a hundred long and five ranks deep. A lone figure stood on the rampart above them.

She nudged the man next to her. "Swap weapons."

He exchanged his sniper rifle for her standard-issue rifle. She peered through the telescopic sight.

Finch held something above his shoulder. Skye put a round in the chamber and exhaled. From six hundred yards she could take him.

Something flashed behind his body and a hissing trail streaked toward the inner circle as a loud bang echoed around the outer wall.

"Get down," somebody shouted.

A split second later, a loud explosion erupted fifty yards to her right. Debris, fire and smoke shot into the air and showered the surrounding area. People near the impact moaned and cried out for help. From here she could see that the rocket had punctured a ten-yard hole in the wall.

She squinted through the sight again. The wastelanders roared and charged. Shouts broke out along the fire step. People rushed to pull the injured away and defend the gap. She would too but not before doing this.

Skye placed Finch's chest in the center of her crosshairs and fired. His shoulder jerked to one side and he fell off the back of the wall. Hopefully head first to his death. She would celebrate the confirmation later if they pulled through.

The northern line opened fire. Wastelanders converged on the damaged section. Ryder and his outlaws rushed through the wooden bungalows and joined the defenders. Skye guessed he decided to leave the southern fire step to join the main fight.

Phillips, his team and Trader streamed through the standing line of thirty mixed brown and royal blue uniforms, and knelt in front of them, increasing the direct firepower. Gunshots continued on the western side. It sounded like the Zeta Forces were holding their own.

Wastelanders continued to fall, but it didn't deter the others. They reached within a hundred yards away and only half of them were down.

She heard Phillips shouting orders, but couldn't hear what they were above the noise. The rate of fire from the wall increased. Skye crouched next to a section of broken wall and pulled back the rifle bolt.

She was out of ammo.

Others suffered the same thing. Ryder and another outlaw produced knives from their belts and braced themselves. One of Phillips' team held broken pieces of rock in both hands. Three of her team grabbed spears from the civilians cowering behind the base of a wind turbine.

Forty wastelanders reached within fifty yards away. Only sporadic shots peppered the enemy. At least twenty would hit the wall at this rate.

"You better take this," a voice said behind her.

She glanced back.

Ross held a loaded magazine forward and drew his pistol. "It's time to fight."

An axe thudded into the center of his chest. He grimaced, dropped the magazine, and fell flat on his back.

Skye grabbed the mag and thrust it into the housing. She didn't have time to consider saving him. Besides, many better men had died today. At least his last act was a helpful one. She put a round in the chamber, turned and fired.

Wastelanders, with bloodstained axes and spears thrust to their front, were almost on top of them. Rage filled their faces. Saliva sprayed through their gritted teeth. Skye took another one down.

Five wastelanders threw their spears forward. An outlaw grunted and fell to his side.

The defenders roared this time. Phillips smashed the butt of his rifle in the face of the first wastelander who reached him. Twenty others charged from the wall and met the advance. Skye leaped over the shattered section and fired at another savage.

Ryder thrust his knife into a wastelander's stomach, and they dropped to the ground in a tight embrace. Another outlaw pulled him free.

More guards and citizens flowed out of the gap. They overwhelmed the remaining enemy, who fell to the ground under a hail of blows. Apart from one.

A single wastelander skidded to a halt and jerked his head in different directions. After probably considering his limited options, he turned and ran. Skye knelt, peered through her sight, and fired. A puff of red mist burst from the front of his head as the round exited, and he fell amongst the field of carrots.

Skye let out a deep breath and realized she was surrounded by silence. Men and women looked toward the outer walls, searching for wastelanders below the darkening sky. A few casualties tried to drag themselves along the ground, but none were left standing.

"Find ammunition from the other sections," Phillips shouted. "Come back here and we rebuild the wall."

Skye looked at his blood-smeared face and saw a real leader. He shook Ryder's hand, and they held a brief conversation. Omega needed both of them to bring about a new era. Off the back of this fight, where so many had lost their life, they could build something honest, capable and strong.

Jake approached her and put a hand on her shoulder. "Great job today. Thanks for responding to my request. We'd have lost that part of the rampart without you."

Skye couldn't force a smile. Not after today. "Do you think it's over?"

"I hope so, but we can't drop our guard."

"I'll take my team to sweep the perimeter."

Jake smiled. "You're a legend."

He moved back behind the wall and knelt next to one of the casualties.

She closed her eyes and sighed, finally believing that Sky Man was defeated.

* * *

Skye patrolled the fields between the two walls for the next hour. Jake sent scouts outside to check the surrounding forest. She heard reports over the radio that only wastelander casualties were still in the area. She climbed the rampart and stared at the scene below. Hundreds of dead bodies were spread around, but she couldn't see Finch.

Wastelander bodies were dragged outside the walls. The stronghold victims were neatly piled inside. They would be buried tomorrow.

Dusk turned to darkness, and she led her team back to the safety of the inner wall.

Her radio, still on the command channel, crackled. "Skye, can you make it to the mansion in fifteen minutes?"

"Sure, Jake. Anything I need to know?"

"Harrison wants a governors' meeting. I think you should be there."

"Okay. Skye out."

She felt confident to stand alongside Jake and give her view. Omega had no official leader, but he organized the joint defense. Harrison's force beat away a small attack of wastelanders from the western edge of the inner wall, but she didn't see him do much else. Herbie went with the plan and lost a lot of men and women. He could hold his head high and justifiably claim that Kappa played their part.

After setting up a shift system between her team to guard a small section of the wall, she walked up the gravel drive to Finch's mansion and slumped on the steps. The ruins of the front gates smoldered in the distance. Citizens met in the street and embraced. Some talked in small groups, no doubt relieved they'd see another sunrise. Skye felt shattered. She couldn't remember her last decent night's sleep.

Finch nearly ruined her life twice. He failed the second time but managed to destroy a lot of others. If she couldn't find him tomorrow, she wouldn't stop searching for him until she returned the compliment.

The two governors approached. Harrison strutted over the gravel with his hands behind his back. Herbie covered his mouth and yawned. His usually smart brown jacket hung open, revealing a stained string vest.

"Is Jake already inside?" Herbie said.

"I think I'm the first here," Skye said.

Harrison looked down his nose at her. "I don't remember inviting you. This is a governors' matter."

Skye shrugged. "Jake asked me along."

"We need someone from Omega," Herbie said. "Let's wait in Finch's study and see if he's left any of that vintage whiskey."

Harrison grunted and walked inside. He now represented the old failed system in Skye's eyes. The last two days had brought about a complete transformation in her beliefs. The population clock hung above her head, but it counted for nothing. If anything, it should be replaced with the number of casualties they took today, serving as a constant reminder to their honor and bravery.

Jake, Trader and Ryder pushed open the wrought-iron gates. All three were in deep conversation. Skye stood and brushed herself down.

"They're already here, in Finch's study," she said.

"Fine, lead the way," Jake said.

Skye led them through the mansion and entered the study. Mary must've cleaned the place up. It was probably all she knew, serving as Finch's housekeeper for the last twenty years. Harrison and Herbie sat on the leather chairs on either side of the shattered glass coffee table.

Harrison stood and pointed at Ryder. "What's he doing here?"

"He's part of us now," Jake said. "You need to accept that."

"That's part of the reason I called this meeting. We need to get things straight before I leave tomorrow."

Trader took a book from the shelf and opened it to the first page. Skye guessed he wanted to listen to how things developed and judge how it would best benefit him.

"So get things straight," Jake said.

"I want you to appoint yourself as the governor here. We carry on under the stronghold treaty, under Trader's arbitration. We've taken a blow, but our system works. He can set new clock values after accounting for casualties."

"Your system doesn't work," Ryder said. "You make your own laws, cast people out, strangle desire, and don't mind killing anyone who doesn't buy into your damned corrupt society."

Harrison scowled and reached for his holster.

Herbie reached over and grabbed his arm. "Go easy. He's entitled to his opinion after today."

"The system in Omega vanished with Finch," Skye said. "We've got a chance to build something better. Why would people go back to working your fields after fighting for freedom?"

Harrison gave her a sarcastic smile. "Because people like being controlled. Isn't that right, Trader?"

"Leave me out of it until you decide on a way forward."

"Here's my proposal," Jake said. "Omega and Epsilon will be run democratically, without any clock. I'll set up a council here, which Ryder and Skye will sit on. The strongholds will still trade, but will not be governed by your treaty rules."

"You can't speak for Beth and Barry," Harrison said.

"I can and I will," Jake said. "You didn't complain at the tower when we went through the battle plan."

"They're a pair of old crows. What use would they be?"

"They're old crows who agree with us," Ryder said. "Omega and Epsilon are both leaving the treaty."

"You're speaking for them too?" Harrison said. He slumped back in his chair and shook his head. "Unbelievable. You know what the punishment is for breaking the treaty?"

"You can't seriously contemplate attacking us?" Skye said.

"Herbie," Harrison said. "Tell them the consequences. You know the other four strongholds won't stand for it."

Herbie rubbed his chin and eyed the group by the door. "I think they're entitled to do what they want. If they carry on trading, it's no skin off my nose. Cut them some slack. If it goes wrong, you can tell them you told them so."

Harrison mumbled something, unscrewed a whiskey bottle and drank from it. A feeling of liberation rose in Skye, like a weight lifted off her shoulders. Their fight would mean something. A better life for the people of Omega and Epsilon.

"So you're okay?" Jake said to Herbie.

"You've proved yourselves today. Compared to Finch, I'd say we've got a pretty good deal out of it."

"They're taking in outlaws," Harrison said. "Trader, how can you control the system if we don't know the numbers we need to produce?"

Trader cleared his throat. "You have a point, but I've already spoken to them. They won't back down. We'll have to run it for a trial period to see if it works."

"And if I refuse to trade?"

"Why would you do that?" Skye said. "What happens if your people want to come and live here instead of working your damned hemp fields?"

"I've had enough of this," Harrison said and bolted from his chair. "You can have your wish on one condition."

"Which is?" Jake said.

"I get to offer everyone outside a chance to come and live in Zeta. We'll see what the people really want."

"You've got yourself a deal. I've spoken to plenty of citizens, and they're all for our plan."

Harrison grabbed the whiskey bottle and stormed out of the room.

Herbie raised his eyebrows. "I think you're on the right track, but it's gonna be a shock to the other places, especially if their people start flooding here. I'll have to make some changes in Kappa."

"We'll help and support you," Ryder said. "Throwing out the failed system doesn't mean ending relationships."

"You're a bit too militant for my liking, young man," Herbie said. "But I'm prepared to give you all the benefit of the doubt."

"You won't regret it," Skye said. "People don't fight for the right to be slaves. We'll prove Harrison wrong."

She couldn't believe those words just came out of her mouth. Her post-battle low was replaced with a flood of optimism. Skye wasn't sure a place on a new council would suit her, but she would do her best to make it work if that's what Jake and Ryder wanted.

Herbie moved along the line and shook everyone's hand. "I'll be leaving at first light with my people. I don't expect you to convince any to stay."

"Agreed," Jake said.

He left the room. Trader shook his head. "You've landed yourselves in a world of trouble. I told you not to go through with it."

"Relax," Jake said. "You need to start worrying about how you break the news to the other strongholds, and how they can support our growth."

"I agree with you, but people will be surprised by the pace of events. The other strongholds didn't see what happened outside."

"You can bring them here and we'll show them the graves," Skye said. She had an idea and turned to Jake and Ryder. "Can you help me do something?"

"Sure," Ryder said.

"What do you need?" Jake said.

"Follow me."

Skye walked along the corridor and out of the front entrance. Jake helped her carry a ladder from the side of the mansion, and they propped it against the front wall. He held it steady, and she climbed the first few rungs.

She turned back and detected a hint of a smile on Trader's face. He lit a cigarette, coughed and thumped his chest. Ryder's smile didn't need concealing. He beamed up at her. Skye continued up and wondered if her parents would be proud. From what Ryder said in the caves, they would approve of the new changes, and she was part of the implementation.

The clock balanced on a small wooden ledge. She used to change these numbers for Finch as a young girl. It never really meant anything to her back then. Pulling it down today would have symbolic value. People in Omega were no longer numbers. Their tags meaningless.

She grabbed the metal frame, shook it loose, and threw it to her side. It crashed against the gravel by Ryder's feet.

Cheers came from behind her. She turned on the ladder and saw a small crowd gathered by the wrought-iron gates. Omega was free.

Chapter Twenty-Seven

Jake spent the night on the inner wall with Trader's team. Leading them through battle didn't mean he could shirk his shift. He decided that Finch's front garden would be a fitting place to bury the dead. Nobody in Omega deserved to live in a mansion overlooking the rows of scruffy bungalows. It would be a place of remembrance.

Two thousand guards and citizens from Omega survived. Out of everyone he encountered that night, only two middle-aged men didn't have a healthy appetite for the new way forward. Both were packing their things and heading for Kappa. He felt sure a few more would leave. A small minority who benefited from the old system and were sold a promise by Harrison. They were welcome to walk through the battered gates.

Plenty of the Zeta and Kappa population asked to stay. Without wanting to poke a hornets' nest, Jake and Ryder both refused the requests, but told them if they were ever made outlaws, they had a place in Omega. He understood that too much rapid change at the other strongholds' expense would likely cause trouble. Although he expected people would flock to Omega once they knew they could live in a free society without tin-pot dictators and population clocks.

The sun rose in the early morning sky, casting long dark shadows of the outer wall across the dew-glistening fields. Barry and Beth left at five in the morning with the people of Epsilon. They were getting straight to work in their foundry to create a new pair of front gates. For a stronghold that went through hell in the last twenty-four hours, a lot had smiles on their faces, especially when Barry ordered them to remove their tags. He planned to melt them down into a statue to commemorate the battle.

Harrison lined up the Zeta SUVs in a convoy formation. Around three thousand of his citizens left the inner wall and surrounded the vehicles. Jake scanned their glum expressions and realized he still had work to do. But not yet.

Trader stood by his shoulder as he watched Harrison shouting orders. "Rome wasn't built in a day, Jake."

"I suppose you're happy to keep some of the old system in place?"

"I carried on the work of Trader four. I know it isn't perfect, but it worked. You have to admit that."

"I'll admit it helped keep pockets of unhappy people alive if you admit there's a better way of doing things."

He laughed and smoothed back his greasy gray hair. Harrison headed over, flanked by two guards.

"We're moving out. You'll be pleased to know that none of my citizens want to stay. Ten of yours are coming with me."

"Fine by me," Jake said, he wouldn't reveal that plenty asked. "We'll bury our dead this morning. Any citizen of Zeta is welcome to come and pay their respects."

Harrison gave him a lingering glare and turned to Trader. "It remains vegetables for clothing and material. I want to know if they start producing something else."

"Business as usual," Trader said. "You'll be the first to know."

"When this little enterprise fails, don't expect me to pick up the slack."

"I think you'll be pleasantly surprised," Jake said.

"We'll see about that."

While returning to the head of his convoy, Harrison glanced toward the barracks, at the pile of over a thousand stronghold casualties, and shook his head. Jake thought even the coldest heart would be moved by the sight. Every one of them had given him and thousands of others their freedom.

"Come to the back of my SUV," Trader said. "I'm cooking up breakfast, and we need to talk."

Jake followed him back through the inner wall. Half of the Omega Force guarded the fire step. Even the most cynical members saw the practicality of letting the outlaws join their ranks, especially when Ryder organized them with an air of efficiency they hadn't witnessed before. Despite victory being confirmed, the stronghold still had to remain vigilant. Not every wastelander would have joined Finch's army, and Jake wanted no casualties today.

Trader had left his SUV parked outside Finch's mansion. Citizens were already digging graves on the front lawn. Others headed out under the protection of Trader's team to gather and burn the wastelanders outside.

He opened the trunk, produced a camping stove and frying pan, and unwrapped a paper packet of anemic-looking sausages.

"Better make it quick, Trader. We've got plenty of work to do today."

"Just give me ten minutes of your time; that's all I'm asking."

Trader lit the stove, and within minutes the sausages sizzled. Jake leaned against the SUV and thought about his ship.

"I still haven't seen Mills," Jake said. "That's the only thing I can't square in my head."

Trader reached inside his breast pocket and pulled out a light green piece of material. He handed it to Jake. "Why don't you ask him?"

He recognized it as a Fleet name tag, with the name *Mills* in faded black stitching. "Where did you get this?"

"When I joined the Fleet. You're looking at him, Jake."

Jake stared at Trader, not knowing what to say. It didn't seem possible. "You can't be. You don't even look like …"

Trader smiled. "Oh, come on. Take off forty years, fifty pounds, thousands of cigarettes, dye my hair and give me a shave, and you'll see it's me."

Jake studied his face and thought back to his old partner on Endeavor Three. Trader appeared nothing like him, but he wouldn't if he'd been out four decades. He eventually saw it in his twinkling eyes.

"Mills ... Why didn't you say?"

"I'm Trader now. This is my life. I wanted to pick the right time." Jake's mind raced with questions. Mills stabbed a fork through a sausage and handed it to him. "Don't you have anything to say?"

"What happened to the crew? Why did you leave me in stasis?"

"We all spent a long time in orbit, Jake. When I woke and brought us down forty years ago, we agreed to leave you as an insurance policy while exploring the immediate area. It was only meant to be a short-term thing."

"Insurance policy for what? You could've asked me."

"I knew you'd refuse. It was only for a few hours until we established the dangers we faced outside. What would be the point in all of us dying? None of us expected wastelanders or strongholds."

"It still doesn't make sense," Jake said. "How did a few hours turn into forty years?"

"None of us were thinking straight. Stasis destroyed a couple of the guys. We were ambushed two miles from the ship by wastelanders. I was the only survivor and got picked up by a Sigma patrol."

"Why didn't you come back for me?"

"I kept my mouth shut and said I was from the north. I planned to come back for you as soon as I managed to escape. Epsilon saw our ship come down, and they dragged it inside their walls after a couple of days."

Jake shook his head. "You're not answering my question. Why didn't you come back for me? You've spent years as the Trader."

Mills bowed his head and took a bite out of his sausage. Jake wasn't letting him off the hook and waited for an answer.

"You were part of Epsilon's economy by the time I had freedom of movement. Quite a popular part, too. I decided to keep you as an insurance policy and integrate you into my role when I neared death's door."

"You seem in reasonable shape to me. I take it you feared an unnatural death?"

"I saw trouble on the horizon. Not exactly what Finch had planned, but I knew something was behind the increasing wastelander numbers. We needed a young military commander and the contents of the bunkers."

Jake suspected his captain's knowledge of the access codes and the weapons inside the bunkers were the main motivation. The requirement of a young military commander was Mills' attempt to sugarcoat and justify his decisions, although he could see the logic behind his words.

"But you didn't stay around after initiating my waking procedure. How did you know I'd survive?"

"I thought Barry and Beth would take you in while I established the source of the wastelanders' movement. I knew it wouldn't take long for you to establish your credentials. I was right about that."

"You could've told me when you picked me up in Omega."

"Baby steps, Jake, baby steps. You had enough on your plate, and I needed you focused on the task at hand. I planned to tell you after a few days, and I have."

"I'm surprised you bought into the system. The Mills I knew wouldn't."

"The story I told you about taking over from Trader four is all true. I aligned myself with the modern world. I never thought one man would be able to change it."

Jake puffed his cheeks. "I guess this means we're working together again?"

Mills laughed. "What do you think we've been doing for the last few days? You can make this a better world. Make sure you do."

Jake gazed around the stronghold at people clearing up yesterday's carnage. Mills' revelation hadn't properly sunk in, but it tied up the loose ends in his mind. He would make sure they built a stronger society, free from oppression, working together again, like previously, as the sixth cycle.

Chapter Twenty-Eight

Finch huddled in the corner of a crumbling stone building and shivered. The morning after the battle should have been special. Instead, he spent the night limping through the forest on his damaged ankle, and sat alone as morning sunshine poked through the surrounding trees outside.

He winced and rose to his feet. His left arm hung limply by his side and his shoulder throbbed with pain. Two bullet wounds, cracked ribs and a damaged ankle were his only rewards for attempting to release humanity from its pain.

Skye's betrayal cut the deepest. He cared for her like his own daughter and arranged her deliverance at the outlaw camp. She repaid him by helping to destroy his glorious future. She stamped on his butterfly.

It would take months to rebuild again. When he did, she'd pay for her insolence, along with the rest of the predators inside Omega. It took more than this minor setback to stop Alexander Finch. Sky Man would return and bring violent revenge.

SIXTH CYCLE

The forest was dense enough to hide in while recovering from his injuries. After that he would head south and gather an army again. Omega wouldn't be able to resist a second attack. He knew the locations of two more bunkers. If people thought they'd heard the last of him, they were wrong.

He shuffled outside, surveyed the area, and laughed. He'd destroyed this settlement ten years ago. The irony wasn't lost on him. He'd been led here by a greater force, to show him his legacy and the path ahead. People didn't understand that he was on this planet for a reason.

Finch plucked a small apple from a tree and bit into the tough green skin. His eyes squinted at the sour taste, and he threw it to one side. They couldn't even make fruit grow properly; that was the extent of the foolishness he faced.

His eyes wandered to a row of scruffy crosses planted in the ground on the edge of the former settlement, and Finch remembered the two pine ones at the end. He'd helped that ungrateful bitch erect them, against his wishes.

Finch picked up a stick, used it to take some of the weight off his left ankle, and hobbled over. He sneered at the wilted flowers by the foot of each one.

He thrust the heel of his shoe against her father's cross and cried in agony. It remained in place and teased him. The memory of Sky Man should be the only thing honored here. Not Skye's worthless parents.

Finch growled and dropped to his knees. He grabbed the arms of her father's cross, clenched his teeth, and ripped it out of the ground. He threw it to the dirt and shuffled over to the mother's vulgar wooden memorial.

A dying rose lay in front of it. He crushed the petals in his hand and vowed to do the same to every one of the backward species who defied him.

He strained, tugged the cross out of the ground, and threw it on top of the other. Both would make a nice fire to warm him this evening.

Finch used his stick to haul himself to his feet and stared at both graves. He smiled to himself and unzipped his fly.

Something hard pressed against the back of his head.

* * *

Skye kicked Finch in the back of his knee, and he dropped to the ground. She remembered him doing it to Sam outside her cell, although this wasn't just about his revenge. Finch had many lives to answer for.

"Who's this?" Finch snapped.

"The daughter of those murdered parents. It wasn't hard to track you."

Finch's head jerked to the side. "Skye, remember all I've done for you. We can talk about this."

Skye knew exactly what he had done for her. That's why she left Omega at first light to find him. She watched Finch closely for any sudden movements and jabbed her muzzle against the back of his head. "Why don't you start by telling me why you did it?"

SIXTH CYCLE

"Did what?"

"Now isn't the time for games, Finch. Why did you arrange the deaths of so many good people?"

"You're just like your father. He couldn't see the bigger picture. I should've killed you when I had the chance. I stupidly thought I could turn you into a better person. You're not trainable, like a wild animal, just like him."

"You killed my parents and destroyed our settlement because he didn't agree with your ideals?"

Finch shrugged, raising Skye's blood pressure. "There's no room for niceties when trying to rebuild a society. Darwin's law: the strong survive. Kill or be killed, my dear."

"You aren't even remotely sorry for what you've done, are you?"

"Why would I be sorry? You're too stupid to see the genius of my plan. If you gave me ten minutes to explain, you'd understand."

"You're delusional."

"Am I? After wastelanders destroyed your home, what happened? Strongholds continued to trade petty goods and built larger walls around themselves. The world was trapped in a spider's web. Blood has to be spilled to get progress. You are naïve if you think otherwise."

Skye felt her hands trembling as her anger rose. "You helped build some of those walls."

"I didn't build all of them, and when someone tries to create God's temple without his permission, he can destroy it. Just like your parents—"

Skye tensed and pulled the trigger. Finch slumped forward as the shot echoed through the forest. She dragged him away from her parents' graves and planted the crosses back in the ground again.

For half an hour, Skye gathered dry wood and used it to build a small pyre. She rolled Finch's body on top of it, lit the kindling at the bottom, and waited.

Wisps of smoke drifted up, and tiny flames took hold of the pieces of wood around the bottom of the pyre.

Skye lay back, resting on her elbows, and watched as fire engulfed the man who attempted to destroy her world. The flames built to a crackling roar and smoke billowed through the canopy. She could finally look forward to a brighter future.

If you would like our next release, or another book by Darren Wearmouth, visit: http://eepurl.com/448r9

ACKNOWLEDGMENTS

We would like to thank our cover designer, Jason Gurley, and our editors, Aaron Sikes and Pauline Nolet. Also, as ever, thank you to everyone who agreed to read an early copy and give us your thoughts. Collectively, you've all helped make this a better book. Thank you!

Darren Wearmouth's Facebook author page.
https://www.facebook.com/darrenwearmouthauthor

Carl Sinclair's Facbook author page.
https://www.facebook.com/indiebynight

OTHER AUTHORS UNDER THE SHIELD OF

WHISKEY TANGO FOXTROT SERIES
The world is at war with the Primal Virus. Military forces across the globe have been recalled to defend the homelands as the virus spreads and decimates populations. Out on patrol and assigned to a remote base in Afghanistan, Staff Sergeant Brad Thompson's unit was abandoned and left behind, alone and without contact. They survived and have built a refuge, but now they are forgotten. No contact with their families or commands. Brad makes a tough decision to leave the safety of his compound to try and make contact with the States, desperate to find rescue for his men. What he finds is worse than he could have ever predicted.
W. J. Lundy

DEAD ISLAND: Operation Zulu
Ten years after the world was nearly brought to its knees by a zombie Armageddon, there is a race for the antidote! On a remote Caribbean island, surrounded by a horde of hungry living dead, a team of American and Australian commandos must rescue the Antidotes' scientist. Filled with zombies, guns, Russian bad guys, shady government types, serial killers and elevator muzak. Dead Island is an action packed blood soaked horror adventure.
Allen Gamboa

INVASION OF THE DEAD SERIES

This is the first book in a series of nine, about an ordinary bunch of friends, and their plight to survive an apocalypse in Australia. — Deep beneath defense headquarters in the Australian Capital Territory, the last ranking Army chief and a brilliant scientist struggle with answers to the collapse of the world, and the aftermath of an unprecedented virus. Is it a natural mutation, or does the infection contain — more sinister roots? — One hundred and fifty miles away, five friends returning from a month-long camping trip slowly discover that death has swept through the country. What greets them in a gradual revelation is an enemy beyond compare. — Armed with dwindling ammunition, the friends must overcome their disagreements, utilize their individual skills, and face unimaginable horrors as they battle to reach their hometown…
Owen Ballie

SPLINTER

For close to a thousand years they waited, waited for the old knowledge to fade away into the mists of myth. They waited for a re-birth of the time of legend for the time when demons ruled and man was the fodder upon which they fed. They waited for the time when the old gods die and something new was anxious to take their place. **A young couple was all that stood between humanity and annihilation.** Ill equipped and shocked by the horrors thrust upon them they would fight in the only way they knew how, tooth and nail. Would they be enough to prevent the creation of the feasting hordes? Were they alone able to stand against evil banished from hell? **Would the horsemen ride when humanity failed?** The earth would rue the day a splinter group set up shop in Cold Spring.
H. J. Harry

Printed in Great Britain
by Amazon